IRRESISTIBLE
FORCE

IRRESISTIBLE
FORCE

D.D. Ayres

St. Martin's Paperbacks

This is a work of fiction. All of the characters, organizations, and events portrayed in this novel are either products of the author's imagination or are used fictitiously.

IRRESISTIBLE FORCE

Copyright © 2014 by by D.D. Ayres

5578 5991
9/14

For information address St. Martin's Press, 175 Fifth Avenue, New York, NY 10010.

ISBN: 978-1-250-04217-0

Printed in the United States of America

St. Martin's Paperbacks edition / September 2014

St. Martin's Paperbacks are published by St. Martin's Press, 175 Fifth Avenue, New York, NY 10010.

10 9 8 7 6 5 4 3 2 1

For Kalia, the newest member of the family

ACKNOWLEDGMENTS

Acknowledgments create a rush of grateful enthusiasm. These are the people to whom I want to say, I couldn't have done it nearly as well without you.

Thanks to my new wonderful editor, Rose Hilliard, who first saw the potential in stories about K-9 partners, and who took a chance on a short story, then helped me shape it into a novel.

Big thank you to my K-9 law enforcement expert, Brad Thompson. He's a 28-year veteran police officer, investigator with the Fort Worth Police Department, and former senior handler and instructor/trainer of the FWPD K9 Unit. And for good measure, he's a two-time Medal of Valor recipient. Best of all, for me, he's an avid reader. The things I got right I owe to him. The things I got wrong are all on me, or a bit of literary license.

Thanks to Loritha Johnson-Hill, a retired investigator with the Fort Worth Police Department, who introduced me to

Brad. In additional to helping with the book, she's a new friend and neighbor.

Last, but never least, my husband, Chris, who puts up with the creative mind. And my family who encourage me even when the work is going off the rails.

CHAPTER ONE

Surveillance was simpler in the South in autumn. It was hunting season in North Carolina. A man dressed in camouflage and carrying a rifle in the woods didn't rate a second glance. The thick canopy of summer had yielded a blanket of damp leaves that made soft whispery sounds underfoot. Sparse branches improved viewing range, even in the darkness. Forecasters had predicted that by dawn, the frost would give way to the promise of an Indian summer day.

It was just the sort of weather James Cannon enjoyed on his day off from the Charlotte-Mecklenburg Police Department. However, tonight he was on the job, alone in an unfamiliar area, and closing in on what might be a desperate character.

James's alertness level ratcheted up as he came to the edge of the woods he had been passing through. The absence of Bogart gnawed at his focus. They were always on duty together, had been until a month ago. That's because James's law enforcement partner had been kidnapped.

The cabin in the clearing just ahead was the purported location where he was being held.

Ever since his partner had been taken, he'd spent a hellish amount of time tracking down useless leads. He'd been afraid, as the days stretched out, that Bogart was dead.

He jerked his thoughts back from that murky water-under-the-bridge reality to the present. Now he had his first good lead, and it had led him here.

He slowed as he reached the clearing. The cabin stood alone and dark in the distance. He'd been told that the woman who rented it lived alone. But he never relied on hearsay when it counted. Two years in the military police plus four years on the job made him cautious. He needed facts. He'd come here, in the wee hours, to check things out for himself.

He eased down into a crouched position to survey the terrain. Almost immediately, something at the edge of his vision caught his eye. It was the absolute stillness of an object amid the natural stirrings of a rural night. He turned his head to discover he wasn't the only one doing surveillance on the property.

Fifteen feet away, a truck sat in the deep shadows at the edge of the tree line on the unpaved track that ran through the forest. Had James not been on foot, he and the driver might have met in the woods.

James rose and moved in a little closer to try to get a better look at the vehicle to determine if it was occupied. It was. A man in dark clothing, unlike James's hunting gear, sat behind the wheel.

Something about the furtiveness of his actions, the way he just sat with headlights and engine off, increased James's suspicion that something illegal was going on here. He wondered if the driver was standing guard. Or, perhaps, waiting for someone?

Even as he pondered his options, a light flared and drew his attention back to the cabin.

A woman had stepped out of the cabin onto the porch. She didn't bother to turn on the porch light, nor did she carry a flashlight. She was simply a slight figure in silhouette for the instant she was backlit by the open doorway. Then a dark furry animal shot past her out the door. The dog was moving at full throttle, coming straight toward the woods, and James.

One bark was all it took to confirm the identification. James's heart squeezed tight, and though he would have denied it to his own mother, he had to blink away the threat of a watery leak in his left eye.

It was Bogart! He was unharmed! He was in good voice. Recovering his partner was going to be easier than he'd thought possible.

James stood to call the dog to him but the sound was lost when the truck's engine suddenly roared to life. Headlights caught Bogart in their full flare but the dog did not hesitate. He was after the truck and his barking increased, signaling that he had found his prey.

"Prince! No! Come here!" The plaintive cry of the woman who'd been on the porch diverted James's attention. She'd left the porch and was running toward the woods. "Come, Prince! Heel! Heel, boy!"

The dog paused uncertainly and turned to look back at the woman just as she entered the circle of the truck's headlights. She was dressed in sweatpants and a hoodie but her feet were bare.

"Heel! Heel, Prince!" Her voice was strained with emotion as she bent down to scoop up something.

Even as the driver threw the truck into reverse and floored the pedal, she stood up.

"Bastard!" She launched what must have been a rock or a heavy piece of a tree limb at her Peeping Tom.

James couldn't help but admire her strength and aim. The missile bounced off the hood of the truck even as it blasted backward.

"Heel! Heel, Prince!" She began running back toward the cabin.

This time Bogart didn't hesitate, he sprang after her, easily catching up and circling her with excited barks as she made her way to the porch. The pair were through the door in an instant, and then it was shut behind them with a force that reverberated through the night.

"What the fuck?" James sat back on his haunches as the sounds of the truck tearing back through the forest became ever fainter, and let his thoughts sort themselves out. First things first.

He'd seen Bogart! Knew he was okay. That was a huge relief.

But now he had other complications to deal with. Something else was going on besides the dog-napping of his K-9 partner. Something he didn't understand. But whatever the something was, he meant to get to the bottom of it.

One thing was certain. Regardless of the events of the night, the woman in the cabin was the prime suspect in the abduction of his K-9.

He should report what he'd discovered to the sheriff of this North Carolina county and ask for help. But after weeks of searching, he wanted the pleasure of confronting the suspect himself. That wasn't exactly legal procedure. Any way he factored it, he was way the hell out of his jurisdiction.

James slid a hand down his face. By nature he was a by-the-book guy, professional, methodical, reasonable. But something had snapped when Bogart went missing. The job of finding him became a personal quest. And he was going to see it through. So then, how best to confront the woman holding his dog hostage?

Maybe the woman who had his dog had abducted him herself, or maybe she had had help. No way to judge that from here.

He had learned long ago that "female" did not equal "easy to best," and certainly not "harmless." Unlike the truck driver, he wasn't going to give her the chance to get the better of him, or escape. He was going in full force and with overwhelming strength, to teach her a lesson she wouldn't soon forget.

He was just going to wait for full light.

Shay Appleton jumped up when her dog, sprawled at her feet, suddenly lifted his head to listen. "What is it, Prince?" She stared into the shiny, alert gaze of her pet with an intensity equal to his. "Do you hear something?"

Prince made a soft nasally sound but his tail did an unperturbed thump on the floor.

Shay glanced at her front door. The bolts were still shoved into place. Was that enough?

For eight heavy heartbeats she stared at the doorknob of her rental cabin, burnished by years of use. It did not turn.

Shay exhaled audibly. Okay, so maybe nothing. Of course it was nothing. Prince wasn't behaving the way he had last night when there had been a real problem.

Not until Prince lowered his head back to his paws did the warmth of spilled coffee permeate Shay's awareness the way it had her jogging shorts.

"Oh damn!" She fumbled to right her mug and grabbed for napkins to catch the steaming liquid dripping over the edge of the kitchen table.

When she was done cleaning, she picked up her empty cup and stared into its depths. She hadn't had enough sleep. And now she couldn't even blame the caffeine she had yet to drink for her nerves.

Hypervigilance. Her condition even had a name. Her doctor assured her that this latest episode would pass. Many women felt unnerved after a nasty breakup. Especially if the ex-boyfriend continued to harass her with text messages and middle-of-the-night phone calls. She was told to ignore the calls and delete the messages unread. Within a few weeks most men moved on.

Unfortunately, that prognosis hadn't made her less anxious for long. Though she had tossed away her disposable cell and bought another so that Eric could not reach her, she could not get rid of the feeling that she was being watched. Again her doctor assured her that only hypervigilance plagued her and it would subside with time.

That was a month ago.

Shay shook her head tightly. Not when it had become freakin' obvious, after last night, that there was a very real reason for it to continue!

Eric Coates wasn't most men. He had not sent angry messages or threats. He was more clever than that.

Eric had found her. Alone.

Who else would have been lurking in the woods watching this place? How had he found her?

Did it matter? He was out there, waiting.

Eric didn't know about the cabin. No one in her present life knew about this place up on the state line. It had been her refuge since age fourteen, the one safe place in the broken world of her teenage years. That was a past she had run from, and was still running from. Even now, she'd do almost anything to protect herself from it.

Shay shook her head to dispel the band of fear threatening to tighten into a headache. She was an idiot to have left the city for an off-season cabin in the woods. She'd just provided him with the perfect place—

"No." She raised both hands as if she could physically chase away the negative thoughts. "No!"

The shock of a wet nose poking her behind the knee jolted her.

She glanced down as Prince pushed his weight against her leg and stared up at her in question, alert to every nuance of her feelings. Her world righted.

She wasn't alone. *She had Prince.*

Relief slid through her as she bent and scratched her new pet behind the ears.

The fairy tales were right. There was a Prince Charming out there for her. He'd arrived in her life the day after she broke up with Eric.

And like in all fairy tales, he'd come into her life from an unexpected place, the animal shelter, in an unexpected guise, wearing a black mask with black ears, and sporting a thick black and golden doggy pelt.

They'd bonded immediately. He was extraordinarily attuned to her moods. While she didn't always trust her own reactions these days, she quickly came to trust Prince's without question. If he responded to sounds in the night, as he did last night, then she knew it wasn't just her anxiety. She needed that assurance badly.

"Good boy." She rubbed his back affectionately a couple of times before straightening up. Prince was the best thing to happen to her, maybe ever. As long as she had him she was safe.

She picked up her cup and moved to put it in the sink. She hadn't been able to force herself to return to bed after her night visitor had been chased away. Instead, she'd curled up beneath a throw on the sofa, where she could sleep with one hand on Prince's back as he lay on the rug beside her, and hold her cell phone in the other in case she needed to call for help. If the sheriff's office would believe her. The Raleigh police hadn't.

The cup rattled hard against the porcelain sink, an indication that the adrenaline-charged anxiety attack had yet to recede. Shame splashed through her at the realization that after all this time, her body could still betray her in this way.

She should have recognized the signs sooner. From the beginning of their year-long relationship she was often uncomfortable in Eric's presence. Yet, she'd never told anyone about her uncertainties concerning him. Life had long ago taught her to doubt herself. Besides, who would believe her? Eric could be outrageously generous and so charming. She was a lowly temp. She was lucky to have attracted the attention of a man with money and good looks, who took her on secret glamorous vacations.

Yet Eric could go from charming guy to complete asshole in the time it took to knock back a few tequila shots. Gradually, he became critical of her, avoided her friends, seldom took her out in public after the first few weeks of their relationship. She gave in more and more to his point of view because it was easier than facing his stern disapproval. But there was a deep well of resentment growing inside her that she hadn't realized was there until a few weeks ago. Even she had a limit.

Rough sex, he'd called it.

Shay clamped her teeth over her lower lip to stop its trembling.

She couldn't quite believe what was happening. Afterward, she'd locked herself in his bathroom and called the police. That brought the next shock.

Eric was so quick to confess that he'd gotten a little carried away, and apologized so convincingly, she could tell the police began to doubt her version of deliberate assault. Still, they said they would take her in for testing and she could file charges and take him to court.

Court. In her fury and outrage, she had forgotten. The last thing she wanted was to go to court where her personal history might be pulled up again for public view.

No, her life would be ruined all over again. Mortified, she had recanted her story.

Shay shivered, recalling her feelings of helplessness and outrage.

It was the sight of Eric's smug expression, knowing he was going to get away with what he'd done, that spurred her to blurt out that their relationship was over, right there in front of the two law enforcement officers who could not help her.

Eric didn't respond but she saw the cold fury in his expression that no one else seemed to notice. There'd been a promise in his last look, and it terrified her. She knew in her bones that he was going to get even. When she let her guard down. When she stopped worrying. When she was most vulnerable.

Shay looked out the window above the sink at the morning light reflecting off the silver surface of the lake. Its serenity didn't calm her this morning.

Since that night a month ago, she couldn't shake the panicky feelings of being followed and watched. Anxiety had her running from her own shadow. Checking and rechecking the locks. Glancing repeatedly over her shoulder until her friends became concerned by her increasingly paranoid behavior. One morning she couldn't even force herself to leave for work until Angie came and got her. Unable to explain the cause of her panic attack, she watched Angie's sympathy turn into concern for her sanity. Two days ago, she had fled Raleigh, seeking refuge in the one place where Eric wouldn't know to look for her.

Yet he had found her.

Shay closed her eyes and took a deep trembling breath.

She had known the drill from age fourteen. Self-control, that was the answer, not meds, to conquer her attacks. Time and self-awareness, those were the keys to control. She mustn't allow small things to get the better of her. She needed to think, be reasonable, and logical. Consider that she was jumping to conclusions.

She let out her breath as a quiver of apprehension rippled over her skin. She resisted it, forcing herself instead to make a mental list of other possible answers for the presence of her night visitor.

She was so certain it was Eric. What if she was wrong? The person in the truck outside her cabin could have been anyone: a camper, a hunter, even a Peeping Tom. Besides, Prince had scared whoever it was away. If he came again, she'd call the sheriff's office. Even if they didn't believe her, someone would show up.

Shay breathed in again, slower and steadier.

Today was Saturday. She'd have to go back to work on Monday. She couldn't afford to lose her position in a job market that wasn't exactly overflowing with prospects.

Get your act together, Shayla Lynn Appleton.

Shay exhaled, longer and easier this time. She could feel her heart begin to slow. She was going to be fine. She just needed to believe it. Or fake it until she could make it a reality.

A sharp, high-pitched bark made her open her eyes.

Prince had come into the kitchen and was watching her from the threshold.

As she walked over to him, his tail began wagging. Then his head swung toward the front door, head cocked as if to listen.

Shay's heart skipped as she followed his gaze. Then she spied his leash hanging by the door. "Oh, you're just trying to remind me it's time for our morning walk."

Prince shot forward with a yelp of excitement.

"Good boy."

It was clear that her pet was better trained than she was. He was trying his best to show her what he needed, but she still often misunderstood. Yet he'd acted without her direction last night, knowing instinctively that she was afraid of whatever was out there in the dark. She really did need to get them both to the doggy-training class she'd looked into, and soon. But not a fancy place like that Harmonie Kennels in Virginia that Angie had suggested she call.

"He's got the attitude of a professional canine. Maybe he's, like, a drug dog that's been retired," Angie had said after meeting Prince.

Angie, her one real friend, was like that, always seeing the extraordinary in the ordinary. Even so, Angie could be very persuasive. She kept mentioning this kennel she'd read about, supposedly the top place in the mid-Atlantic states. So, after arriving at the lake, Shay had called just to find out how much the training would cost.

The woman who answered had been much too nosy for Shay's liking, asking if her shelter dog had any distinguishing markings or ID tag. That's when it hit her that the woman who had brought Prince to the shelter might not have been entirely honest. If something was amiss, she might lose him. So she had hung up quickly, sorry she'd made the call.

As Shay came up behind him, Prince began pawing at the door, making little excited whimpering sounds.

"Fine, but you'll have to slow your pace this time." She pulled back the dead bolts then reached for the doorknob with one hand and his leash with the other. "Yesterday you nearly— Oh!"

One moment she and Prince were alone. The next she was staring into the gaze of one very stern-looking man in camo.

CHAPTER TWO

"Excuse me, ma'am. I need to talk with you. Now."

The man's tone left no room for debate as his combat-booted foot moved to block any idea Shay might have about closing her door. "Step back into the room and leave your hands where I can see them."

"What?" Shay stared stupidly at her assailant. She should be terrified but in some distant place the situation hadn't caught up with her head. Not when Prince had rushed forward and was jumping and yipping and play-pawing her attacker's arm as if this were some sort of game.

Finally, she said the only thing that came to mind. "Prince, down!"

To her surprise, the dog paused and looked at her. "Heel," she commanded, and pointed at a spot on the floor beside her right leg.

Prince moved dutifully over to her side and sat down, heavy tail thumping out a staccato rhythm of high spirits. She gripped a handful of his fur, just behind the collar, feeling the warmth of the animal as proof they were okay. This was another of Eric's sick campaigns to frighten her, she told herself. Like the night before. Only this time she'd had enough. Hiring a thug to scare her was one step too far, even for him.

All the anger of the night before came roaring back as she looked up into the scowling face of the man accosting her.

"Who the fuck do you think you are, scaring my dog like that?"

The man's gaze flickered, as if taken aback by her language. But that surprise didn't modulate his voice. "Move back into the room."

Shay bit her lip, the delayed reaction of surprise beginning to pump up her heart rate. Advice from an article about self-defense popped into her thoughts. *Never let an assailant take you to a secluded place.* Her cabin was as secluded as it got.

Shay folded her arms across her chest, tucking her hands into the folds of her elbows so he couldn't see that they were shaking. "This is my property and I haven't invited you in. You're trespassing."

A smile spread beneath the shadow of his hat brim but it was nothing like friendly. "I wouldn't be worried about my actions when yours are about to land you time in jail."

Shay slowly lowered her arms as she felt surreptitiously for the cell phone she kept hooked in her waistband for easy access.

His smile vanished. "What are you doing?"

She stilled. "Trying to scratch an itch. You make me nervous."

"Put your hands where I can see them and back up!" His voice had an edge that could cut stone. "Now!"

Though she was determined to hold her ground, when he produced a rifle and held it crosswise before him as if he might swing the butt of it at her head, Shay found herself propelled backward in spite of herself.

The man came through the door and slammed it shut with a kick of his boot.

Until this moment, she'd thought herself frightened. Now the sick wash of fear roiling up through her stomach gave her a sense of what true terror felt like.

A little hiccup of fear escaped as she bumped up against Prince, who had positioned himself behind her. What was the command for attack? Why didn't she know it? Didn't Prince realize what was happening? He hadn't required any prodding to go after the trucker lurking in the woods the night before. She had to do something.

Her shoulders slumped forward, her arms tightening against her waist, as if her stomach hurt. Her voice was subdued when she spoke. "What do you want?"

All the fight seemed to go out of the woman before James. His gaze did a quick perimeter search of the room before it came back to her. She was standing with her eyes downcast.

He lowered his rifle. "I'm going to ask you a few questions. You better give me all the right answers. Do you understand me?"

The woman merely nodded. He took her by the chin and raised her face to his. "Do you understand me?"

"Yes." It was a whisper of a reply. Terrified eyes gazed up at him, eyes as golden brown as the morning autumn forest he'd just stepped out of. He felt like a bully staring into them, but dammit, she deserved no pity. She had started this mess by kidnapping his dog.

He released her. "Is there anyone else here with you?"

She looked sideways, as if assessing her options, then shook her head.

"Good answer. It better be truthful. Are there other dogs on the premises?"

Suddenly, she pulled her hands from their tucked position and began yelling into her cell phone. "Help! Help! He's got a gun!"

"Fuck!" He dropped his rifle and grabbed her from behind as she tried to get away. Bogart took this as his cue to once again join in the fray, and began jumping and barking in unbridled joy.

"Brouza Hund! Platz!" James's drill-sergeant tone caused the dog to obey instantly. He moved several feet away from the pair and dropped into a submissive crouch. Too bad the woman in his arms wasn't so easily mastered.

He had dropped a hand over her mouth to stop the shouting but she continued to kick and twist, rubbing her body against his in ways that made him register that she was young and in good shape, and smelled like the kind of fresh-brewed coffee he'd give his left nut to have a cup of right now.

For his peace of mind, and before she hurt herself, he overwhelmed her protest by scooping her up off the floor with an arm about her middle. "Settle down, dammit, or I'll cuff your hands and feet. Do you understand?"

She stilled but didn't respond. But of course, he realized, she couldn't speak with his hand over her mouth. He lifted it.

She sank her teeth into the meaty edge of his hand. As he released her, she twisted and lifted her knee in a quick jab to his groin.

If he hadn't been a police officer she might have caught him off guard, but he was accustomed to dealing with suspects. The bite hurt but her knee bounced harmlessly off the thigh he lifted to deflect her jab. He did lose his hat as she swung a slap in his direction before dancing away.

The hellcat palmed her phone and began jabbing numbers into it.

"Shit! Give me that!" He jerked the phone from her hand.

Shay stumbled back out of his reach but lifted her chin in triumph. "Too late! I've already called 911 once. You'd better leave. The police will be here any minute."

"Dammit, lady! I *am* the police!"

As his roar of rage died away, James glanced at her phone. Sure enough, she'd dialed the emergency number. He ended the call and tucked it in his pocket. He had to give her credit. She had balls.

He swiveled his head in her direction. For the first time she came into focus as a person, and it was a revelation. She was about five six, with a thick mahogany ponytail that had been skewed to one side by their struggle. Thick dark bangs framed her eyes, which appeared darker than before and were narrowed in calculation. But to be honest, he was more interested in the fact that her hoodie had come unzipped and it was spectacularly obvious that she wasn't wearing a bra.

She followed his pointed gaze to where the vee of her jacket had widened to the waist and the globes of her breasts were trembling with the heated rise and fall of her breath.

"Pervert!" She jerked her zipper up, her cheeks coloring with emotion, anger, or embarrassment, he couldn't tell. The zipper didn't budge. Cussing under her breath, she yanked again, and then a third time before it moved, locking the plastic teeth back together all the way up to her chin.

James stood staring at her a moment longer, wondering whether she'd yanked open her jacket to distract him or if it was just an accident. Either way, he was distracted. None of this had gone the way he'd expected.

He glanced over at his long-lost partner to help him regain his balance. Bogart sat up and gazed at him with a lolling-tongue expression that looked for all the world like a big fat grin.

James's attention switched back to the woman. She had recovered her composure with surprising speed. But her expression caught him totally off guard. She wasn't just angry; she was dead furious and ready to do battle.

He watched her judge the distance between herself and the door and then between herself and him, before she spoke. "You say you're police? I want to see some ID. Now."

He reached into his jacket for his badge and then held it out toward her. "Charlotte-Mecklenburg Police Department, Special Operations Division."

Shay glanced at the shiny badge and then up into his face. If she'd been asked before this moment what her attacker looked like, all she could have described was a very angry male in camouflage clothing with a rifle.

Now she needed a whole new vocabulary.

He was young, maybe not even thirty, and tall. And he was gorgeous. He had that old-fashioned handsomeness with a broad brow and strong jaw, baby blues, spiky short dark hair, and the kind of mouth that made bad boys so irresistible. Not that it made any difference. So what if his muscular shoulders and tapered hips gave him the look of an Abercrombie & Fitch model? He had attacked her. In her home.

Shay tore her gaze away. *Stop staring.* Where was her sanity?

She drew herself up and found a safe place halfway between his chin and his belt buckle to stare at. "Why the hell would you break in here like that?"

"You're in possession of a canine belonging to Charlotte-Mecklenburg law enforcement."

Shay's gaze jerked up to his face. Even his scowl was, well, damn sexy, now that she didn't feel her life was in danger. Then understanding dawned.

She moved quickly over to stand by her pet. "I don't know what you're talking about. This is my dog, Prince."

"The hell he is! That's my dog, Bogart."

Both turned to gaze at the dog who had been silently watching them. The K-9 barked twice, thumping his tale in good spirits, but didn't move an inch.

They seemed to be at an impasse.

Which was just as well, because the siren wail of a law enforcement vehicle closing in fast was filling the morning with sound.

A minute later a sheriff's vehicle rolled to a stop in her yard.

CHAPTER THREE

"Hello, Shay." Chief Deputy Sheriff Elijah Ward stood wide-legged on the porch of Shay's home, surveying her through the mirrored lenses of his shades. "You make a 911 call?"

"Yes!" The deputy was one of the local enforcement officers she'd known since she was a teen. He was a big man, twenty years her senior, with a polished-pecan complexion sprinkled with chocolate freckles across his broad nose and cheeks. "I'm glad you got here so fast."

"I was just round the bend in the lake, checking on Malcolm's house. Everything okay?"

"No." Shay pushed her door wide and pointed inside to the man standing in shadow several feet behind her. "This man just forced his way into my house. I want you to arrest him."

The deputy whipped off his shades with a crooked finger as he entered the room. The stranger in question stood at ease but slowly lifted both hands as the lawman approached. "Ms. Appleton says you forced your way in here against her will." He squinted at the man dressed as a hunter. "What do you have to say about that?"

"It's a misunderstanding, Deputy." James turned his right hand palm out so that his badge was in view. "I'm on a case. My name's James Cannon, Charlotte-Mecklenburg police."

"You got a driver's license, son?"

James duly produced it.

The deputy examined the badge and license closely then nodded in seeming satisfaction. "What brings a Charlotte officer over to this part of the state?"

"The theft of a K-9." James lowered his hands as relief flooded through him. The deputy could have made things hard for him if he had wanted to. "This young woman is in possession of a canine in service with my police department. I came to arrest her for dog-napping."

Shay took a step toward James. "You lying son of a—"

The deputy cut her off with a raised hand. "Dog-napping." He continued to stare at James. "Is that a real crime?"

"Yes, sir." James reined in his annoyance. There were still people even in law enforcement who saw K-9s as little more than tools instead of valued partners. "My canine partner was kidnapped from a vehicle in Charlotte a month ago. I doubt you got a bulletin about it all the way up here. But I've been following leads for weeks. It led me here. I should probably have come to the sheriff's office first, but when I saw Bogart in this yard last night—" He noted Shay's jerk of surprise at his mention of the night before, and filed that reaction away for later. "You could say I lost perspective."

"Over your pet." The deputy's tone was still skeptical.

"Bogart's a highly trained and crucial member of the K-9 service."

The deputy turned his gaze on the big-eared dog who

sat happily panting away at Shay's side. "What have you got to say about this, Ms. Appleton?"

"This is my dog. I adopted him from animal control last month."

"The hell you did."

Shay took an instinctive step back at James's hard tone. His expression was neutral but the tension in his body could not be interpreted as anything other than coiled strength under stress.

Deputy Wood moved his considerable bulk between James and Shay. "Easy, Officer. Go on, Shay. Tell the man your story."

Shay shot James a rude look. "I volunteer at one of the animal shelters in Raleigh. I was at the desk when a woman came in with Prince." She reached out to rest her hand territorially on her dog's head.

Her accuser shifted his weight, as if uncomfortable. "What name did she give?"

"She didn't."

"Keep talking."

Shay sucked in a breath of annoyance. She'd never done well with authority. His every word sounded like an interrogation. It was reminiscent of Eric in a bad mood. It worked her temper. "The woman said her dog had mauled a child's pet. That's why she had a muzzle on him. She said he was vicious and uncontrollable, and needed to be put down before he could hurt someone else."

James swiped a hand over his mouth to block the vulgarity he couldn't quite squelch as he gazed down at Bogart. The eager interest in his partner's black eyes and happy thump of his tail highlighted the absurdity of the accusation. Bogart was too well trained to attack without cause. Yet his partner was capable of becoming a very dangerous adversary if commanded to be so. Had Bogart gotten frightened and attacked a child's pet? He doubted that. Yet his heart tripled its beat. Everything he learned from now on could be crucial to protecting his partner's future.

When James's gaze rose to meet Shay's again, it was the opaque, official stare of a lawman on duty. "She told you specifically to put him down?"

She nodded.

"Shit!"

Shay decided she couldn't have worded her own response to the idea any better.

"Continue."

"I told her our shelter doesn't destroy an animal unless it's so sick or injured that a vet recommends it. Or we have a formal complaint and court order. That's when she got all huffy and said she didn't have time for all that. If we wouldn't destroy him, then she'd find a place that would."

"Why didn't you ask for verification of her accusation?"

Shay folded her arms protectively across her chest. "We aren't the animal police. When a person walks in the door with a pet, shelters don't ask them to prove ownership. We allow a person to surrender their pet without question. It's better than trying to catch animals after they've been abandoned."

"Go on."

Shay glanced away, flushing with annoyance. Definitely, this guy was a cop.

"She was leaving when I decided something wasn't right. Prince wasn't showing any signs of aggression or anxiety. He even ignored a kitten that got loose from its owner and wandered over to brush up against him before being retrieved. So I stopped her and said that I'd fudge a few things, and personally take care of her dog."

"You let her think you'd destroy him?"

Shay smirked at her interrogator. "I let her think what she wanted to think so she'd leave him with me. She actually gave me a ten-dollar tip."

"That was fast thinking, Shay." The deputy looked at James for confirmation.

James nodded. "No argument with you there."

Shay let the deputy's praise wash over her as she knelt down and hugged Prince's neck.

The action exposed a collar James had not seen before. It was royal blue with rhinestones and silver studs. He winced at seeing his partner decorated like some kind of show dog. Yet he couldn't fault the instincts of the woman before him for recognizing what a great dog Bogart was.

As for Bogart's would-be executioner, an ugly suspicion had begun to creep into his mind. "Describe the woman who brought him in."

Shay was really beginning to hate the way this man talked in commands. "Tall. Lots of blond hair and makeup. With big boobs. Your type, right?"

Shay was surprised to see her interrogator blush. Then she realized it wasn't embarrassment but the seething complexion of a man about to blow his top.

"Any of this making sense to you, son?" Deputy Ward watched James with a raised brow.

"Yes, sir. Though I never would have thought—" James quashed the expletive that accompanied any thought of Jaylynn Turner. She had been a three-month nightmare in his life. He should have listened to . . . hell, everyone. His friends, his sisters, even Bogart seemed to find fault with her. She was just one of those dumb things men sometimes succumb to when they were following their dicks.

But never in a million years would he have thought she

would stoop so low as to steal Bogart, and then try to have him put down.

Another thought struck him, one that made him queasy. He eyed Bogart with some anxiety. "They neuter animals before they're allowed out for adoption."

Shay seethed under the glare of his stare. Even his questions didn't end in question marks. "It wasn't a formal adoption."

James's exhale of relief was audible. "I guess I owe you a debt there."

She snorted. "I didn't do it for you. The shelter people agreed that because she handed him over to me, personally, there was no need for an adoption."

"Well, then, no harm done." The deputy hooked his thumbs in his belt, all smiles to have the matter settled. "I've known Shay a long time. I can vouch for her."

Shay felt the hair rise on the back of her neck. "Excuse me, Deputy Ward. I'm not the one who needs a character reference here. He broke into my house."

As she said this Prince decided he'd been obedient long enough. He leaped up on her, barking and wagging his tail.

Trying to hold on to her outrage under the onslaught of Prince's doggy affection, she hauled him in by the collar. "My dog needs to go out before he pees all over the place. Excuse me."

She walked over to her door and reached once again for the leash, and a net bag that she slung over a shoulder. To her consternation Prince wasn't the only one to follow her. Her intruder crossed the room toward her.

After she snapped on Prince's leash, she turned on him, thunder in her expression. "We don't need company."

James reached down and scratched Bogart behind the ears, smiling despite his anger at the situation. Bogart answered his affection with long wet licks of his hand and wrist. Happy for actual physical contact with the friend he'd thought he'd lost forever, he bent to allow Bogart to lick his face. No matter how awful the day, how tired or weary or worried he was, having Bogart within reach calmed him down.

It worked. In fact, his voice sounded almost mild when James stood up and spoke to Shay. "I'm coming with you."

"Hold up, son." Deputy Ward waved James toward him. "I'm calling this in. I may need some additional verification from you." He stepped away from them as his radio crackled to life on his shoulder.

James bent down again. "I'm taking this damn decoration off before Bogart catches it on something and chokes." He unsnapped her leash, released Bogart's fancy blue collar and tossed it aside. He shoved a hand into one of the deep pockets in his camo pants and pulled out a nylon service collar with the word "police" spelled out in block letters. He strapped it around the dog's neck.

When he stood up, James gave Shay his most intimidating look. "Don't do anything stupid."

Refusing to give him the satisfaction of an answer, Shay simply opened the door. Bogart shot through it like a furry cannonball. Without a backward glance, she followed at a more leisurely pace.

James stood in the open doorway to watch. His well-honed instincts about people told him that she wouldn't skip out on the local deputy, yet he remained unable to take his eyes off her.

Once across the grassy expanse of lawn into the edge of the woods, Bogart went about taking care of his needs in rapid order. Only then did he come bounding back to Shay, who waited patiently in the middle of the yard.

The morning had turned into one of those glorious autumn days with bright golden light spiking between the trunks of bare-limbed trees near the horizon. The odor of freshly cut grass drifted in from across the lake, and James knew the chill of the crisp-smelling air would soon give way to the deep-South warmth of a buttered sunshine afternoon.

Bogart was loving it.

James watched in affection as his partner raced back toward Shay in long loping strides. He was a bit small for a Belgian Malinois, sixty-five pounds compared to the average size of the breed, whose weight could range upward of eighty pounds. The usual golden coat of the breed was in Bogart's case so heavily peppered in places it looked as if he'd been rolling in ashes. And, like the most famous characters played by his Hollywood namesake, Bogart was often underestimated by strangers until put to the test. He was capable of staring down any suspect, leaning his slightly oversized head to one side as he assessed a situation, ready for action when intimidation didn't work.

James smirked. His partner was a bit of a rascal, too. He liked to hide things and wait to be ordered to find them. And when he didn't like someone—for instance a competitive girlfriend like Jaylynn—a shoe, or a purse, or even a cell phone might get "accidentally" chewed.

As James watched, Shay produced a brightly colored tennis ball from her bag and tossed it with the same good right arm she'd used to lob that branch at the mystery vehicle the night before.

James frowned as Bogart took off after the ball, wondering what that episode the night before had been about. He glanced back at the deputy who was busy calling on his radio, wondering if he should mention it. Of course a better question was, why hadn't *she* mentioned it? One would have thought she'd have connected his intrusion to her unwelcome night visitor. Unless she knew who the visitor was.

His attention came back to Shay with renewed intensity. She was hiding something. He could feel it in his gut. She'd been afraid the night before but attacked anyway, just as she'd done with him. His hand still throbbed where she'd bitten him, even though she'd barely broken the skin. Scared but not cowed. Who was this woman?

She was athletic, no doubt about it. As she chased after dog and ball, she moved with the unconscious grace of a person who was at home in, not at constant odds with, her body. He was surprised to see her produce another ball. K-9s were taught to chase and hold, not play chase and retrieve. How had she discovered that?

She also obviously understood that Bogart had high energy and needed to be exercised regularly. Her second throw was long and high. Bogart went after it at top speed.

James turned back and scanned the cabin's central room, noticing that the only personal property on view was a laptop on the dining table. Had she looked up Belgian Malinois on the Web? Maybe that's how she knew he needed to be managed with exercise and companionship.

Jaylynn never got that. The time he spent with his partner was not to slight her but to keep Bogart from becoming anxious and frustrated, which would lead to him becoming bored, and making mischief. For instance, chewing up a pair of her five-hundred-dollar shoes because Jaylynn couldn't be bothered walking him on the one rare occasion when James wasn't there to do it.

Shay's cries of approval, as Bogart ran down another toss caught on the wind and came sailing back, snared his attention once again.

Encouraged by her responses, Bogart began to show off. No longer content to chase a ball after it landed, he ran out ahead of her throws. Then he stopped short and leaped high to snag the ball out of the air. Pretty soon he had lined up a group of six balls on his side of the field, placed side by side.

James couldn't blame his partner for wanting to show off for this woman. Her laughter was full throated and a little husky in a way that made it a pleasure a man wanted to hear repeatedly, and often. It settled in his belly and moved lower down until it reached his groin.

Get a grip, Cannon.

When her supply was depleted, she walked out to retrieve the balls. As she picked up the final one, Bogart jumped on her, using his strong back legs to propel him forward. Shay fell sideways onto the grass.

Heart leaping into his throat, James jumped off the porch to go break up what could so easily turn dangerous for a dog trained to catch and hold a suspect. But before he covered more than six feet he again heard her laughter. It came in gurgles and spurts as she covered her face to keep her companion from licking every inch of it.

James paused to watch them with more than a little surprise. Never in a million years would Jaylynn have gotten down and dirty in the grass with a dog, especially not one who had a mouth full of teeth that could tear flesh. Or one that drooled in her hair as he playfully tugged Shay's ponytail. It struck him that this was not something spontaneous between the two but a game they must have played often during the time they'd been together.

An alien feeling not unlike jealousy whipped through him.

At that moment Shay looked back at the cabin and noticed him watching her. She sat up, her smiles dissolving into a mask of dislike as she wrapped her arms protectively about Bogart's neck.

Annoyed, James turned away. He didn't like the feelings she'd stirred up in him. Even less did he like the fact he had noticed how her breasts jiggled beneath her hoodie, reminding him how he knew that she wasn't wearing a bra.

How long since I've gotten laid?

James rubbed a hand down his face. He was exhausted. Not thinking right. Whatever was running through his mind and body was nothing more than the result of fatigue and casual lust. He needed lots of hot coffee. His stomach growled, reminding him that some eggs and pancakes and maybe a thick slice of ham wouldn't be unwelcome, either.

Surprisingly, Shay came in right behind him with Bogart at her side, ears alert with interest and his tongue lolling from his mouth in satisfied fatigue. He came up to James and bumped his leg with his big head, which James immediately patted.

A little winded and even more disheveled than before, Shay ignored James as she walked over to the deputy who had just finished his radio conversation. "So what happens now?"

The deputy's gaze shifted between the parties before him. "I suppose you can produce some paperwork with proof of ownership, Officer Cannon?"

James nodded. "I have it in my truck. It's parked at a gas station about two miles from here. I can bring it by your office."

Shay swung around on him. "He wasn't chipped. We checked at the shelter. If this is your dog, and a service animal, why isn't he chipped?"

Rather than answer directly, James made a gesture

with his hand. Instantly Bogart went prone and then rolled over.

James knelt and reached for one of Bogart's hind legs and pulled it wide as his fingers delved into the fine fringe of golden pelt at the base of his partner's belly. There, just inside the hairline, were a series of tattooed numbers.

Shay glanced away. She knew about the tattoo but— dammit!

James looked up at the lawman bending over his shoulder. "Bogart was chipped in Germany. U.S. scanners can't read them. That's why I had my driver's license number tattooed backward here. You can compare them if you want."

The deputy straightened up. "I'm satisfied, Mr. Cannon. But there are formalities. So let's go get your paperwork."

"Wait just a minute." Shay stepped forward. "I don't care what kind of proof he has. He can't just come in here and take my dog."

The deputy sighed like a man who was accustomed to dealing with the public at its most illogical. "Now, Shay, you understand what happened and know what's right. He's got proof of ownership."

"But Prince was abandoned!" Shay heard the rising anxiety in her voice but she couldn't stop it. She turned to James. "I own him by right of—of salvage."

James looked up at her. *Doesn't she know when a fight is over?*

Forcing himself to remain detached, he rose to his feet. Yet he couldn't block the effect her golden gaze had on him. Though he doubted he'd ever see her again, he knew he'd be a long time forgetting the righteous fury in her oh-so-expressive gaze.

"You're right, Ms. Appleton. I owe you my thanks. You saved Bogart's life."

"You're damn right I did." Shay blinked back the very idea of tears, horrified that he might notice the telltale gleam. "And his name is Prince."

Deputy Ward laid a hand on her shoulder. "The fact is, this man can prove the dog's his. I'm sorry but that's the way it is."

James watched Shay chew the inside of her lip. He knew she was trying hard not to defend her position again. Despite the fact that he was sympathetic to her point of view, it wouldn't alter the outcome. Bogart was his partner. They belonged together.

Still, that chewing got to him, on several levels, not the least of which was the feeling stirring in his pants. Standing there with her skewed ponytail and tousled bangs, she looked like an abandoned creature herself.

James turned away from the raw emotion in her face, as much to protect his peace of mind as her feelings.

Shay backed up against the wall as the lawman from Charlotte took her Prince by the collar and snapped on a leash he had produced from his pocket. She crossed her arms to rub the goose bumps that had arisen. She was an adult. She'd learned much too early how very unfair the world could be. She'd learned to expect less than most people from life. Yet . . .

Until this moment, somewhere deep inside her had lived the ridiculous hope that Prince really belonged to her, that it was all a misunderstanding and that, at the end of the day, he would be curled up against her as she slept. Now she could no longer deny it. Prince belonged to someone else.

The unfairness of it all overwhelmed her good sense, rising as a stinging heat up through her legs and thighs into her stomach and then up into her chest and neck and face. She couldn't breathe. The only action inside her was the hard hammering of her heart. As the sensation ebbed away, taking her hope and leaving behind a great sense of loss and impotence, fury once again flared up within her.

"I want to press charges against this man, for trespassing."

CHAPTER FOUR

Shay swung around on the deputy. "I want him arrested! I can demand that."

Deputy Ward sighed the sigh of a man who sometimes hated his job. "You can. But I wouldn't advise it."

"Why? Because he's a police officer?"

Deputy Ward tucked in his chin. "That's not the issue."

"He admitted to you he broke in. You're my witness."

The deputy looked even more uncomfortable. "Can I speak with you a moment? In private."

James looked around. "Do I smell coffee?" Without being invited, he headed toward a doorway through which a range top could be seen. Bogart followed obediently on the leash.

The deputy hitched up his pants before he began speaking in a low voice. "I know you're fond of the dog but you don't want to do this, Ms. Appleton."

Shay breathed through her nose before replying. "All I want is my dog. I'll drop the charges if I can keep Prince."

"*Uh-huh*. But that's not how it's going to go down. And I got to warn you that attempting to take a law enforcement officer to court will be a sorry business. You've got a history of . . . let's just call it unreliable behavior."

"You mean because of what happened when I was a child?"

The deputy shifted from one foot to the other but there was sympathy in his gaze. "We've known you a long time, Shay. The sheriff and your mama were close friends. Did all he could for you two." His gaze strayed away. "But we haven't seen you in, what, three years? And last time you were here you reported seeing individuals on your property. That all turned out to be nothing."

The heat of indignation flared so hotly Shay could scarcely draw breath. "So you think I'm either a liar or a nutcase?"

His gaze came back to her, his expression apologetic. "What I'm saying, Ms. Appleton, is you've got a history of being high-strung. Your mother, God rest her soul, did her best to protect you back then. But you've got an established pattern of erratic behavior. Heck, I almost didn't rush over this morning on account of that. A good lawyer, if he did a little digging . . ." He lowered his voice. "Now you don't want that."

The word "digging" stopped Shay's next argument even as it was forming. Heart hammering in rage, she looked away.

"All done?" James stepped out beyond the wall that had shielded him, no coffee cup in sight. As much as he craved that cup of coffee, he'd opted for information about Shay Appleton instead.

The pair broke apart like conspirators caught in the act. Shay turned an ugly glare on him, as if she had guessed he was spying on her.

The deputy stepped up, as if to once again shield Shay. "All done. Ms. Appleton isn't pressing charges."

Half in shadow behind the officer, Shay didn't respond, yet James could feel the hostility radiating off her.

He wanted to ask a dozen questions about what he'd just overheard. Then common sense nudged him, hard. *Do you have time to dick around, waiting for answers that probably won't come and wouldn't mean anything to you if they did?* No, he did not. Time to go home.

"If we're done here, I'd like to get on with the formalities, Deputy, so I can head back to Charlotte."

Shay moved to stand between him and the door and folded her arms, defiance in her cocked hip. "Are you really going to take my dog?"

James had dealt with a lot of suspects, furious that they had just been arrested. Some were riddled with disbelief they had been caught. Others were so whacked-out on drugs they thought they were Batman, Iron Man, and the Hulk all rolled into one. Yet the singular anger in her golden eyes seemed to scorch him right down to his short hairs. It was a real and very personal thing. Nothing like the irrational anger of a strung-out, maddened, or intoxicated suspect. Her gaze was clear and focused and aimed at him.

It hit him like a punch in the gut. What had happened to make such a pretty woman capable of so much hostility?

For an instant he thought she might attack if he moved even a toe toward the door. It was a raw moment. He wasn't afraid. He just didn't know how to defuse the situation.

The impact of her defiance changed shape in that moment. Suddenly his discomfort wasn't about besting the woman before him. It was a purely sexual response.

He noticed how her thick fall of shiny bangs framed the most expressive pair of eyes he'd ever looked into. He saw her full lower lip tremble and wondered if she knew what that kind of thing did to a man's libido. Her old-fashioned, fresh-scrubbed prettiness might not be popular in a world that demanded long, lean, and edgy. Yet he was intrigued. He wondered what she was like when she didn't feel under siege.

He saw her eyes flare slightly in awareness of the attraction that must be showing through his stare. Her pupils went supernova, the black eating up the gold until he felt as if he were staring into her soul. It was a hungry, lonely soul, one that overwhelmed his senses.

James stomped on his emotions as he looked away first.

He felt sorry for her, he did. But whatever was wrong was Deputy Ward's problem. He'd done what he came to do, recover his partner. He wasn't going to let a pair of golden-brown eyes make him feel guilty and horny and— *Shit!*

He reached into his pocket, pulled out his wallet, and withdrew all thirty-four dollars. He held it out to her. "For your trouble."

Her gaze shifted from his hand to his face. He saw her mouth go tight, pinching off its lush natural fullness until all that was left was a white rim of mute rage.

He put the money away, so unnerved that his hand shook a little.

"Bogart. *Hier!*" The sound of James's command voice snapped his partner to attention and he trotted over to his handler's side.

"No, Prince! Heel!" Shay stood with her hand held out, a red rubber ball balanced in her palm. "Let's play, boy. Come on." She bounced the ball with a whack against the wooden floor.

Bogart paused, looked back at her and then at James.

Months before, James had worked out a nonverbal secret signal with Bogart after a fleeing suspect—who he later learned had once worked in the K-9 corps—had almost succeeded in calling Bogart off the attack. When he made that hand signal, only he could countermand.

He signed. *"Hier."*

The dog sprang to his side.

He felt a surge of triumph to have won his dog's loyalty back, but when he turned to Shay he saw the sick look of humiliation on her face and felt like a bully. Damn! She was breaking his balls one minute and his heart the next.

He picked up his rifle and his hat and headed for the door. As he reached the threshold, music began issuing inexplicably from his pocket. He reached in and pulled out an unfamiliar cell phone playing Katy Perry's "Wide Awake" as its ringtone. It was the disposable he'd taken from Shay.

"That's mine."

The heat of embarrassment stung his neck as he handed it over.

Shay snatched it and answered. Her face went white and then she whispered into the phone, "Go to hell!"

She punched "end" and turned around to face her audience. She didn't look at the deputy. She shot James a look hot enough to scorch ground. "Telemarketer."

CHAPTER FIVE

Shay realized too late that she should have been paying more attention.

She had been holed up in the cabin most of the day, mourning the loss of Prince. Yet the afternoon's warmth had drawn her out into the sunshine. Needing some exercise, she had walked along the perimeter of the lake to a convenience store/bait stand two miles away where she'd bought fresh-shucked oysters packed in ice to make for dinner. She was nearly to the cabin porch before she saw the truck turning into her drive.

Eric!

The cold fear of the night before swept over her again, leaving her weak and tingly. She reached for her phone only to discover it wasn't in her pocket. Her heart did a sickly double thump. She'd left it to charge in the cabin.

She nearly ran inside and slammed the door. Yet it was too late to do that without showing him exactly how scared she was of him. Besides, there was no Prince there to protect her. She'd have to depend on the sheriff's department again . . . if they would even respond this time.

She grabbed her left elbow with her right hand, hugging her icy package to her body as she stood in the yard, and waited. She was all alone. She'd better get used to that.

He climbed out of a truck so old and beat-up she would not have thought a bank executive like Eric Coates would be seen dead in it. Was that the point? No one would suspect he'd be driving it?

He looked the same, totally put together in jeans and a jacket and loafers. Hard to believe that underneath that polished exterior was an asshole who enjoyed making waitresses cry. That was one of his specialties, finding fault and then humiliating servers he decided weren't up to his standards. It shamed her now to remember how she'd said nothing.

As long as it's not aimed at me. That pitiful excuse seemed unthinkable now.

He paused a few yards from her and struck a casual wide-legged pose. No doubt, for her benefit. Then he smiled. "Hey there, Shay. How are you?"

"How did you find me?"

"Your phone's GPS."

"What?"

"Come on. You're supposed to be the techie." He made quote marks with his fingers for emphasis. "There's an app for that."

She frowned. There were several location apps. Except that she always kept her GPS on off. She certainly didn't need it to come up here. He must have discovered her whereabouts another way, and was trying to hide the truth.

Alarm zinged through her. *Not an app.* "You put a tracking device on my phone!"

He grinned. "I like to keep up with my favorite people. Lucky, huh, or I wouldn't be here."

Shay breathed in slowly. *The crazy-making sensation*

of being watched hadn't been her imagination. "You've been stalking me from the beginning."

Instead of showing irritation he continued to smile. "I like to think I was looking after you. You've always kept secrets from me, Shay. Like why you change phones every six months. I let you think that was okay because I'd know if you were lying. So, yeah, I knew you left Raleigh three days ago. But, with all the responsibilities of my job, I had to wait until the weekend to follow you. Now we can talk uninterrupted."

Feeling violated gave her courage. "We have nothing to say to one another."

"That's not how I figure it." He flared his coat to place a hand on each hip, his tone the reassuring one she heard him use when dealing with bank customers. "I just can't leave you thinking that I am some sort of monster. I never meant for things to get out of hand the way they did the night you walked out on me."

He made it sound as if his behavior had been no worse than ordering two desserts after a huge meal.

The tension running between them was familiar, if unwelcome. It made her accusation a stammer. "Y-you raped me."

He shrugged. "So, we got a little kinky. Everybody's trying things these days. I saw those books you've been reading. So don't try to make this about me because you decided you didn't like it. I even tried to protect you from your mistake. My apology to the police sounded absolutely believable, didn't it?" His tone of voice practically begged her to toss him a bone of compromise.

Shay ground her teeth together to keep from giving in to the old impulse to make excuses for his cruelty. He could be a very persuasive man, twisting things just enough to make her doubt herself. Over and over, she'd caved in, only to feel like a fool later after he had gotten his way. But not anymore.

"Just go away, Eric."

Did she see a hint of annoyance before he looked away?

He took a moment to survey his surroundings, the cabin and then the lake beyond. "Nice place. Have you come here before?"

Her silence seemed to encourage him. He took a few more steps toward her. "You never mentioned that you could afford to rent a cabin. Why didn't you tell me, Shay? You know how much I like to get away from the city on the weekends."

He glanced around a second time. "Of course, the cabin's not much. All a temp's salary can afford. But I like to rough it once in a while."

The look he gave her made Shay suck in a breath.

The sound of a snapping twig caused a sharp jerk of his head toward the woods. "Where's your dog?"

For a split second she thought about lying. But he'd realize soon enough that Prince wasn't here. "Due back from the groomers." She made herself hold his stare. "Any minute."

He hunched his shoulders against her words, a sullen look creeping into his expression. "You got a dog when you know I have allergies. That was thoughtless."

"I didn't—" Shay took a deep breath. *No more explanations. No more apologies.*

But she knew she'd shown her vulnerable side as a smile tugged at his mouth. "It's cooler out here than in the city. Mind if we step inside?"

Everything in her cried, *Don't let him in.* Yet that's where her phone was, and she needed to get to it.

A nervous tic jerked the edges of her lips. "No. We don't need to talk. I've heard your apology. Let's part as . . .

friends." She turned away, not too quickly so as to seem frightened.

She stepped up on the porch, refusing to look back over her shoulder for fear she would give her nervousness away. If she could just get inside, she'd be okay.

The moment her key turned in the lock, he moved behind her much more quickly than she had thought possible, and pushed the door wide.

Shay leaped away from him. Spying her phone on the table by the chair, she lunged across the room and scooped it up in her free hand before facing him. "Get out before I call the sheriff."

"Okay, okay." He lifted both hands as if he were under arrest. After a quick glance around he shoved at the door with his foot. It didn't quite close but he didn't seem to care. "Did you like my flowers?"

"No." She decided not to provoke him by saying she threw them away, along with the note signed "Mine forever." It had sounded to her more like a threat than a lover's promise. "We're exes, Eric."

He gave a little jerk of his head, as if to dismiss her words. "You wanted me to work for it. I got that message. Here I am. Aren't you glad I didn't give up? Most men would have, a long time ago."

The wet chill from the oyster bag she still clutched had seeped into her tee and made her shiver. "Then you should be glad to be rid of me."

He paused and stared at her. "Yes. But I'm the loyal sort. Why aren't you the loyal sort, Shay?"

He sounded wounded, as if she really had hurt him. It tugged an old reaction in her, one that made her want to make things right. Then she remembered the tracking device.

Never taking her eyes off him, she made herself remember a week ago, when he'd shown up unexpectedly at a bar and grill where she was having dinner with Angie and Henry, friends from work. He had slid into the booth beside her and put an arm around her as if they were still a couple. Her friends had said nothing. Embarrassed and not wanting to make a scene, she said nothing, either. But when she slipped outside, on the pretext of going to the restroom, she had discovered that two of her car tires were flat.

Before she could call for help, Eric had appeared in the parking lot. He pressed her to let him drive her home, saying how dangerous it was for a woman to be out at night alone. It was the gleam in his eyes that gave away the truth. He had slashed her tires. But she had no proof, and he knew it.

So she'd run back into the restaurant and asked Angie and Henry for help. When they came out, Eric was nowhere to be seen.

A shiver rippled over Shay's arms. She was isolated, nowhere to run this time, and he knew it.

His gaze shifted to the fireplace where wood had been laid for a fire, and the sheepskin rug before it. "Nice. Cozy. Almost like you were expecting me."

He looked back at her, his eyes a little sleepy in that way he had when his thoughts had turned to sex. "You hurt me, Shay. I don't mind admitting it. I keep thinking, what if we had a whole weekend alone to talk about things? I know we could work this out."

"We're over." Her finger slid over the emergency key of her phone in warning.

"Yeah, about that." He rubbed his forehead. "I've got some news you need to hear from me." When Shay didn't bother to respond he said, "I'm engaged."

Shay opened her mouth and shut it. And opened it. "Who?"

"She lives in Atlanta. Daughter of a state senator. We were seeing each other before I met you. But then she started jerking me around, wouldn't commit. So I told her I needed a breather. It worked. She didn't last a month before she called, saying she couldn't live without me."

Shay absorbed this information without an outward reaction. *Eric had been back together with the woman who is now his fiancée for nearly the entire year I had thought I was exclusive with him.*

Shay swallowed her resentment and disgust. "Does she know about me?"

He shrugged. "Women. They screw with your mind. Want to call the shots in a relationship. But in the end, what they want is a man who's in charge. You know the feeling, right?" He glanced at her from beneath his brows, a bad-boy-with-a-please-forgive-me pose.

Shay knew she should just agree with him, in the hope that he would leave. But then he'd have gotten everything his way. As usual. The heavy thumps of her heart weren't just from fear. Anger spurred that pump, too. She'd just spent a miserable month fighting her own self-doubts and vulnerabilities. That was his fault. She just couldn't let him get away with thinking he had bested her.

"Why were you seeing me if you had her?"

He looked a little annoyed. "Her daddy's had me dancing a damn two-step courtship these last ten months. You were my no-strings revenge fuck."

Shay didn't even feel insulted by his crude remark. Instinct told her he'd come here to do more than gloat, and that's where the danger lay.

She dropped the bag of oysters on the table and clutched her phone to her chest where he couldn't miss noticing it. "You need to leave."

His head jerked up, annoyance spoiling his good looks. "Now see. I'm asking you to understand my situation. But you won't even try to understand. You'd rather jerk my chain." He folded his arms casually across his chest.

"Get this straight, Shay. I'm not leaving until I get what I came for."

"You don't get to make threats anymore."

"Threats? I'm not threatening you." His tone of voice ratcheted up to angry before he caught himself. He paused and unfolded his arms, his expression showing the strain of dialing back his temper.

He took another step toward her, his voice dropping in tone. "The truth is, Shay, I just can't forget how you walked out on me. And called the cops on me. That wasn't very nice. I need you to apologize."

A spurt of anger made her brave. "Don't hold your breath. We're done."

His face lost animation. All that was left was an icy glitter in his narrowing gaze as he approached her. "Who the fuck do you think you're dealing with? You don't call the shots in this relationship."

In that moment everything clicked into focus for Shay. *He's going to hurt me. Really hurt me this time.*

The thought shocked her so much she immediately shied away from it. Yet there was no avoiding his expression. She'd seen that look once before on a man's face, and it had ruined her life.

Shay backed up, trying to avoid him as her finger pressed the emergency button. But he grabbed her wrist and wrenched the cell phone out of her hand then tossed it away before she could be certain the call had gone through.

Panicked by memories, she swung at him wildly, her fist connecting to his jaw with a force that snapped his head back.

"Shit!" He pushed her back so hard her body slammed into the cabin wall. Then he seized her shoulders and her head snapped back against the wall with a sickening thud.

"You stupid bitch!" He began shaking her with enough force to cause damage.

Panicked and unable to free herself, Shay gripped his biceps to steady herself and hung on. She had no family to protect her. No one ready to smack down the man hurting her. Eric knew that. No one would come to rescue her.

A whimper escaped her, drawing her deeper into remembered terror.

CHAPTER SIX

"Let's haul ass!" James swung open the door and Bogart bounded into the passenger seat of his pickup.

What should have been a mere formality at the sheriff's office had turned into an all-day marathon of waiting while the Charlotte-Mecklenburg police department "checked" their facts in the matter. He suspected this was his chief's way of expressing disapproval of the manner in which he had rescued Bogart. His unit leader was going to tear him a new one, too, when he got home. That didn't matter. Bogart was back where he belonged.

As he tightened the seat harness especially designed for dogs, Bogart happily licked his face.

"Oh, now you want to make up." James playfully pushed his muzzle away. "I don't forget that easily, you turncoat. You chose the pretty girl over me."

Bogart tilted his head to the side, black eyes regarding James with soulful interest. This meant, James knew, that Bogart was trying to figure out his partner's state of mind.

For the year and a half they had been together James had been continually surprised by his dog's intelligence.

Bogart would often sense and size up a situation as quickly as he did, sometimes more quickly. Yet they were still figuring each other out. One veteran of the K-9 force had warned him that Bogart was his "learner dog."

"It won't be until you're working with your second dog that you'll feel as if you know what you're doing most of the time."

James stroked Bogart's back, an action that was almost second nature when they were together. While he hadn't liked to hear it, he was beginning to understand what the seasoned handler meant. For instance, he didn't quite get why Bogart had sided with Shay Appleton, even after he appeared. Was it because he had sensed which of them was more in need of his support?

Or was his partner feeling abandoned and untrusting of the man who'd allowed his at-the-time girlfriend to give him away?

James winced as regret sucker-punched him. What the hell had he been thinking to let Jaylynn into their lives? He'd let her screw up everything.

No, he wasn't going to think like that. He and Bogart just needed to get back to their routine and they'd both be fine.

James took his dog's muzzle in his hand and wagged it. "Okay, you win this one. I might even have been tempted if Shay Appleton had looked at me the way she looks at you." He scratched his partner behind the ears. "But that's over now. 'Prince' has had his day. Bogart is a working stiff. We're going home where we belong."

The ringing of his cell phone caused him to pause before climbing into his truck.

"Hi, Mom."

"Hello, James. How are you, sweetheart?"

"Great. What's up?"

His mother hesitated and James came instantly alert.

His mother wasn't the type to let small things bother her. Something was wrong. "I just wanted to remind you about Thanksgiving. It's at my house this year."

James frowned. "It's always at your house, Mom. Thirty-something years."

"That's just it. Allyson has got it into her head that, as the eldest daughter, she should have it at her house this year. She said something about all the preparations being too much work for me."

James had never thought about that. "Well, is it, Mom?"

"I'll have you know I can hoist a twenty-pound turkey in each fist. I don't go to the Y three times a week for nothing. I can certainly handle a meal for nine adults and two children. Of course, we'll probably include a few last-minute people, too."

James smiled. That sounded like Thanksgiving at the Cannon house. The numbers increased as the day drew closer. "So, great. I'll have my feet under your table on Thanksgiving."

There was a pause. "You won't let Allyson change your mind? You know she's not the best cook but she can be very persuasive about things she wants. She's got almost three weeks to work on everyone."

"Sic her sisters on her."

"Yes. I could do that." There was that hesitancy again.

"Is there something else on your mind, Mom?"

"I was just wondering how you're doing, son. Alone."

James frowned. "What's with the sad tone, Mom? Given how you felt about Jaylynn, I thought you'd be jumping for joy that I'm single." Before his mother could respond he glanced at Bogart. "Oh, great news, Mom! Bogart's turned up. Just this morning."

"Really? James, that's just wonderful! A miracle. How did it happen?"

James gave her the quick, clean version of Shay having

taken his partner in at a shelter in Raleigh and then him finding out about it. No point in laying out the whole shitty mess that involved Jaylynn's part in Bogart's disappearance.

"So, is he all right?"

James scrubbed Bogart hard behind the ears and he barked in response. "Hear that? He's fine."

"Okay. You be careful driving back to Charlotte. It'll be dark out."

James smiled. He was a cop. He carried a gun. His life involved the daily possibility of danger. Yet his mother worried about him driving a major highway after dark. "Sure thing, Mom. Love you."

James hung up with a smile on his face. The family always ended every call with "I love you." Only in his teens did he balk. A guy couldn't say "love you" to his mother— forget his dad—if anyone else was around. But he'd always known he was loved, and surrounded by enough family to make a man sometimes wish he could hide out from them. But mostly it was just good to know that they would always have his back. Time to go home.

Yet once behind the wheel, James just sat without putting the key in the ignition. He couldn't forget the look in Shay Appleton's gaze as they walked away. She looked more than defeated, she looked abandoned.

The setting sun slanted down through the trees in the parking lot, highlighting the warm colors of the autumn leaves. The colors reminded him of her dappled gold and brown eyes. Those eyes held secrets he didn't begin to understand but they moved him just the same. The look said she didn't have options, or someone to back her up. And that resurrected an old and painful memory he thought he'd successfully buried.

It happened his first year on the job. A domestic-abuse

call from a neighbor who'd heard a woman's cries coming from the apartment next door.

He'd responded with his senior partner to find a young woman, plain and thin and wearing little more than a man's shirt, and a bruise the size of a fist that had spread across her cheek to swell her eye shut. She wouldn't let them in and wouldn't answer any questions except to say that she had fallen over a toy and struck her face on the coffee table. There was a small child crying in the background. If there was a man behind that door, menacing her, they could only speculate.

His senior officer had tried everything to get her to open that door, cajoling her, offering to settle the crying child, to take her to the emergency room. She wouldn't budge. But the gaze of fear and pain from her one good eye had branded James.

As they turned away, he'd been hot with frustration, calling his partner unfeeling.

His partner had waited until they were back in their squad car to speak. "You got emotionally involved. That's not the job. If they don't ask for our help, we can't force them. If they say no, then you leave a card and walk away. They aren't your problem anymore."

His seasoned partner would repeat this speech several times in other vastly different circumstances his rookie year, but he never completely bought it. It didn't help that, a few weeks later, they were called back to that same address to find a dead mother and child.

James massaged his brow in weariness. Shay Appleton didn't want his help. She couldn't have been clearer about that if she'd told him to eat dirt and die.

"You leave a card and walk away."

His murmur drew a whimper of response from Bogart. James shook his head as he gazed at his partner. "You don't get a vote this time. You've become emotionally involved."

He started the truck. He had become a good police officer. Otherwise he wouldn't have been able to win a spot on the K-9 force after just three years on the force, the minimum. That required the hard-won ability to be unemotional in emotional situations. And to know when to step away from a situation when it didn't call for his intervention. Shay Appleton wasn't his problem by any stretch of the imagination. He was out of his jurisdiction. Hell, out of his emotional comfort zone. He had only one obligation at the moment, and that was to get back to Charlotte to square away the details of his actions so that he and Bogart could return to active duty.

Still, the sight of her standing on the porch as they drove away, clutching the railing as though without it she might collapse, made him feel like one cold bastard.

During the course of the day the deputy had offered his opinion of Shay being a "high-strung little gal." Later the sheriff confided that Ms. Appleton had lived in the cabin for a time during her teens. Later, whenever she came up, which hadn't been in more than three years, she always made calls about some nuisance or another. One year it was a supposed lurker. Another time a stray rock had been thrown through a window. When pressed for the reason for her fears, he ducked his head, saying only, "She's city folk now. Crickets and such make 'em skittish."

James sighed. Law enforcement officers, himself included, were often too jaded to see a stray rock thrown through a window as anything more than mischief. Yet he couldn't shake the feeling that the sheriff, deputy, and Ms. Appleton weren't being completely honest with him. Something lay just under the surface of the events of the day that none of them were willing to discuss.

Not that they should confide in him. After all, *he* had been the one to wage war on her doorstep. Besides, he had his own secret. He hadn't told them about the stalker of the night before.

Because he didn't want to be further involved.

James's conscience jumped up to body-slam him. Ms. Appleton had handled his intrusion with more grace and courage than many a suspect he'd arrested. She didn't seem the victim type. Nothing like that worn-out young mother, in too deep to crawl back to life before it was too late. Yet her wary gaze held the suspicion of someone who had been through something hard, and no longer trusted the world to be on her side. Did it have something to do with the man in the truck?

Something nudged the back of his mind. The fact that she'd seemed prepared for trouble. If not from him, then from something equally unpleasant. Yet that, too, was none of his business. She had Deputy Ward to watch over her.

Life was tough. He had his own problems.

He rolled down the windows for a breath of country air, put his truck in gear, and headed down the rural lane that led back past the lake to reach the highway. He didn't need to pass Shay Appleton's cabin to do that. He could have taken the shorter route.

Ten minutes later, when the cabin came into view through the trees, he could have swerved right and hit the tarmac and headed toward Interstate 85 and home. Instead, he stepped on the brake to roll past at a speed that barely registered on his odometer.

There was a truck in the yard. It looked suspiciously like the one that had been parked at the edge of the woods the night before. Of course, it might be coincidence, or his imagination working overtime. Or a maintenance man, or a—

Bogart suddenly lunged forward in his harness; his ears pricked forward, and from deep within his chest came a low guttural growl. He'd caught a scent.

"Shit!" James turned into her drive. Bogart on alert was good enough probable cause for him.

The door was ajar, wide enough for James to see inside before he even reached the porch. In seconds, he took in every pertinent detail.

A tall man in jeans and a blazer stood facing the far wall, legs apart as he leaned forward. Shay was behind him, forced tightly against the wall by his body. James's pulse ticked up at the sight. Was this a threat, or a sexual encounter he was about to disturb?

The man was speaking, his voice so low James couldn't pick out words. Shay suddenly turned her head away as if to avoid looking at him.

James saw her expression. It was one of a small animal cornered by a larger one. Before James could react, the man seized her shoulders and her head snapped back against the wall with a sickening thud. "You stupid bitch!"

James tensed, equally angry and relieved. The man's threat gave him every right to enter without invitation.

He released Bogart's leash and said firmly, *"Geh weiter."*

Bogart shot through the opening, barking in alarm.

The sounds of an angry dog stopped the man from shaking Shay. He glanced around and into the jaws of a snarling Belgian Malinois.

He whipped his head back to Shay. "You said your dog wasn't here."

Without seeking to explain Prince's appearance, Shay seized the moment to try to free herself. "Let go of me, Eric. If you don't, he'll tear you to pieces. I swear."

"Shit!" Eric shoved her away, freeing her.

James pushed the front door wide, his gaze fanning the perimeter of the room as he entered. Satisfied no one else was present, he gave his partner a new command. *"Pass auf!"*

Ordered to guard the man, Bogart moved in, head low.

James watched his canine doing his job. Bogart was getting details he couldn't sense, like the odor of pheromones flooding off the pair. The man would be running high, giving off pheromones of an aggressor. Shay would be shedding fear. The man began backing slowly away.

"I'd stand still, if I were you." James kept his voice calm though his own emotions were running high.

The man stilled, eyeing the dog warily as Bogart sniffed his pants leg. When he gave a soft growl and bared rows of flesh-tearing teeth, the man involuntarily stepped back in alarm. "Call him off!"

James waited a beat, just to make certain the threat had been delivered and received, before giving the command to back off. *"Fuss!"*

Instantly obedient, Bogart trotted back over to James.

"Good evening, Ms. Appleton." He spoke to Shay as a courtesy. His attention was focused totally on the man beside her.

"What is this?" Eric's head swung from Shay to James. "Who the fuck are you?"

James braced his legs apart, arms slightly flexed. "I'm the police. Who the fuck are you?"

Eric shifted toward Shay. "You tell him."

Shay shook her head.

James kept his gaze on Shay's guest. "Step away from Ms. Appleton. Now." When the man had moved grudgingly a couple of feet away, James spoke again. "I'm going to ask you one more time, nicely, who are you?"

The man smiled a professional's smile, all charm and confidence-building. "I'm a friend of Shay's."

That brought a sound of derision from Shay as she rubbed her upper arms. "We're not friends, Eric."

James shifted his weight. "Want to try again?

The man's smile dissolved. Obviously, charm had a short half-life with this guy. "I don't have to answer your questions. I haven't done anything wrong. She let me in. Tell him, Shay."

"Why do you keep telling Ms. Appleton what to say?" James cocked an eyebrow. "Afraid she might say something not so flattering about you?"

The man's gaze narrowed as it moved from James to Shay, and then the dog. "What's going on here?" He looked back at Shay. "Is this guy really a cop? He's not in uniform."

James moved back the edge of his camo jacket to reveal his badge, hung on his belt, and then the gun on his hip. The man's demeanor changed from intimidating to nervous. A muscle flexed just below his left eye while, at his sides, his hands began flexing and unflexing. Maybe he was the kind of jerk who saved his rage for women.

"Is that your truck outside?"

The guy's gaze shifted toward the door. "Why?"

James reached into his pocket and retrieved his police notebook. He thumbed through it until he found what he was looking for. "I've got a partial of a license plate and a description of a vehicle just like the one you're driving. It was reported as a prowler in this neighborhood last night."

The man sucked in a breath and turned to Shay. "Unbelievable!"

James let a smile ease into his features. He had the bastard. "Ms. Appleton didn't make the complaint. Added to that, I just witnessed you shaking her in a manner that could constitute assault. I need to see some ID, Mr.—"

The man let out a heavy sigh as he reached for his wallet. "Eric Coates."

James took his time as he made a note of the information on the license, letting the man stew as he pondered what he was going to do next. So far, Shay had contributed four words to the conversation. He was going to have to get rid of the guy to get her side of the story.

When he raised his gaze from his notepad he was pleased to see a sheen of sweat had formed on Eric's upper lip. Definitely nervous. "You need to know I can arrest you right now for harassment and assault." He waited a beat to allow the man time to absorb his situation. "If Ms. Appleton wants to press charges, I'll be happy to add a laundry list of other offenses."

Eric's head swiveled toward Shay. "You can't do that. Not if—" He seemed to catch himself before he finished.

James glanced at her. "Shay?"

She offered a stiff lift of one shoulder. "Stay away from me, Eric." She looked at James, a small frown pinching her brows together. "No charges."

James didn't take his eyes off Coates. "But Shay—"

"I said no charges."

James suppressed his annoyance with her decision while noting that relief flooded Coates's expression. "In that case, I'm issuing you a citation." He signed a sheet and ripped it off his pad and held it out.

Looking smug, Eric took it, then turned to Shay. "Remember what I said. We'll talk later."

"I wouldn't advise that." James came up behind Eric, close enough to make his physical presence a direct threat. "On a personal level I'm telling you to leave Ms. Appleton alone. Permanently."

Eric swung around, his eyes widening. James let him look. "So . . . what? You're the new boyfriend?"

Bogart stood up, his ears flicking forward in response to the man's aggressive tone toward his handler.

Eric looked down and his expression changed. "So that's where the dog came from." He looked back at Shay. "You cheating slut."

Bogart bared his teeth in answer.

Shay lifted her chin against the insult. "You should leave, Eric. Now."

Eric's gaze flicked between man and dog. "Okay. Right. I'm done."

James didn't plan to block Eric with his shoulder as he passed, but somehow the man was thrown off balance, stumbled into the sofa, and fell.

Unsmiling, James held out a helping hand. "Sorry about that."

For a split second the heat of testosterone-fueled challenge shimmered between them. Then Eric's gaze shifted to where James was holding the harness of an angry barking dog.

Ignoring James's offer of a hand, he quickly righted himself, and lurched through the front door, slamming it behind him.

The second the door closed the remaining pair turned and spoke at the same time.

"Are you okay?"

"How did you know about last night?"

CHAPTER SEVEN

"Go ahead."

Shay rubbed her palms up and down her denim-clad thighs. "No, you."

James smiled, slipping out of police mode. "Ladies first."

"Wait a sec." Shay crossed over to lock her door.

As James pulled Bogart's favorite ball from his pocket and tossed it as a reward for a good job, he noticed that she had three locks where most people could have been satisfied with one. The first was oxidized with age. The other two were shiny and new.

When she turned back to him, it seemed she had reconsidered her first question because she substituted another. "Why did you do that?"

"What?"

She folded her arms and stared.

Busted. "I saw what he was doing to you, Shay. You should have let me arrest him. Since you wouldn't, I sent him that message in a way he'll remember."

Her chin shot up. He didn't need words to translate that into *I can take care of myself.* Trouble was, it was obvious that she had been doing a lousy job. Not that that was his business, but—whoa. Wait. Not. His. Business. Even so . . .

"Want to tell me why you won't press charges?"

She looked away. "I have my reasons."

"Whatever they are, they aren't going to keep him from putting his hands on you, again, like when I walked in."

Shay reached down to Bogart, who had come up to her, and scratched him behind one ear. "News alert, Officer Cannon. I'm not your concern."

"Come on, Shay." He said her name softly, as if he had used it before, and it sounded wonderfully comfortable in his mouth.

Shay straightened up, feeling a little shaky from running on adrenaline. "Are you asking as a police officer or a friend?"

James felt himself shifting onto uncertain ground. "Whichever you need."

Shay searched his face for a moment. What she needed was someone to believe her. But she couldn't explain why without explaining the very things she wanted most to keep hidden. So even the compassion in his expression couldn't help her.

Shay snatched her gaze away, searching for her security blanket of hostility. "Why did you come back, anyway? Looking for a little pat on the back to make you feel like a hero?"

Annoyance jerked at James's patience. He'd swung by on a hunch. Yet after his graceless entry into her life, what had he expected, a parade?

"Fine. My bad. I thought maybe since we share a fondness for Bogart that we might become . . . friends." James made a business of putting his pad away. "So, who is that asshole?"

Shay almost smiled at his description. "He's my ex. Boy-friend."

"Your decision?"

She nodded. "I broke it off a month ago, but he hasn't taken the hint. I think now he will."

"Don't count on it."

Shay pushed a hand up under her bangs, using her fingers as a comb. "Is that why you let Eric believe you had more than a professional interest in me?"

She caught that, did she?

"It'll make him think twice before he tries to force his way in on you again. The least I could do."

"Or you just pissed him off in a way that will make him an even bigger threat when you're not around."

Reminded of Eric's violent actions, Shay moved her hand to the back of her head, probing the place where it had connected with the wall. *"Ouch."*

James frowned. "Are you hurt? Here. Let me look at that."

"No, it's okay."

But James didn't pause. He spun her around lightly and then his fingers were in her hair, parting it carefully at the crown. He wanted to lecture her on the dangers of violent men but he sensed that right now the last thing she needed was to be pressured by a man. He felt her flinch as he revealed a red bruised area. "You've got a knot developing back here. You should be looked at."

Shay slipped free of his touch and danced away from him, as if being close to him could breach her defenses. "No. I'm fine."

"Are you nauseated?" He held up two fingers. "What do you see?"

"V for victory. Okay?"

"Has he gotten rough with you in the past?"

Shay stared at him, not knowing what to say. No one had ever taken an interest in her claims before. Then she realized that no one had ever seen Eric in action before.

She licked her suddenly too-dry lips before she found her voice. "Once." She looked away. "I don't want to talk about it."

"Fair enough. But you should think about pressing charges. It's not too late. I can go after him. You call the sheriff while I track him down. I'll bring him in and you have him arrested for assault. I'm your witness."

"No." She didn't even give his suggestion a moment's consideration. "Eric's gone. That's what I wanted."

James waited a beat, weighing how hard to push her. He decided he needed to ease up before she shut him down completely. Maybe another approach would work. "Coates doesn't seem the sort to take directions well. What would have happened if I hadn't walked in?"

Shay jerked her gaze up to meet the full impact of his blue eyes. What she felt emanating from them was a genuine interest and something surprisingly like warmth. Then his question boomeranged back through her thoughts. *What would I have done?*

The sudden sick look in her expression twisted James's gut. She was trying to tough it out but clearly she had known she was all but defenseless against that bastard.

He took a step toward her, keeping his voice soft. "A guy who likes to manhandle women is likely to circle back as soon as he thinks he safely can. That might be a day, or a week. You should at least get a restraining order against Coates so you will have serious backup if you need it."

"Is that your professional or personal opinion? Because what I really didn't need was for Eric to think I left him for a hunky new boyfriend."

She turned, picked up the soggy packet of oysters she'd dropped on the table, and headed toward the kitchen.

James stared after her. *Jeez!* Where had he gone wrong? He'd meant to reassure her. Now she was pissed.

When she disappeared through the doorway, he glanced around to call Bogart to heel, but his partner was already at his side, staring up at him as if he were about to hatch.

Bogart looked back over his shoulder toward the kitchen and then again at James, his brows twitching up and down, signaling confusion.

"Yeah, yeah, I know. I need to fix it."

Reluctantly, he headed after her.

Shay didn't release her breath until she was all the way into the kitchen. She'd been unforgivably rude to the man who'd saved her and was now just trying to help. What was her problem?

Oh hell. She knew what was wrong.

Struggling to regain control over her stressed-out emotions, she emptied the container of iced oysters into the sink. She was so grateful that James had appeared when he did that she was tying knots inside herself just to keep from showing it.

Because her emotional reaction had ranged far beyond simple relief.

It had been nothing short of thrilling to see his tall silhouette filling her doorway. Even unshaven and still dressed in wrinkled camo, James had the look of capable protector written all over him. Her very own Avenger.

Get a grip, Shay.

She couldn't afford to think that way, for even a second, about Officer Cannon. He wasn't hers. Nor was Prince . . . Bogart. Just because they had unexpectedly appeared as the tag-team rescuers she had been praying for didn't mean she should let her emotions run wild. In a few minutes, she'd be all alone again.

And James was right. Eric would show up again in her life, sooner or later.

Shay's throat began to constrict with mounting anxiety.

"No! Not yet!" she whispered under her breath. There'd be plenty of time for an anxiety attack over her future once she was alone.

James found her standing before the sink. He paused in the doorway, propped a shoulder on the door frame and crossed his arms, trying his damnedest to look less like a cop and more like a regular guy.

While he decided what to say, he took in all the details of her he hadn't had time to notice when he walked in.

He liked the way she looked in skinny jeans shoved into hand-tooled cowboy boots so scuffed and creased that they appeared to have been her favorite footwear for a long time. A teal-blue turtleneck sweater covered her from chin to the tops of her thighs. He knew from wrestling with her that it hid a body with plenty of feminine curves. Not that he should be thinking about her in that way. Yet nothing he'd done so far today fell into the *should* category.

Unable to think of anything intelligent to say, Shay tried to ignore the man standing in her doorway. It wasn't easy. Her gaze kept straying halfway toward him before she could snatch it back. Each foray made her more fully aware of his presence. The easy grace of his long body draped in camo reminded her of the hard muscles beneath. Of the way he'd effortlessly lifted her off her feet this morning. She could still recall the hard band of his arm pressing under her breasts.

Oh crap. She needed to stop thinking altogether.

Desperate for distraction, she looked down at Bogart, who had come up to her with his tail wagging, certain that his presence was welcome.

She squatted down and hugged his neck. "My hero." She didn't dare glance at James for fear he would realize that she was referring to him. "I don't know what would have happened if you hadn't shown up."

Finally, she peeked at James as she leaned her cheek against Bogart's back, stroking him with long slow glides of her hand. "Thank you."

James sucked in a long breath. Her stroking hand was damned distracting. He leaned away from the wall. "You're welcome. Glad we could help out." He glanced around, uncertain of what to do next. "So, I guess we should be going."

He signaled to Bogart, who whined and lay down at Shay's feet instead of obeying.

A chill shot through James. Bogart had never disobeyed him before. Just how badly was their bond ruptured by their weeks apart? Or was Bogart still feeling very protective of Shay? The color had come back into her face but her expression was as wary as ever. Maybe his dog understood her needs better than he did.

"Have you fed Prin—Bogart today?"

James shook his head. "He shared my package of peanut butter crackers at the station but . . ."

Shay stood up. Trying to ignore the fact that he was watching, she leaned up on tiptoe to take down a bag of food from an overhead shelf.

James was paying attention, not only to obvious things like how her sweater lifted to reveal her nicely rounded butt, but to how hard she was trying to push past the trauma of the last minutes by finding ordinary things to do. Her hands shook as she poured hard nugget chow into a bowl, but he hadn't yet seen a single tear. Many victims dissolved into a puddle the instant they were safe. Shay's reaction was to retreat into a porcupine ball of thorny hostility.

"What's that?"

Shay paused in pouring liquid from a jar she'd taken from the refrigerator. "Chicken soup left from last night." She put the bowl in the microwave for several seconds then stuck a finger in to test the temperature. When she put the bowl on the floor, Bogart gave her hand a quick lick and then began wolfing it down.

James shook his head. "It's embarrassing what that dog will do for food."

Shay turned to James with a grin so wide he had to laugh.

When the laughter subsided they were left standing looking at one another. Shay's eyes were wide, speculative, as if weighing every ounce of him for clues. To what?

On James's side at least, there was an undercurrent of something coming to life, something remarkably like sexual attraction. It made no sense. But then nothing about the day had made sense. He'd just ended the worst relationship of his life. And Shay, from what he could gather, was still trying to end one. Neither of them needed another entanglement. He groped for a way to break the moment.

"You should have told Deputy Ward about last night's visitor."

She gave him a startled look. "How do you know about that?"

"I was in the woods, doing a stakeout, looking for Bogart. Saw someone watching your cabin. The way you went after him, I'm guessing you already knew it was Eric. Why didn't you mention that to Deputy Ward?"

He saw her internal struggle reflected in her expression. Definitely hiding something. In the end she just said, "I was about to make dinner. I suppose there's enough."

James decided that might just be the most ungracious invitation he'd ever received. But he wasn't offended. The excuse would give him time to learn a little more about her. "Thanks."

"It's nothing special. A little Hoppin' John and fried oysters."

James's mouth watered in anticipation. "Sounds great."

She looked him up and down again in a way that made him suddenly very aware of every slept-in wrinkle and blade of grass still clinging to his clothing, and the hard scratch of stubble on his face. "You really slept in the woods last night?"

"Yeah."

"Then you probably want to clean up."

"That would be great."

James wasted no time in striding out to his truck and grabbing his gear stuffed into an old army-issue backpack. When he came back in, she was waiting for him in the living room. Her expression was once again guarded and her hands were sliding up and down her arms as if she were cold. He wondered if Eric had left marks on her there, a thought that made him wish he'd done more than shoulder-check him.

He noted wood stacked in the fireplace, ready to be lit. He wondered if she would think he was making himself too much at home if he offered to light it for her. Yeah. Better wait.

As soon as he moved away from the door, she hurried over to lock it.

Then she turned back to the room, tossing her hair over her shoulder as she walked past him. "The bathroom is back here." He followed.

She came to a stop in a narrow hallway and pointed. "On your left. Through the bedroom. Towels are in the cabinet. The shower takes five minutes to deliver hot water. Dinner in twenty minutes."

She tried to let him pass, backing herself up until she was flat against the wall.

James turned sideways, too, but it didn't quite work.

The backpack slung across his shoulders wouldn't allow him to press against the opposite wall.

Things were fine until his chest grazed her right breast. He heard her softly drawn breath on contact and sucked in his stomach in response. That only inflated his chest another inch, making more surface to brush against her. She began trying to slide past him, her gaze strictly on his chin. He was free to gaze down at her, to inhale the ginger scent rising from her hair. The mere brush of her against him, muffled by his clothing and hers, was enough to make him instantly hard as concrete.

He levered his body forward, jamming his butt against the wall in the hopes that his chest would be the only thing brushing her. If his johnson touched her she'd know he was ready for action.

"Sorry." He murmured the word in a husky voice as he closed his eyes and tried to think of *nothing*.

Contact lasted only a few seconds but it seemed forever. Shay held her breath as she stared at the camo design of his jacket only a few inches in front of her nose. Her mind was fully on the rough drag of his jacket across every inch of her breasts. The contact was unexpectedly arousing as his buttons grazed first one and then the other of her nipples. To back him off a bit, she pressed a hand flat against his chest.

He felt rigid in places she didn't expect, as if touching her were a test of his strength. And damn, every muscle in his body seemed to be trying to impress her with its definition. He was firm and contoured and—something moist and smooth and hard poked her!

Shay looked down. Bogart had stuck his wet nose into her open palm.

A second later, James was past her, moving into the bedroom with a swiftness she could only interpret as the desire to get away from her.

It struck her as she headed back to the kitchen that all she'd had to do was back up into the bedroom to let him by her.

Sure. Now her brain was working.

Shay rolled plump shiny silver oysters in cornmeal and spices before adding them to the skillet, glad she had decided to buy more than she thought she could eat in one sitting. Frying messed up the stove so she'd planned to cook enough to last for a couple of days. Now, of course, she had a man to feed. The thought made her smile. Immediately she banished the warm feeling.

She couldn't afford to like James. He was an A-type take-charge personality. Just what she didn't want or need after Eric. Not when the self-respect she'd worked so hard to build for herself the last few years had just come apart at the seams. Timing. Timing was everything. Hers had always been lousy.

As she forked the oysters to turn them over in the grease, she began to analyze her feelings so that they could be brought to heel before James emerged from her bathroom. She needed to think of something to talk about over dinner, nothing too personal. And maybe she should go brush her hair. She must look a mess after—

"Crap!" Shay glanced guiltily at the kitchen doorway. She was making plans for the possibility that the man in her bathroom might care how she looked.

As if she had just found a new prospect for her love life.

As if the last disaster hadn't just stalked out her door.

No! James made her uneasy. For instance, why had he come back? Just because he had turned up in time to stop Eric before things got completely out of control didn't mean her silent pleas for help had worked. He must have had some other motive.

She glanced down at Bogart. "I don't suppose you'll tell me what's up with your partner?"

Bogart thumped his tail, his tongue lolling out of the side of his mouth.

She tossed him a fried oyster which he caught and swallowed without even rising from his prone position.

Afterward, he sat up and barked and offered her his paw.

She laughed and shook it. "Yeah, you're cute, my charming Prince. But it seems you come with attachments I can't afford to have in my life."

When the last oyster had been fried and a salad of kale added to the table to fill out the menu that included black-eyed peas over rice, she glanced at the clock.

He'd been in the bathroom thirty minutes. How much water could one man use?

On the way through the living room, she glanced at her front door. She knew she had locked it after James came back in but she found herself checking, just in case.

All three locks were in place.

Her breath came out in a whoosh of relief. As she turned into the bedroom she heard music coming from behind the bathroom door. No wonder he hadn't heard her call. He was singing rather loudly to a Jake Owen country and western song.

His rather nice baritone was crooning "can't be alone with you," as she tapped on the bathroom door.

No response. She rapped more loudly, saying in a near shout, "Dinner is—"

CHAPTER EIGHT

Shay had seen naked men. But not one quite this impressive close-up. He was bigger than he appeared when clothed. As the steam curled out of the room behind him, he seemed to have emerged from some primitive grotto. Muscles she'd felt in their morning struggle and later brief encounter in the hallway were covered in smooth tanned skin lightly furred in a golden pelt that still held a few drops of water from his shower.

Instantly embarrassed to be staring with lips parted in surprise, she looked down. That didn't help.

The hair on his torso turned darker and sleeker as it arrowed down his flat abdomen, skirted his navel and then sank out of sight behind well-used jeans left unsnapped and half zipped. In fact, the denim seemed precariously hung on the hook of one jutted hip.

"Yes?" A voice from somewhere over her head delivered the word in a quiet, deep register.

Shay closed her mouth. She'd come here to say something. She was pretty sure she had.

"Dinner ready?"

"Yes." It took her another second to lift her gaze to his face.

A single slick of shaving gel covered the last patch of uncut whiskers. Where he had shaved, the smooth skin of his lower face was drawn taut in a grin.

He must have seen something in her face because he glanced down at himself then muttered, "Oops! Sorry!" He tossed the razor into the sink and used both hands to yank up his zipper.

"And don't leave a mess in my bathroom." She spun quickly, and stalked away.

He was watching, she could feel his gaze slide warmly down her spine to her behind. That made her aware of the way her boots made her hips sway.

She turned the corner into the living area before she let herself slump against the wall. Her mouth was dry, her breath tangled up between "oh my God!" and "hot damn!"

The details of him still simmered in her overstimulated senses. The swell of his shoulders, still damp from the shower, were freckled. He smelled of soap and shower steam. There was a small scar on the swell of his right bicep and a small mole above and to the right of his left nipple. Her palms still prickled with the ridiculous urge to touch the whorls framing those flat brown male nipples.

Shay felt her skin ignite as her body betrayed her attraction. Officer Cannon was getting in under her guard. Just by being here, he was taking up valuable space that she desperately needed to keep herself whole.

She struggled with the impulse to turn around and tell him to get out. She didn't want to share her meal with him. He made her uncomfortably aware that what she really wanted to do was go back in there and join him in that steamy room, and show him what a slutty mind she had.

Shay took a deep breath. If only she had the same courage she did in her imagination. But she was not a wild girl. At least, not outside her head.

She could hear her counselor now. The exaggerated intensity of her emotions was simply because Officer Cannon represented safety and order. And his confident sexual attractiveness was easy to appreciate. She needed to stop fantasizing in order to face her anxieties.

Those thoughts sobered her. Yes, James Cannon was a babe magnet. Probably accustomed to women going all gooey at the sight of him. That's why he'd thought nothing of opening a door half naked. It wasn't a come-on. It was a comfortable fact of his life.

She needed to keep it together. An hour and he'd be gone. Plenty of time for a full-blown meltdown after that.

Lifting her bangs from her damp forehead, she straightened up and headed for the kitchen.

Bogart was there waiting for her by the stove, all innocence with his bright eyes trained on her. That's when she knew there was a problem.

"Oh Prince! You didn't!"

Prince had gobbled up half the platter of fried oysters.

Shay stirred her iced tea in silence as she watched James eat. He was nearly done and they hadn't yet exchanged more than half a dozen words. The silence was worse than talking would have been; it gave her brain nothing to do but be acutely aware of every inch of the man sharing her table. He wore a Henley shirt of waffle fabric and, over that, an unbuttoned flannel shirt to ward off the evening chill. His hair, still damp from the shower, molded to his head in dark wet spikes. She wished she was bold enough to catch on her finger the single bead of water hanging from his right earlobe.

No, she mustn't touch. Out of her league.

Annoyed with her thoughts, she got up and turned on

her digital music player plugged into its dock across the room. It blared to life with a driving beat that scattered the silence.

Bogart sat up and glanced at her, his head and ears cocked to take in the unfamiliar music.

James continued to eat in silence because every time he looked up, his hostess was staring at his plate as if he were her last customer whose idling over his meal was keeping her past the end of her shift.

When he'd opened the bathroom door he hadn't thought about the fact he was shirtless until he saw the blush flare in her cheeks and her top teeth catch her lower lip. She looked vulnerable and wary, and yet he knew she could be tough and bold. Because there, behind the surprise and instinctive modesty, was the shimmer of sexual interest. He'd felt himself expanding in reaction to the curiosity in those tortoiseshell eyes.

James swallowed, hard. He was thinking way too much about things he shouldn't. Her interest died soon enough. He saw it the second she began to recoil. She must have thought he was being deliberately provocative with his un-zipped jeans.

When he'd entered the kitchen, he half expected her to change her mind about him staying for dinner.

He stole a look at her plate, empty but for a smear of black-eyed peas and three rice grains. She'd said he'd taken so long to dress that she'd eaten her share of oysters ahead of him. He wondered if she had lied about having enough to share, and was forgoing the oysters so that he could eat the plateful she'd served him. If so, it was too bad for her. Honest to God, it was so good he wanted it all.

"When is the last time you had a meal?" she asked, as if she had read his mind.

A corn bread muffin paused halfway to his mouth.

"Yesterday. I was too busy trying to keep my ass out of a sling today to think about food. According to the sheriff's office and my sergeant, I broke enough rules today to get me fired."

"Sounds intense."

He shook his head. "If I was in serious trouble I'd have been sent home by escort."

"That kind of stuff happen to you often?"

"Never before."

James put his muffin down and gave her a level look. "I'm a by-the-book police officer. You don't make the K-9 unit unless you're above average in performance. That's not a boast. It's a fact. I made it on my first try. Even harder. What happened here today, that was about Bogart."

"What about Pri—Bogart?"

James felt deep emotion push up through his police armor of professional distance when he thought about how long and hard he'd searched for his partner.

Embarrassed, he took a long gulp of his iced tea. He remembered being told the first day of training that when a K-9 officer served what was often a graveyard shift, night after night, just you and your dog, a bond of mutual respect and interdependence developed as tight as with any human partner. He and Bogart lived alone, ate alone, patrolled alone. How to explain a connection like that and not sound obsessive?

Then he remembered how fond she'd grown of Bogart in their few weeks together and knew he would be revealing their relationship to a sympathetic listener. Even so, he found himself staring at his plate as he spoke.

"He's not a pet. I mean, Bogart's my friend and I take care of him, feed him, and I enjoy his company off duty. But he's really something special. Not one dog in a thousand can do what he does and do it as well, every time he's asked. He's tenaciously loyal and I completely trust him. He would die for me so I try to make certain that won't occur because of a mistake I made. I'd give my right arm to protect him."

He glanced at her to see the effect his words were having. She was still looking at him expectantly.

"I don't expect you to understand but when I saw him last night, alive after I thought he could be dead . . . Something snapped." He ran a hand across his mouth. "I'm not proud of it."

"That's some speech. You practicing it on me for your sergeant?"

That forced a chuckle from him. "How'd I do?"

"I'd cut the 'right arm' crap. Sounds lame." She reached for the last oyster on his plate and stuck it in her mouth.

He smiled, almost accustomed to her contrariness after a day of exposure.

"Who is the woman who stole him from you?"

James shrugged. "A mistake. You ever make a mistake in a relationship?"

She glanced away at that. "All the time."

"If you want, next time I see this Eric guy I can clear up any misunderstanding about our relationship."

"We don't have a relationship."

"No?" He forked a last mouthful of peas and rice into his mouth, his gaze never leaving her face.

Shay felt a quiver run through her. From the moment she met him, she'd thought James Cannon was one unemotional son of a gun, except where his partner was concerned. But gazing across less than two feet of space into eyes so ridiculously blue they made her think of heat-blasted summer skies, she knew she'd made a mistake. Behind the cool law enforcement exterior, there was a lava flow of emotion held in check by a cocky grin. At the moment, all of that was directed at her.

Run. You don't need this. You can't handle it.

Needing to put distance between them, she picked up their plates and carried them to the sink before she spoke again. "You should be getting on the road."

James nodded and tossed Bogart the last bite of his muffin. "You're a great cook. Don't know when I've eaten better. Only I won't tell my sister Allyson."

"You have lots of family?" She didn't know why she asked when she was trying to get rid of him.

"Yes. Three sisters. All older, all married. So, two nephews and two nieces, plus my folks. And that's just the immediate family. You?"

"No one." She busied herself scraping plates with nothing left on them. "Mom died three years ago. Cancer."

"I'm sorry to hear that. So, what do you do?"

She shrugged. She knew she shouldn't have started another conversation. It had just spawned questions she didn't want to answer. That's what cops did, ask questions.

But he was persistent. "What do you do for a living?"

Her expression flattened out as she turned around. "Nothing special."

James came to his feet. Obviously the casual chitchat was over. Still, his ever-professional gaze narrowed in on her posture.

She was leaning her hips against the sink, a seemingly relaxed pose. But she was also twisting a dishrag between her hands as if she were trying to strangle it. Intuition said she was hiding something more than anxiety over Eric. She certainly didn't like to answer even the most casual question. Experience said that he wasn't going to find out why.

Sometimes you hand them your card and walk away.

He pulled one of his professional cards out of a pocket and held it out. "You have any more trouble, don't hesitate to call."

She came forward and took it in two fingers, careful not to touch his hand.

James shook his head and turned toward the living room.

"What are you going to do about your ex taking your dog?"

James looked back over his shoulder. Trust her to go to the heart of his remaining problem. "I'll have to give that some thought."

"She's pretty. You'll probably forgive her."

He didn't respond but the change in his expression made Shay suddenly a little sorry for the woman who would have to face this man.

She glanced over at Bogart.

But not that sorry.

She bent down to hug him one last time.

James saw the telltale sheen of unshed tears when she rose to her feet. *Damn.* He wished he could offer her something as consolation but he knew better than to sympathize with her again. "You should think about replacing Bogart with a dog of your own."

"No one can replace him."

"Right. But if you decide to look for real protection, you're going to want a dog trained to act on command. You weren't getting half the use you could have outta him. Want me to show you?"

She jutted out her chin. "What would be the point? You're taking him away from me."

James was rendered silent. It was those deep-set eyes framed by her bangs. Even though her mouth was saying back off, her gaze was vulnerable, heartbreaker sweet. Naturally, something stupid popped into his head.

"Tell you what. It's Saturday night. We don't have to be back on duty until Monday evening. Why don't you keep Bogart until tomorrow? Say your good-byes."

She studied his face for several seconds, trying, he suspected, to figure out where the trap lay in that offer. She must be accustomed to disappointment. "Where will you sleep?"

He glanced at his watch, hiding a smile. "Charlotte's less than three hours away. I can still make it home in time to catch the end of a ballgame on TV."

"You'd drive all the way back here tomorrow to pick him up?"

He racked his brain, trying to figure out why he'd opened his mouth in the first place. But now that he'd done it, he didn't want to argue.

"Feed him in the morning, early, and then again about eleven A.M. He's off his schedule and it's important that he be back on it by the time we're on duty Monday night."

He turned and reached for his backpack, which he'd left by the kitchen door.

"Wait!"

It was only a whisper of a breath but James felt the fear in her voice slide up his spine like ice. And then he heard it, the faint creaking of floorboards on the porch, almost drowned out by the music.

He glanced down first at Bogart, who stood expectant but not at full alert. Then he looked back at Shay. She stared past him at the cabin door, eyes wide. He turned his head in that direction as Bogart issued a low growl. The front doorknob was turning slowly.

James motioned her back with one hand as his other went for the Sig P239 he'd tucked into a pancake leather holster attached to his belt in back. He watched the doorknob jiggle as someone tried to force it open. If this was Eric again, he wasn't going to be restrained in his response.

The hard rap of knuckles on the door made them both jump.

"Ms. Appleton! Shay, you in there?"

The voice of Deputy Ward came loud and clear through the wooden door.

"Yes!" Shay expelled the word in a harsh breath but her face was bloodless and she seemed rooted to the spot.

"Shit!" James let go of the butt of his weapon and went to unlock the door. "Evening, Deputy Ward. You might have knocked first."

The deputy's eyes widened at the rebuff. "I did knock a minute ago, and got no answer." He lifted his chin to aim his line of sight past James's shoulder. "You okay, Ms. Appleton?"

"I guess it was the music." Shay glanced at James. "We didn't hear you."

The deputy moved his bulk through the door, gaze moving from one to the other. "I thought you'd have left this area by now, Mr. Cannon."

James shoved his hands into his pockets, letting his annoyance slide away. "I came back by to allow Ms. Appleton the chance to say a final good-bye to Bogart."

The deputy eyed the dog that had come forward to sniff his leg. "I see. Seems like a big to-do over a dog." Then he seemed to catch a whiff of something. "You frying oysters, Shay?"

"Yes." She unfolded her arms, forced them to her sides. "We just finished, or I'd offer you some."

"That's all right. Does smell good." Even though he spoke conversationally, James could tell the lawman was assessing a situation he didn't quite understand and wasn't sure how to respond to. "Just wanted to be sure everything's okay. I felt kinda bad about what I said this morning. About your false alarms, Shay. Turns out you did have cause. Wanted you to know I'm going to take your complaints seriously from now on. Even if it looks like I don't have to worry about your guest here." He tilted his head toward James. "That's a nice jacket you got there, Mr. Cannon. Roomy."

Ah, the deputy had noticed his change of clothing, and that the jacket was a good cover for a concealed handgun.

"I stopped by to let Bogart say his good-byes, and Ms. Appleton was kind enough to allow me to use her shower."

"I see." The deputy smirked. Definitely, he was getting a picture of things. More than what was going on. "That's real neighborly of you, Shay. Most folks wouldn't be quite so kind to a man who had broken in on them. "

Shay folded her arms under her bosom. "As Mr. Cannon explained earlier, it was a mistake."

"I see." The deputy's mouth twitched again. "Nice music. And you look very nice, too, Ms. Appleton. Things look downright cozy. You two take care now. Have a nice evening."

James watched the deputy let himself out before he turned to Shay. "I think—"

She had turned away from him. But she could not hide the fact that she was shaking. No doubt she was embarrassed, probably angry, too. He hoped she wasn't crying. He hated it when women cried, though she didn't seem the type.

He came up behind her and placed a hand on her trembling shoulder. "I'm not sure what that was about but you shouldn't let it upset you."

To his surprise, she turned into him and moved forward to lean her forehead against his chest. She wasn't sobbing but gasping, as if she couldn't get enough air.

His hands slid up her back, trying to rub away the tremors that rippled through her. "You can tell me what's wrong, Shay. I won't judge. I want to help."

She lifted her head and looked at him. Her eyes were wet but her face was creased with laughter. It escaped her now in little hiccups. "Deputy Ward," she gasped between chuckles. "In one short day I've gone from nut to slut in his eyes."

It took James a second to make the emotional adjustment from comforter to coconspirator in her little joke. "You think? Maybe I should—"

She placed her hands palm flat against his chest, her fingers dragging lightly against the fabric to bring her into closer contact. "Maybe you should stop trying to help me."

He gazed down at her, his hands curving without his consent into the contours of her back, his fingertips divining her spine through the heft of her sweater. "Maybe I should. Still, you should have told him about Eric's visit."

She held his gaze. "Why didn't you?"

He opened his mouth but she didn't let him get out a word.

"You really want to help me?" She lunged up on tiptoe and kissed him.

The moment her lips met his, he felt a current of electricity leap from her lips to his and run straight as lightning down his spine to his cock.

The sensation seemed reciprocated in her female parts.

Shay moaned and reached up to hold his head down to hers for another few seconds. For weeks she had been battered and bewildered by circumstances over which she had no control. In this moment, she was in control and it was a glorious, heady feeling that she wanted oh so much.

But good things don't last.

She tore her mouth away from his reluctantly, closed her eyes and swallowed. Another mistake. But such a thrilling one.

Why didn't he say something? Let her go. His hands remained warm and persuasive on her back. What was he waiting for?

She leaned away from him and opened her eyes. He

was staring back at her, his breathing a little labored, his own eyes now dark with an intensity that had all but swallowed up the blue. He wanted her. Equally shocking.

She put a hand on his chest to hold him off. "Don't kiss me again."

"I'm not going to." And James meant it, right up to the moment he said it.

Then he knew he lied.

CHAPTER NINE

Something broke open inside Shay at the second touch of James's lips to hers. The release sent the scorching heat of lust flooding through her body.

From the moment her scuffle with the intruder at her door stopped and she looked into his face, the confrontation between them had altered. Regardless of the circumstances, her resentment of James had been fueled in part by the need to fight the inexplicable surge of hunger she felt for a stranger and to cling to her good sense.

She sighed as he dragged his firm mouth back and forth across hers. She'd never felt instant attraction before. It was absolutely wonderful! And scary.

Could she? Should she?

For once her mind and body were in sync, luxuriating in the pleasure she didn't want interrupted. Her mind offered up all kinds of reasons she should submit to the excitement raging through her body.

He is a stranger.

He doesn't know about my past, about my failures, or my lousy luck.

I will never see him again.

He only knows me here and now, the today of my life.

I can be anyone, even a really wild woman who takes what she wants, and what I want right now is him.

Shay trembled as James's hands found new areas of her back to explore. Then she thrust her tongue between his lips. He tasted different, delicious! Oh hell! Nothing was going to stop her now, even if she had to tie him down.

James, at least the small part of him still paying attention to reason, suspected he was making a mistake. The rest of him was fully along for the ride.

Some women's kisses were flirtatious invitations. Some planted a kiss on a man that went straight to his dick, raw and raunchy and promising more.

Shay Appleton was kissing him like her life depended on it.

He fought for objectivity. He was accustomed to dealing with women of all sorts in every stage of emotional distress. Shay was overwrought. This was just a physical reaction from emotions strung out too far for her rational mind to conquer. But he knew it would. Eventually.

He waited for her to recover, not really kissing her back but not pushing her away. Lord, but she tasted good.

Logic fought for the upper hand. She didn't like him. Hell, he had no business liking her. Too prickly. Not his type.

His libido counterpunched with a physical argument. It dropped his heartbeat to his groin where it pumped up his dick with every pulse.

Firmly ignoring the sensations lower down, he tried to lift his head to gulp a breath of sanity but she reached up and held his mouth to hers.

This time her kiss was one of complete abandon, open-mouthed and wet with lots of tongue. *Damn!* She moved closer, her hips pushing forward against his in invitation. She had more moves, too. Like rubbing her pelvis against his groin as her breasts massaged his chest.

His restraint was shredding. All the years of being a by-the-book officer who broke no rules, gave no favors, and accepted no bribes, not even the occasional freebie blow job offered by a working girl, counted for zilch. His professionalism was wilting under Shay Appleton's sexy assault. Everything else about him went rock hard with lust.

Calling on the last shred of his self-command, he reached out to try to hold her away. Yet when his hands reached her hips in anticipation of giving her a gentle shove, they grasped her instead and hauled her in until she was up on tiptoe.

She moaned into his mouth and then caught his lower lip in her teeth and sucked it into her mouth.

Ah damn! This wasn't what he expected. Still, nothing much had happened . . . yet.

His hands weren't paying much attention to his head. They shifted from her hips down to encounter the firm curves of her ass. He could feel the heat of her through her clothing, and wanted more. His hands slid up, his fingers slipping under the hem of her sweater, and found the warm soft skin of her back.

What the hell?

He turned his head and slanted his mouth across hers, giving in to the impulse to see just how far she'd go. Because, deep down, he'd been fighting his attraction to her since he walked in her door.

Shay didn't retreat. She reached for his shirt jacket and pushed it back over his shoulders. Then she was pulling at his Henley, trying to get it up out of his pants.

She felt him shiver as she ran her hands under his shirt-front and over the warm contours of his chest. The crisp hair she'd longed to touch earlier tickled her palms. She heard a little sigh escape him as she walked her fingers down his ribs and smiled under his kiss. The man who'd been in control of every encounter between them so far didn't feel so much in control at the moment. The heavy thud of his heart under her palm said he was far from it.

That made her want to push him further.

She slid her hands up to his nipples, hard little nubs that grazed her palms, and plucked them with her fingers. This time he sucked in a quick breath. And then he took charge. One hand moved from her back, down over the full curves of her butt, fingers flexing to cup her low. He pulled her to him in a quick motion that spread her breasts across the hard planes of his chest and her sex against the proof of his arousal.

Things became pretty chaotic after that. She jerked his shirt off and then she lost her sweater and jeans as he waltzed her backward toward the nearby sofa, all the while connected by hot wet kisses. It was like a struggle with only one goal, mutual satisfaction.

When they reached the sofa, he sat back, pulling her down with him. She threw a leg over his thighs and sank down onto his lap, all the while never losing their lip-to-lip connection.

Mind smoked by the heat of lust, James retained just enough police discipline to remember his weapon. He reached behind his back, found the gun tucked into the holster at the small of his back. He pulled it out and reached as far away as possible to tuck it barrel down between the cushion and the arm of the couch.

He saw her eyes widen as she followed his actions, and when she looked again at him, there was a question there. He'd seen the question before, in other women's eyes. Some were excited by the fact that he carried a gun. Others found it a complete turnoff. He couldn't gauge Shay's response, only that she had one.

After a second she looked down.

Operating strictly on autopilot, because his head was now definitely in his pants, he leaned forward and whispered against her ear. "Shay?"

"What?" She looked up at him. Those autumn eyes of hers were smoked by desire but her expression was now guarded.

"We can stop right here."

Caution turned to misery, the sexual flush in her face fading. Her response wasn't even a question. "Don't you want to?"

Hell yeah! his dick demanded.

His head told him not to give in to the urge to lick the drop of sweat streaking into the deep cleft between her breasts. White cotton had never looked so naughty as it did cupping her breasts. As it was, his zipper was going to leave teeth tracks in his shaft if he didn't release it soon.

He cupped her face in his hands and lifted her face up so that she had to look at him. "I'm there. If this is what you really want."

Shay didn't want to think about *want*. She could only feel. And what she felt was the frantic feminine *need* to screw the balls off this man. And that frightened her.

She closed her eyes. This was stupid! Another mistake! But she'd made so many, what was one more?

When she looked again she saw the expression of a man ready for sex and hoping like hell he was about to get it.

James went perfectly still under her glare, his cock throbbing in insistent need in time with his heartbeat.

She did not move away. The warm damp seat of her panties pressed against his groin. The heat of her crotch caressed his dick through his jeans. It was a risqué position for a woman who a second ago was about to screw him six ways from Sunday but now looked like she wanted to extract his tonsils without administering anaesthetic.

Shay reached down between them and brushed her hand with slow deliberation across his turgid fly. "This is not any rescued-damsel-in-distress thank-you bullshit. Okay?"

"Got it." The only distress she seemed to be in was over the decision of whether to throttle him or screw him. By the expression on her face, the outcome was still up in the air.

She wriggled back on his thighs so that she could fold her hand over the thick length of his dick beneath his jeans. "It's just a one-time thing. So don't be a bastard about it later. Okay?"

"Okay." He grinned. She had chosen to screw him.

When she leaned in to kiss him again, he decided to take further decisions out of her hands. He caught her by the waist while his other hand slid up under her hair and cupped her head to hold her still under the sensual assault of his kisses.

Shay yielded control, concentrated her attention on the in-and-out motion of his tongue between her lips. Kissing had never felt better, sexier, hotter.

As her mouth opened wider under his, James began a slow grind, his engorged cock rubbing insistently against her through the barrier of their clothing.

After a moment he slipped a hand between her thighs and pushed aside the crotch of her panties then sank a thumb deep into her hot juicy wetness. Desire doubled with a jerk of his dick. He'd give her the best he could manage.

Shay whimpered as he parted the wet silk of her lips with his fingers. Her body shuddered, grinding her sex against his hand, frantic for release and afraid it would be snatched away too soon. It wasn't.

She couldn't catch her breath but it didn't matter. She didn't need to breathe. She only needed to feel James inside her as quickly as possible.

She lifted herself up so she could reach for his zipper. She jerked it down and then her hands were inside his waistband, pushing jeans and shorts down. To her surprise, he levered easily off the sofa with her astride, allowing her to push his clothing down over the rock-hard contours of his butt.

"Hold it." He dove into the back pocket of his jeans and pulled out a foil packet.

Shay looked at it, brought back from the frenzy of the moment. James was prepared. He had produced a condom.

"I—uh." *Am always prepared* would sound a little too overconfident.

"Boy Scout?" She was giving him an out.

They locked gazes. "Yes."

"Better that way."

James quickly sheathed himself and then grabbed her by the waist with one hand. Reaching down between them, he directed his shaft at the right angle, felt the slick heat of the outer folds of her sex part against its head, and shoved toward the goal.

A faint cry escaped Shay as the fat head of his cock entered her. He was bigger than she had expected. She took a couple of quick breaths, telling herself to relax.

"Shhh!" His voice was a thick whisper. "Take it slow."

"No. I want all of you. Push harder."

Grinning, he took her firmly by the waist, and drove her hips down on his swollen cock. With an upward thrust of his hips he slid into her, balls deep.

A series of little inarticulate cries erupted from Shay as he slid home. The sounds exploded in wonder by his ear as the ripples of her climax massaged the length of his shaft.

Damn! He hadn't even begun to move. She was so responsive he almost lost control. She might need only one thrust, his body demanded many more. Now. While her body was sucking him in.

He bucked under her, pounding into her hot wet depths like a jackhammer. She grabbed him by the shoulders and held on, riding his rhythm with eagerness.

Seconds later she gripped him hard, her fingers digging into his shoulders as he continued to pump her. He felt her climax rising again as she called his name in little breathless whispers that feathered his ear.

Afraid her cries would upset Bogart, who had wandered off in the direction of the kitchen, he reached up and stuck his thumb in her mouth. Her lips clamped down on his finger as she began sucking it like a lollipop.

Until that moment, he hadn't known he was wired from thumb to cock. The clutch and caress of her sex, echoed by her firm sucking of his thumb, wrung from him a helpless, "Aw God."

He was running hot and wide open. He wanted her so badly he thought he'd bust a vein. And yet . . .

Just a few more strokes, he promised himself, gasping for air that had suddenly deserted him. Just a little more pleasure. One, two, three long slow pumps in and out. He savored the sweet agony of suspense until it wrung from her a feminine moan of protest.

Then he lost control.

He buried his head in her neck to keep from shouting as he pumped out his climax.

For a moment the world stopped. When it came back it was distant, vague, muffled, a dim shadow beyond the vivid touch and scent of their coupled bodies.

Sweat ran into his eyes and trickled down his back. Her breath was hot against his damp neck. Her skin glistened with perspiration where his hands still held her. Her hair smelled of dinner and coconut conditioner. At that moment, it was the sexiest smell ever.

After a few more slowing breaths, he became aware of the cool evening air in the unheated cabin, and thought about the unlit fire. Yet it registered as a distant thing. Something he would worry about later.

From the corner of his eye, he spied Bogart. He lay parallel to the cabin door, guarding instinctively against intrusion at a moment when his handler was far from alert and ready.

He smiled. *"Gute Hund!"*

Bogart lifted his head then lowered it back to his paws, thanks accepted.

Finally James looked down at Shay. Her forehead was propped against his chest. Her shoulders were quivering and he thought he heard little sobs. He lifted her face up to his. Her cheeks gleamed with tears.

"Did I hurt you?"

"No. It was just so . . . intense."

"Yeah." He wiped the tears from her cheeks with his thumbs. "You're sure you're okay?"

"I never—" Shay shook her head. She wasn't much of a sharer. And he didn't seem the sort of man you admitted all your weaknesses to. "I'm okay."

It took her a moment to rise up off him. When she did, it was to slip on her sweater, which he noticed only came to the top of her thighs and revealed the lower curves of her naked butt as she walked away.

"Where are you going?"

She turned back from the entrance to the kitchen, her expression unreadable as she avoided his direct gaze. "You look like you need time to recoup. Want a beer?"

He grinned. "Whatever you got, I want it."

* * *

James lay awake in the darkness, staring at the LED lights on the clock radio across the room. It was 1:41 A.M. Shay lay curled against him on the bed they'd moved to sometime during their second session. So deeply asleep, she snored like a truck driver. Bogart, too, could be heard dream-woofing softly now and then as he slept on guard by the front door.

What the hell had happened tonight?

He'd had good sex and bad sex. And a lot more in between. He'd never had sex quite like this. It was like sex at the end of the world, all desperate need and raw hunger and . . . anger. Shay Appleton defined enigma: an intense defiant contradiction that attracted him while messing with his head.

She didn't want to talk. She didn't want to hear words of praise or tenderness. She wanted what he wanted, sex. Lots of it. Hot, eager, pulse-pounding, body-rocking sex. Until, exhausted, they could no longer remain awake.

He should have guessed. She did nothing halfway. Angry, hurt, scared, all her emotions were expressed straight up, in your face. Now he knew what it was like to have sex with her. And he wanted to be reminded again and again.

He closed his eyes. Tomorrow. Tomorrow they'd have to talk.

Shay gazed straight ahead. It was very dark, so dark that when she shut her eyes and opened them again she couldn't tell the difference. A moment later, she realized the covers were over her head. She flung them aside.

She lay on her stomach, head turned toward a doorway. Pale moonlight came from beneath it. A finger of dread slid up her spine. Was the bathroom door blocked? She always blocked it at night.

Even as she stared at it, the shadow of a pair of feet

appeared at the bottom, partially blocking the interior light.

A moan escaped her. No! This couldn't be happening!

Still half asleep, James opened the bathroom door.

A scream split the dark, lifting every hair on his arms and along his spine. Instinct made him reach for his weapon. But he was naked. No gun. In the sofa cushions. Too far away.

"No! No! Stay away! Stay away from me!"

He heard Bogart's bark, bright and sharp. An alarm that meant he was coming to help.

James reached back and flipped on the bathroom light, adrenaline gushing through him so quickly his heart seemed to expand in his chest.

The light angled sharply into the bedroom, in stark relief to the shadows. He looked first toward the bed, empty. He swept the room, looking simultaneously for Shay and a makeshift weapon.

She stood in the far corner, only her feet lit by the partial light.

Bogart streaked in, barking loudly as his big head swung from side to side, trying to detect an aggressor. After a second, he paused, black eyes gleaming as he stared at James.

James shared his confusion. *What the fuck?*

He groped along the bedroom wall until he found a light switch and flipped it.

Shay stood with her back to the windows. Her eyes were wide and both hands covered her mouth.

James took a few steps toward her. "Shay?"

Her gaze did not track to him. Instead, she stared at the bathroom door. That's when he realized she was still asleep. In the midst of a nightmare he did not share.

Bogart barked again, running up to press against his partner's leg in confusion. James bent to stroke him.

"Gute Hund." He pointed. *"Geh raus."*

Bogart turned away and after a quick glance at Shay left the room.

James's attention was still on Shay. He moved into her line of vision and said in a sharp, commanding voice, "Shay Appleton!"

She jerked and blinked, then her hands slid away from her mouth as her gaze focused on him.

"That was you?" The words sounded forced out of her, almost airless.

"Yeah. I needed to take a leak. Sorry if I scared you."

"It was you." She shook her head tightly then pressed her palm to her forehead. "This was a very bad idea."

He smiled. "I thought it was really nice."

She lifted her head, her expression empty. "You need to leave."

"Now?" He glanced at the clock. "It's 4:38."

"I don't care." She moved across the room, seemingly unaware that she was naked, and began pushing him. "You have to go. Now. Please."

"Okay, okay. I get the idea. Just let me put my clothes on."

Shay backed off but only as far as the bed. She grabbed up the sheet and wrapped herself in it.

James shoved a foot into one leg of his jeans he had scooped up off the floor. "Look, I understand if you're a little weirded out by how fast this all happened."

She shook her head. "You don't understand. You won't ever understand."

"You'll never know if you don't give me a chance."

"You don't know anything at all about me." Her voice was suddenly all challenge.

"Fair enough." He paused to wrestle himself into a sweatshirt he'd pulled from his backpack. "But that doesn't mean I don't want to know you better."

He straightened up to look at her. "Because I do, Shay."

She shook her head again, not looking at him.

He thought about saying something else. But then he realized the argument was over. She'd told him to get out. The message was loud and clear.

James finished dressing in silence.

When he was done she followed him into the living room. "Don't come back. Don't call. Don't text. Don't anything."

James swung around. "Why? Just tell me why. Was it something I did?"

She just stared at him, her expression as closed as a fist.

"Okay. Right." James glanced down at Bogart, who had been watching them. *"Hier."*

Bogart trotted over to his handler's side.

James made it to the front door before turning back to Shay. "I don't know all that went on between you and Eric, but don't judge me by him. Not all men are assholes."

CHAPTER TEN

Yardley Summers, owner of Harmonie Kennels, held a hand folded over her eyes to shade the rising sun as she watched K-9 partners Officer James Cannon and Bogart go through their paces. It was a drill they had been through so many times they should have been able to do it in their sleep. Yet something was off today. James didn't seem to fully trust Bogart, keeping him on a short leash. Bogart was clearly insulted by the lack of freedom and giving attitude.

"Let him run. Get out of Bogart's way." Her voice carried rapid-fire across the otherwise quiet, misty chill of the morning. Weather was never a factor when they drilled. It only made things more interesting.

She watched as James let out the leash but it wasn't enough. She'd chosen a routine task for them, pick up the trail of a suspect and track him down. They were botching it.

Clamping down on the temptation to say more, she watched in mute exasperation as two of her best graduates fumbled around like newbies.

Bogart seemed unable to settle down to the task. He kept looking back at his partner for reassurance, as if this were his first trial.

James wasn't giving back confidence. Instead of smiling and encouraging his partner verbally, his expression was tight and his hand too heavy on the lead.

Bogart began jumping and leaping around James, clearly riled up for the hunt but frustrated by the lack of direction.

Yardley muttered under her breath then gave vent to her feelings. "Just unclip him. Dammit. Give him the scent again and then get out of his goddamn way."

James did as she directed.

Finally, after another sniff, Bogart swirled around, long tail moving in slower loops as he sniffed and then ran on ahead, free now to find his way. Suddenly he paused and lifted his head. His panting ceased. Two seconds later, he wheeled and headed off into the brush where the culprit had been told to hide.

James ran after him, offering encouragement in a high-pitched rapid tone now that they both knew they had the scent.

Yardley didn't bother to follow. She knew the conclusion so well it wasn't necessary. She swore under her breath as she set her cap on her head and then folded her arms, one booted foot thrust forward so that her hips were cocked, to wait for her students to return.

Through sweat, determination, and by what her grandmother called "just plain cussedness," Yardley had made Harmonie Kennels one of the top breeding farms for K-9 service dogs on the East Coast. Teams were sent here for her rigorous training programs. Using her sterling reputation in the business, she insisted on having the final say-so in the pairing of her animals with their human partners.

She had put this team together because they shared similar natures. James had the same energetic yet tenacious quality as Bogart, and good instincts. Good instincts couldn't be discounted. Partners who trusted their instincts often solved cases using details that by-the-book partners missed. She was certain James and Bogart could become one of the finest K-9 teams she'd ever produced, but only if they learned to trust each other completely. Just now, they were acting like a couple who'd had the Big Fight. The bond between them had been disturbed and they were both the worse for it. That made her furious.

James and Bogart came back from their trial at a trot. The sight of the pair of healthy male specimens drew a half-smile of begrudging admiration from their coach. She pinched if off immediately and placed a fist on each hip. It was time to chew their asses.

James stopped before her, not at all winded. "Sorry. We're a little rusty."

Yardley ignored the gorgeous smile he slanted her way. "Rusty can let a suspect escape. Or get you killed."

He sobered instantly. "Yes, ma'am."

"How long have you and Bogart been off required training?"

"Four weeks, ma'am."

"Eight hours a week minimum, times four weeks. Well, hell. You've missed thirty-two hours of training. That's enough to ruin you as a team."

"Yes, ma'am. That's why I came out here first thing. To be assessed."

Yardley walked slowly around the pair, assessing the tension running through the young officer's body and the concern expressed by the way his canine companion was watching his partner's every twitch.

"You youngsters get a few takedowns under your belts

and think you don't need to learn anything else. But without constant discipline and training, you're not K-9 officers. You're just a boy and his dog."

"We'll do better tomorrow, ma'am. I'll work him day and night between shifts."

"Did you not hear me? You're not fit for street duty."

Stung by her assessment, James had to bite back the comment that came to mind. It wasn't Bogart's fault he was rusty. It wasn't his . . . Hell. Maybe it was.

"Come with me."

They were both silent as they walked back to the main office. Hard as she could be, James was grateful for Yardley's close connection to the partners she paired up. Without it, Bogart might not have been found.

Aware that Bogart was missing, Yardley had paid special attention when she received a call from a young woman who said she had recently adopted a Belgian Malinois from a shelter. The caller said the dog was so well trained she thought he might have professional abilities. Yet when Yardley asked her to describe the dog, the young woman hesitated. That hesitation was enough to prick Yardley's curiosity. When pressed for details, for instance where exactly she had adopted the dog, she'd only say it was near Lake Gaston. When asked if the dog was tattooed or tagged, the caller had hung up. Even more suspicious. Following a hunch, she had called James.

They agreed. Why would the caller contact Harmonie Kennels unless she was aware of some connection to the dog in question? It could be a setup. Someone who'd steal a police dog might have a vendetta against the owner or the department. Worst-case scenario was the go-to mode of operation. The benefit of the doubt could get a law enforcement officer killed.

James and his sergeant had come up with a plan. On his own time, James would do some investigation in the general area of Lake Gaston, by pretending he was a civilian with a missing pet.

It was amazing what a local gas station or café owner knew or observed about her or his customers. One glance at the photo James carried of Bogart, and the owner of a café located on a farm road off Interstate 95 just east of Littleton gave him the location of a recent customer with a dog that fit the description. But, he added, she wasn't a local. Just visiting. Using one of the old 1950s cabins located on a cove on Lake Gaston. Sure enough, that's where he found Bogart, and Shay Appleton.

James found himself wondering what Shay was doing now.

"That's your problem right here."

James paused, looking guiltily at Yardley. "What?"

"Your mind just wandered. That single-minded obsession to do your best, it's missing today."

"Yes, ma'am. I was just thinking how lucky we were that Shay was the one to get custody of Bogart."

Yardley noticed that he called the woman by her first name but let that slide. "Did she know anything about handling a dog with Bogart's special talents and needs?"

"No, but she has good instincts. They developed a relationship very quickly." He told her about the incident in the woods the night he'd discovered Bogart was alive and then, the next day, how his partner had alerted him to the man's return. "Both times Bogart understood without prompting that she was in danger."

She regarded Bogart thoughtfully. "That's quite remarkable."

James grinned with pride. "Bogart has a sixth sense about such things."

"You need to keep that in mind." Yardley then bent down and gave the Malinois a big hug. "Good boy! Such a smart boy, too."

James waited patiently as Yardley lavished affection on his partner. Her voice became light and girlish when she dealt with the dogs. Then her smile would betray the sensuous woman behind the military posture. She was an enigma in a male-dominated field of K-9 law enforcement. Once in the armed services, she had left to train K-9s. Yet she commanded the respect of a general whenever she entered a room or came on the training field. It didn't hurt that she was one helluva good-looking woman.

Not that you could mention that around her. She was tall and lean but with curves in all the right places. She had eyes so black rumor was she was part Apache. But then there was that long dark red hair, almost mahogany, usually stuck under a fatigue cap. Her strong-boned face held a hint of sensuality most often disguised with a no-nonsense expression. Her friends called her Yard. Everyone else called her ma'am.

James wondered from time to time what sort of man would be able to get behind those defenses and claim the woman only rarely glimpsed, like now? So far, he'd seen every man who tried get shot down. He hoped he'd be around when that changed.

Yardley came to her feet, produced a ball from her pocket and threw it. Bogart was off like a missile, chasing it. "What happened with Ms. Appleton's boyfriend?"

"Her ex." James flexed his shoulders, revealing more than he knew. "I leaned on him a little."

"Can't she take care of herself?" Yardley's tone was that of a woman who wouldn't need a dog or a man's help to put anyone in his place.

That question had been on James's mind, too. "She was doing okay with Bogart around."

Yardley frowned. "You think she's still in danger?"

He retrieved a ball from his pocket as Bogart waited

patiently for another toss. "Not really my business. She made that clear."

Yardley nodded. "Then she's got some grit. Good."

She took the ball from James and sent it sailing away. Bogart hustled after it as if it were a sirloin steak.

Yardley used the pause in conversation to think about what she should do next.

She knew more about her K-9 teams' private lives than most trainers. It was that kind of a business. Man or woman, and dog, needed to be part of a support system, an extended K-9 family, which included keeping up with one another's business, even if it was personal. Everything affected the bond between officer and canine. Nothing could be allowed to come permanently between that. When something did, they often needed help to work it out quickly, or they would fail.

While visiting a German breeder two years ago to observe their methods for selecting dogs to be trained, Yardley had had a chance to watch Bogart come into his own. And fell a little in love with this scrappy runt of the litter.

Bogart needed a master who knew when to hold him back, and when to get out of his way. From the beginning, James seemed to have an intuition about that delicate balance. But today, everything possible had gone wrong. Now there was something else in the mix.

She could tell James's preoccupation had something to do with the young woman named Shay. Bogart had bonded with her quickly. Perhaps James had, too. There was no way to know how important she was to them. And neither man nor dog was going to be back in top form until that issue had been worked out.

She seldom made command decisions for her teams, but she wasn't above steering from the rear.

"I'll sign off on your readiness for duty, temporarily,

but I'm going to recommend sending you and Bogart down to a place near Raleigh where you can get an intensive week of retraining. A sort of K-9 boot camp."

James looked startled. "I'd prefer to work with you, ma'am."

"I'd like that, too, James. But I've got a special forces team coming in to learn parachute jump techniques with their K-9s starting on Monday. I won't have the time or manpower to spare for you for several weeks."

"I don't know how my chief will react to the idea of giving me more leave after all the time I took off to look for Bogart."

"You leave Joshua to me."

It surprised James that she referred to his senior officer by his first name. He didn't know what her relationships were or how high up they went in both law enforcement and national security. But clearly, she had access to every power security player who mattered. If she wanted him at a K-9 boot camp for a weeklong refresher course, that's where he was going.

But first he had to settle the matter of his partner's disappearance.

CHAPTER ELEVEN

James made sure he saw her first.

Engrossed in conversation with a station employee, Jay-lynn Turner stood at the far end of a hall on the third floor of the building that housed one of Charlotte's TV station offices. A former Miss North Carolina runner-up, she was a long leggy blonde with a bosom that impressively filled out a swimsuit. The cascade of long blond hair dipping to the center of her back made her instantly recognizable in a crowd. Dubbed "Charlotte's Sweetheart" after viewers voted her their favorite local morning-show host, she wasn't particularly good at news delivery, often flubbing a line. But she had the charisma to cover slipups with a girly "oops, I did it again" kind of glance. The camera loved her. And the right demographics tuned in to watch her. She was on a trajectory for bigger things.

When he was growing up, hot girls like her had not been within his reach. He'd been a late bloomer, not top-ping five foot seven and a hundred and thirty pounds on high school graduation day. Homecoming queens, cheer-leaders, and other popular girls thought him nice, smart, and funny; a social death sentence that relegated him to friend status.

He'd sprouted during his first year of college. He'd played soccer since first grade so his fit physique just proportioned up with him. Now that he was a combination of nice guy and stud muffin, the dynamics shifted. Suddenly, women were eager to give him the sexual experience he had lacked. The short, skinny kid without confidence remained. So he had treated sex like it was a competitive sport through his early twenties until he adjusted to his new self-image. Things were different now.

He would be thirty next April. Most of his friends were either married or engaged. And he'd begun to feel the need—which had nothing to do with his mother's unsubtle prompting—to settle down.

He had thought he knew what he wanted. It was a fantasy he hadn't even fully let himself in on until he'd found her. He was looking for the kind of woman who would turn heads and gain him the envious admiration of his male friends. And be willing to become his wife and, in time, mother to their children.

When "Charlotte's Sweetheart" singled him out with her flirtatious attention during an appearance on her morning show with Bogart, for the Charlotte K-9 service, he was so flattered his hard-on lasted the next three hours. He even started thinking about how to make payments on a diamond ring that first day.

James felt the heat of a rare blush sting his neck. The memory made him want to kick his own sorry butt around the block.

She's so beautiful but so boring. Wasn't that a song lyric? He'd always thought: *Screw boring. If I could nail a woman like Jaylynn I wouldn't care if she couldn't add four plus four.*

Only that was no longer true. Not even great sex could

prevent his quick disillusionment with his fantasy girlfriend. That was because Jaylynn had only one topic of conversation: Jaylynn.

After an initial fuck-o-rama weekend, even their physical relationship began to have limitations. She didn't want him to tangle her perfect hair that was, he discovered, not really all hers. She didn't want to stay up late or wake up early for sex on his days off. She needed to be "fresh" for the camera. She couldn't do "it" the day she got a bikini wax. "It doesn't look good."

Turned out, she was great at faking emotions, too. She wanted him on her arm for her public appearances but she couldn't make time for a barbecue with his colleagues, let alone spend time with his family. After one too many arguments on the subject, she admitted that she didn't like any of them that much. She even let slip that her dating him had been a calculation. The obvious chemistry between them on-screen, not to mention Bogart's appeal to dog lovers, had tracked well with her demographics. Being a couple raised her profile. And she was always on the lookout for people and situations that gave her more publicity.

Just before they broke up, she was bragging about the fact that she had a new following in the Virginia penal system. She'd visited a correctional center as part of a morning-show segment on rehabilitation of the incarcerated. Their fan mail, she told one and all, just made her day. She told James that the thought of a building full of horny incarcerated men thinking about her made her feel all hot and kinky.

She turned away from the colleague to address an underling who had approached, long hair rippling with her every move. James felt his nut sack tighten. She'd betrayed him. He wasn't ever going to forget that.

James let his anger rise a bit. He'd been one sorry-ass

fool, letting pride keep him from ending it. How long would it have gone on if Bogart hadn't disappeared?

Jaylynn had never even tried with Bogart. She didn't want him around. No, Bogart couldn't be kept in a kennel outside when they were together. Yes, his partner shed, but it wasn't that bad. If Bogart was part of the deal, then James couldn't stay at her place overnight.

Not surprisingly, the feeling of dislike was mutual. Oops, sorry, Bogart chewed up her favorite purse. Oh no, you can't find your cell? Yes, look, Bogart hid it. He does that when he's bored, or being ignored. Maybe if she didn't leave her things lying around everywhere. If she just tried to be friends with Bogart . . .

Instead, Jaylynn had tried to destroy him.

The memory of Shay laughing and rolling in the grass with Bogart flashed through his mind, tugging a smile from him. Shay's love of Bogart had no calculation. He doubted she was capable of fake emotions.

He thrust that thought aside as Jaylynn started down the hall.

She didn't notice him until she was within half a dozen steps. "Well, look who's turned up? If you've come to apologize, it will have to wait. I'm busy."

James smiled but it held no humor. "I didn't come to apologize." He signaled with his hand and Bogart, who was sitting out of sight, padded softly into view.

"Oh my God! How—I mean, you found him." Her voice was full of false emotion. "It's a miracle. Hey there, boy."

She reached out a hand as if she meant to pat him but Bogart rolled back his muzzle until all his teeth showed. She jerked her hand back. "Where—I mean, how did you find him?"

"Cut the crap, Jaylynn. I know. Everything." James's voice was pitched low so that others moving through the hall couldn't hear him. But she got the message.

She blinked twice. "Okay, I have an admission to make." Her perfect posture slipped as her shoulders rounded in feigned regret. "Your dog wasn't stolen." She glanced across at him. "I was too ashamed to tell you the truth. So I kind of made up that story about him being stolen."

"Really?"

She nodded, staring now at a spot on the floor halfway between them. "I stopped on the way to the groomers to pick up a new nail polish. When I opened the door, he took off." Her lower lip, scarlet-lipstick perfection, trembled. "He never liked me, you know. I think he ran off just to upset me."

"Cut the shit, Jaylynn. You drove him all to the way to an animal shelter near Raleigh to have him put down."

She straightened her spine, thrust out her perfect breasts, and shook out her hair. The stare she leveled at him said she was done with explanation. "Like I said, I'm busy. If you want to discuss this—no, you know what? We have nothing to say to one another." She tried one last time for her "Charlotte's Sweetheart" smile. "It was good while it lasted but it's over. Let's not waste each other's time and spoil it by making bad memories."

James watched her take three steps to the nearest doorway. "If you leave this hallway before we're done, I'm going straight to the station's general manager to tell her the story you don't have time to hear."

She turned around slowly. "What do you mean?"

He gave her the "come here and sit" hand signal he used with Bogart, and he was pleased to see by her insulted expression that she recognized it.

All pretense of flirtatiousness vanished as she retraced her steps. "Make it quick."

James gave her the account of how he'd found his animal, his voice level and unemotional. She grew paler with every sentence but her expression remained neutral.

When he was done, she gave him her trademark blink and then a coy big-eyed "oops" glance. "So, I made a mistake. What do you plan to do about it?"

"It's not me you have to worry about. You lied to the police, alleging the false charge of dog-napping. You could be cited for false allegations, for starters."

Her expression relaxed. "What is that? A fine? I can pay it."

"You also stole and tried to destroy police property."

Her gaze flicked to the very much alive Bogart, panting by his side. "But I didn't actually do anything."

"Then there's your public relations problem when this gets out. People love their pets. Your ratings soared when Bogart was on. Remember all those crayon pictures of him you got? 'Dog killer' isn't going to look so good on your resume."

"You and that damned dog." Her voice was bitter. "I wish I'd never set eyes on either of you."

"Ditto." He held her glare. "I could press civil charges, too. But I won't."

Jaylynn closed her eyes for a moment, as if in prayer. When she opened them the old Jaylynn was back, the silky siren pose slipped into place.

"So, you're just toying with me, trying to make me sweat. I should be very mad at you." Her lashes fluttered and her mouth turned pouty as she placed a hand on his chest, nails bent to make playful indentations in his uniform. "I forgive you. I knew you were a good guy."

"I'm not that good." He brushed away her touch. "I have a police report to file. Specialty-trained dogs like Bogart are worth upward of twenty thousand dollars. The department could bring charges against you for grand larceny."

"My God!" For the first time she seemed to understand that she was in jeopardy. "What can I do?"

"Turn yourself in and throw yourself on the mercy of the department."

"But I can't do that without exposing myself to . . ."

James finally smiled. "Yeah. Public opinion. Maybe it's time to bite at one of those offers you say you're constantly getting from other stations."

She stared at him. "You can't prove it was me. I'll say you lied, that you're a jealous ex."

James turned and walked away.

"I'll get an attorney." Her voice carried after him, making the few people passing in the hallway turn and stare. "A good one who can make anyone look like a liar."

He paused to look back. "I can prove it was you. There's a witness."

He and Bogart quickly turned the corner before he said something he'd regret.

CHAPTER TWELVE

"Must be nice to have the kind of job security where you can just take off without notice."

Shay gave Henry an obscene finger wave as she passed his cubicle.

He laughed in response. "Lunch?"

"If we're still here then."

Henry was one of two friends she had at Logital Solutions, a tech temp agency. Angie was the other. Though "friend" was more a term of mutual likability than time spent together. They were seldom in the building since temp agency employees were only doing well if they were out of the office. LS supplied the IT sprawl that was Raleigh-Durham-Chapel Hill with high-tech workers. On any given day, they could be cities apart.

"Hi, Shay."

She glanced over at Angie who occupied the cubicle directly across from hers. Five foot two and amply proportioned, Angie was one of those lucky creatures with lots of curves, a sweet face, and long golden curls that made her look like Alice in Wonderland with an addiction to peppermint white hot chocolate from Starbucks.

Then there was her costume habit.

Shay leaned against the entrance of her friend's tiny cubicle, taking in the shimmering deep blue and silver fabric tacked to the walls, and then Angie's blue star-spangled oversized sweater and navy tights with ankle boots. "What's this week's theme?"

Angie dimpled in delight. "Goddess Diana." Shay pointed to the globe light on her desk. "In honor of November's hunter's moon. Perry wouldn't allow me to hang anything from the ceiling. Said it violated safety regulations."

Shay smiled. That was about the only thing their boss Perry wouldn't let Angie get away with. She was Logital Solutions's star. Aware that traditional employers might disapprove of her eccentricities, Angie worked remotely, delivering excellent work even while wearing a tutu.

"How was your vacation?" Angie studied her face. "You look like you haven't been to bed since you left. Tell me those huge bags under your eyes come from sleepless nights screwing a yummy new guy."

Shay shrugged. "Actually the week sucked. I lost Prince."

"Oh no! Hit by a car?"

"Taken by a Charlotte police officer. Turns out he was a stolen K-9 police dog."

"K-9 officer? Like this?" Angie turned and opened a file drawer and pulled out a calendar of K-9 officers and their dogs. She flipped it open. "Isn't this July shot hot?"

"Yeah, gorgeous pelt." Blushing for reasons that had nothing to do with the gorgeous male officer in the picture, and everything to do with the one who'd shared her bed over the weekend, Shay handed back the calendar. "See you later."

Shay had promised herself that she wasn't going to go

over it again in her mind, for maybe the zillionth time.
Screw that.

Sex with James had been—well—fan-*fucking*-tasic!

For once in her life, her overeager brain cells had
checked out and let her just feel every way, every move,
touch, pressure, quake, and rush of the desire that ran between them like lava.

James had smelled good, of soap—her soap—and the
faint scent of shaving gel. He'd tasted of her dinner and
desire. He was hot everywhere she touched, as if there
were a secret fire ablaze beneath his skin. When he em-
braced her, he felt solid, capable, and sexy as hell. And he
wanted her.

She had always wanted to be wanted like that. It was
urgent and sweet and hungry. In his arms was the safest
and most secure place she'd been in a long, long time.
She was gloriously happy, pretending for a night that she
was capable of a normal relationship with someone who
wouldn't hurt her. Only it hadn't worked out that way.

She'd gone all "Psycho Shay" on him, and thrown him
out. All because he had used the john in the middle of the
night.

Shay cringed. It had been a long time since she'd had
that particular nightmare. Seeing the shadow of feet beneath her bathroom door had set it off.

Now she'd never see James again.

She dragged a hand across her cheek, wiping away a
tear she had not given her body permission to spill.

That was her only consolation. She'd never have to look
James Cannon in the eye and see the expression of fear
tinged with revulsion that had made her high school years
a constant misery.

She eased into her chair in her cubicle. Her space was
pristine compared to Angie's. That was because she didn't
leave clues to her life around. No pictures, cards, memora-

bilia. For an IT specialist, she was very low-tech in her personal life. No social media or tweets, not much e-mail outside of job necessity. Today the only thing on her desk was a shiny brochure.

The hair on Shay's neck lifted as she recognized it. It was for a private luxury island resort in the Caribbean.

She snatched it off her desk and glanced around quickly. It was a souvenir of the most recent of several weekend getaways Eric had taken her on, at his bank's expense. No one else was supposed to know about it.

When her gaze came back to the brochure she noticed the slanted spidery script in the upper left-hand corner. It read: "Ready to make up?"

"Shit!"

Angie's head popped up over her cubicle wall. "What's wrong?"

Shay thought fast. "Ah . . . paper cut." She stuck an uncut finger in her mouth for emphasis.

"Hate that." Angie slumped out of sight.

Shay bit her lip to keep from asking Angie any of the questions chasing each other in her head.

Eric had been here? When? And why, of all the trips, would he think she'd want to repeat that weekend?

A searing flash of their final night at the private resort lasered its way into her consciousness. Eric had brought her along to an international banking convention. The executives at the after-hours party were wasted on expensive booze and cocaine when one of them suggested a dance-off with their female companions as contestants.

She had suspected many of the women were paid companions. But when a dozen of them gamely shimmied out of their clothing to bump and grind in sexy barely there undies and less, she knew.

Shay closed her eyes, remembering how humiliated she'd been when Eric had pulled her to her feet and pushed her out on the impromptu dance floor, hissing in her ear, "Act like you're begging for sex. Don't embarrass me. Make them believe it."

He expected her to swing her ass for the amusement of a bunch of drunk strangers.

Worse than stumbling through suggestive dance steps to music with crude sexual lyrics was withstanding the expression on Eric's face as he watched her efforts. Because she wouldn't undress, she was voted off the floor first.

On their way back to their suite, in defense of his scathing review of her poor performance, she'd burst out with, "Unlike some of those women I'm not a whore."

"True," he'd answered. "You're not skilled enough to survive as one."

Shay rubbed the too-tight sensation between her brows. There were so many memories she wished she didn't have. Then, using two fingers, she picked up and flipped the brochure into the wastebasket. If only she could lob Eric in there with it.

To distract herself, she pulled open a drawer to survey its contents. There was a half-eaten bag of chips, a partially eaten power bar, and three pieces of candy that were at least eight weeks old. She tossed them after the brochure.

The tactic didn't work. Memory ambushed her a second time before she could steel herself.

One second she was sitting in her cubicle, the next her world was imploding, sucked into the deep shadows of an unlit apartment bathroom on a night when she was fourteen years old.

She began to vibrate as the memory moved and settled with disturbing familiarity into her psyche. Fingernails bit into her palms as her stomach cramped in fear. The phantom smells seemed to fill her nostrils until she was near suffocating.

She was alone in a new place, an apartment over a Chinese restaurant. Years of orders of stir-fried vegetables and General Tso's Chicken had soaked into the carpeting and drapes. The odor made her feel either constantly hungry, or queasy. It was supposed to a short-term solution, until her mother got established in Raleigh.

Her mother, an LPN, was working extra shifts at the senior care nursing facility so that Shay could finish another school year without needing to get a job, too. "You make the grades that will take you out of this life, Shay. I'll support that."

Always a sensitive child, she locked her bedroom door when her mother was away at night and never ventured out until dawn. But tonight that extra large Slurpee she'd insisted upon with a burger dinner was pressing hard on her bladder. She needed to go. Bad.

She slipped out of bed and turned the knob.

The bathroom floor was cool under her bare feet. She didn't turn on the light, feeling her way along to the toilet. It was ugly, cracked on the rim and stained in ways her mother couldn't scrub away. Better to pretend it was okay than to see that it wasn't. She had finished her business and reached for the handle to flush when she heard it.

Heavy footsteps stopped before the bathroom. Not Mom.

"Ms. Appleton?"

Shay jerked upright and twisted in her seat toward the opening of her cubicle.

Perry Deshezer, entrepreneur and owner of Logital Solutions, stood there in a dress shirt with rolled-up sleeves, cords, and Nikes, his standard office attire.

"You okay?"

Shay blinked. The solid world disappeared for a nerve-racking fraction of a second before returning. "Yeah. Sure."

"Good." He sounded unconvinced. "How was your vacation? Catch any fish?"

"What?" Shay focused on the items on her desk. *In my cubicle. In my office space. Grown-up Shay is here.* "Oh, I don't fish."

"But you enjoyed yourself?"

"Yes. Why—" She glanced up into his slight frown. Then she remembered what Angie had said about the bags under her eyes and used the same excuse. "I, ah, lost Prince."

"Oh no, Shay. What happened?"

She gave him the sanitized version of Prince's return to his rightful owner. By the end of it he was shaking his head. "That reeks."

She looked away, feeling a little ashamed for having manipulated his sympathy. "I just need time to get over it. To work."

"You're in luck. Halifax Bank's IT customer service person went on maternity leave last week. It's way beneath your skill set but they asked for you by name. "

Shay had begun to recoil at the beginning of his speech, her stomach clamping down hard on her coffee-only breakfast. "They asked specifically for me?"

He nodded. "I told them you were out until today. They said they'd wait. You must have impressed the hell out of them when you worked there last year."

"Un-huh." Shay avoided his eye, her stomach roiling.

Eric was a regional manager for Halifax Banking Corporation. They'd met while she was temping as a techie at the main branch. Now Halifax Bank had asked for her again. Coincidence? Or part of Eric's new scheme? "Who exactly asked for me?"

"The HR person."

Shay glanced guiltily at the brochure sticking out of her wastebasket. "No one came in person?"

Perry chuckled. "Who would send a messenger to hire a temp?"

"I just wondered." She looked up. "I'd rather not take this one."

He crossed his arms. "Shay, you're one of my best workers but that doesn't benefit either of us unless you're earning an income. We don't have anything else that fits your skills at the moment."

"Right." Shay looked away from him. Perry was a stellar boss. He tolerated a lot, but when it came to the work ethic, he was all business. As for Eric . . .

She felt good old reliable anger coiling inside. Eric worked out of the main branch in downtown Raleigh but his position as a regional manager kept him on the road. She might not even see him. And if she did, it would be in a public setting.

You don't have to be afraid. James saw Eric in action. Eric won't want the police involved again.

Of course, Eric wouldn't know getting in touch with James was the last thing she planned to do. But more than that, she needed to prove to herself that she was once again in control of her life. She couldn't do that by hiding.

"I'm just bummed. The job sounds like a bore." She gave an elaborate shrug and rolled her eyes. "Sorry."

Perry glanced at his watch. "You can start today, then, say by 10 A.M.?"

Her gaze strayed to her computer where the time displayed was 8:41. "Sure."

He gave her the once-over, taking in her jeans and sweater and unmade-up face. "Enough time to stop by home and change?" He never missed a thing.

"On my way."

"The paperwork is done. It'll be at reception. Just sign it on your way out."

"Oh, I have a new phone number. I lost my phone."

Perry frowned as she handed him a slip of paper. "Isn't that the third time this year?"

Shay shrugged.

As he walked away, Shay grabbed her tote, the tremor in her hand the only giveaway of her state of mind. All she had to do was sit before a computer and talk to customers on the phone all day for six short weeks. She wouldn't even interact with most of the other employees.

I can do this.

The shiver working its way down her back was only anticipation, she told herself. Then her gaze slipped sideways to the brochure.

Eric had set this job up. She was certain. That meant he had something in mind.

So what?

She'd be in a public place, doing a job she could handle in her sleep. If he did come near her she would show him that she was no longer afraid of him. He had more to lose than she did if their relationship became public knowledge.

Screw him! He wouldn't be allowed to keep her from making a living.

CHAPTER THIRTEEN

Mumbling something about "shit for brains," James corrected a mistake he'd made in his daily report. Paperwork was his least favorite part of the job, even if it was done on computer. He hit ENTER then massaged his eyes with his fingers.

Asleep beside his desk, Bogart stirred and growled, deep in doggy dreamland.

A smile tugged at James's mouth. After four nights on patrol, he felt they were back on top. But that wasn't his call. Instead of heading home to sleep, he was about to go home to pack. He'd gotten his orders for a week of training not far from Raleigh, beginning on Monday.

If he left early, he could spend the weekend in Raleigh. He needed a little R & R where no one knew him as a cop. It was just lucky coincidence that Raleigh was where Shay lived. A coincidence he had every intention of exploiting.

Yes, she'd tossed him out and told him never to come back. But he hadn't been able to get her out of his mind. It wasn't just the sex. It was her loneliest-soul-in-the-world gaze. For a few brief hours, she'd let him in, and it had been magic. He needed to know if their connection was as real as his gut told him it was. Or, just a strangers-in-the-night fantasy.

He pulled a thumb drive from his pocket. He had only one other thing left to do before his shift ended. That was to file his report on Bogart's disappearance. Every officer in his unit would recognize the description of the suspect as his ex. That was going to be damned embarrassing, but he could tough it out. The department would make the decision to file suit. If so, Jaylynn was about to be hit with a shitload of trouble. On the other hand, the chief might decide to avoid calling attention to potentially embarrassing publicity for the department. Either way, it wasn't his call.

He pushed the drive into his computer to upload it, needing only one more bit of information to make the report complete.

"Here's that info you asked for." Dwight Meyer handed him a folder. Dwight worked fugitives, which specialized in finding people and mining information.

James nodded. "Took a while."

Dwight shrugged. "Ms. Appleton's got the lowest social profile of any twenty-something woman I ever came across. Practically off the grid. You'd think she was on the job. No social media pages, no tweets, no blog. Not even a regular cell number. Bet she uses disposables. Yet she jobs for a high-tech temporary employment agency."

James frowned. "Really?"

He nodded. "First flag, Cannon. She changed her name at eighteen. Legally."

That didn't totally surprise James. He had run into a wall trying to track her information down on his own. Shay wasn't in the Raleigh phone book and had no police record that he could locate, not even a traffic ticket. Was that even possible?

Then there was her almost paranoid need to reveal nothing about herself.

An uneasy feeling moved through him as he indicated the folder. "What's the second flag?"

"You tell me." Meyer didn't like to categorize his finds. "She's got a sealed juvie file. That's all I could find out without a warrant." The final word vibrated in the air between them. Meyer was willing to go deeper, if asked to.

"It's not that kind of case. Thanks."

James picked up the folder, unusually slim in that it contained all readily available information on an adult woman's life. It was also a concrete reminder that he had already behaved unprofessionally with her, in more ways than one. They'd met under extreme circumstances, known each other only a day and one hell of a memorable night. But once back in Charlotte he realized he knew squat about her. Not her full legal name, home address, phone number, or where she was employed, all information needed to complete his report.

What he did know was that they fit together like Legos, even if she had decided to toss him out despite it. Or, because of it.

A lewd grin tugged one corner of his mouth. When he was balls-deep in her neither of them had cared about anything else.

"You hearing this?"

James looked up. "What?"

Sheila Hooper, another K-9 officer, pointed to one of several TV monitors in the report room. "Your ex is going to make a big announcement, right after the commercial break. You aren't getting married, are you?"

"Fuck that." He said it without heat. All the same, he moved toward the nearest TV monitor where the local morning news show was on the screen.

Jaylynn appeared on-screen. She sat behind the news desk dressed in uncharacteristic somber shades of navy and gray, usually reserved for when some prominent person had died. No megawatt smile today. She made eye contact with the camera and began speaking, her voice tight with emotion.

"It is with deep regret that I announce today that I am temporarily leaving my position as co-anchor of Charlotte's top-rated morning show. I'm making this selfless gesture in order to address the vicious campaign of false accusations that have begun to circulate about me."

Tears welled in her eyes as the camera moved in for a close-up. James knew they'd never be allowed to fall. Jaylynn had told him that welling worked on camera. Tears made mascara run, a no-no.

"As a celebrity, I am aware that some people think I'm fair game, but they forget that lies can tarnish a person's reputation, even if they are completely false. Therefore, with the help of the legal team I've assembled, I intend to get to the bottom of this and clear my name."

Sheila elbowed him. "What's that about?"

Game face in place, James shrugged.

Jaylynn has gone on the offense!

Legal team? Was she serious? He doubted it. Yet she had turned a strategic retreat into a fake noble ride into the sunset. When the truth got out about what she'd done, half the town was primed now not to believe it.

That was slick, and so Jaylynn.

He glanced down at Shay's file and shoved aside the uncomfortable feeling of having her investigated. He had the best of motives.

Right. Dudley Do-Right to the rescue.

His father didn't give a lot of advice, especially about women and relationships. Most of that was about navigating a household where the women outnumbered the men 4 to 2. What advice he did give lingered in his son's mind.

Once when he was twelve or thirteen, while they'd been camping out under the stars, his father had waxed philosophical. "Some women smell like forever. You don't get a whiff of it often. Once, maybe twice, in a lifetime. If you're ever lucky enough to get a whiff of that kind of woman, Jay, stop. And think. 'Can I live without this fragrance for the rest of my life?'"

At the time James had thought his father was talking about the smell of a particular perfume or lotion or conditioner. Now he knew better.

Shay's skin in the soft folds and hollows of her body captured and held the scent of her. There were no words really to describe that womanly perfume. The impressions that came to his mind were of warm buttered bread, caramel apples, and a faint pleasant musk. Shay smelled uniquely female. It was a fragrance he couldn't get out of his mind.

He knew that beneath her prickly armor was a woman capable of real and deep emotions. She had good instincts, had developed a deep attachment to Bogart even after being warned he was dangerous.

And she made love like she had invented it. That was the woman he wanted to get to know better. If she'd let him. But first, he needed to file his report on Bogart's disappearance.

He opened the folder again, typed in the pertinent information from the first page into the report on his computer, and hit upload.

After he was home and had taken care of Bogart, and showered and packed, he turned to page 2 of Shay Appleton's folder.

When he was done, his world was a lot more complicated.

CHAPTER FOURTEEN

"Yes, Mrs. Stockton. You get to choose your password. No, I can't keep it handy in case you forget it. It's very important that no one else know it."

Shay listened for a few seconds, closing her eyes so no one would see her eyeballs rolling back in her head.

"No, ma'am. Using 'password' for your password is a very bad idea. It's the first thing thieves try. Yes, they're clever. Do you remember your first phone number? No, don't tell me. That's not your number now, is it? Great. Use that as your password. You're welcome. Thank you for banking with Halifax Second Bank and Trust."

Shay glanced at the phone bank. For the first time all day, there were no calls waiting. Fridays were the worst. People still tried to do last-minute banking before the weekend, as if online weren't 24–7.

She whipped off her headset and reached for a bottle of water she kept close at hand under her desk. As she lifted her bottle for a first swallow, Eric Coates passed through her peripheral view. The bottle paused, suspended at her lips.

Unable to take her eyes off him, she could feel her heart thumping heavily beneath her suit jacket. For the past five days she had been waiting and dreading the possibility of this moment.

He sauntered over to her cubicle, pausing here and there to shake hands with one customer and pat another on the back. She tried not to fidget as nerves made a double-twist pretzel of her insides. He was deliberately prolonging the moment of meeting, making her aware of his complete control of the situation.

No. This was different. They were in a workplace environment. Besides, everyone knew he was engaged.

The official announcement had been in the Monday morning online Bank Weekly distributed to all Halifax Bank employees. There was even a picture of Eric squeezing the waist of a pretty blonde in a silvery cocktail dress. Underneath were the words "Felicitations to the Happy Couple."

He came right around the corner of her glass partition. "Hey, Shay." His voice was pitched in the low intimate register she once thought he reserved for her alone. Now it sounded rehearsed.

Shay raised her voice. "Congratulations on your engagement, Mr. Coates."

The smile pleats at the corners of his eyes deepened. "Just because I'm engaged doesn't mean we can't still have some fun. We just need to be more discreet."

Shay lowered her gaze, trying not to choke on her disgust. How she could ever have been so blind? He was a total douche. "I'm seeing someone."

"The cop? Drop him. I've upgraded your tastes beyond his pay grade."

He leaned in, a casual brace of his hands on her desk as if they were colleagues discussing an issue. "We've got a sweet little deal going here for the next five weeks. My office is right over your head." He glanced up. "I like the idea of that, you beneath me."

Aware of the people moving past them in the lobby, Shay leaned in before she looked up into his face. "Fuck off, Eric."

He leaned in a fraction closer, too. "I'd rather fuck you."

Shay waited until he was out of range before she took a deep breath.

She picked up her water, thirstier than before. She missed her mouth and spilled an icy trickle into her lap. She ignored it. Tilting the bottle again, she swallowed and concentrated on the sharp cold of the water as it traveled all the way down into her stomach. It was like jumping into an autumn lake, only from the inside. After her conversation with Eric, she wanted to shower.

She should get up and leave right now, and never come back. Perry would be furious. Probably fire her. So then she'd move out of Raleigh altogether. There wasn't anything or anyone holding her here.

That thought was as depressing as it was supposed to be inspirational. Anger came in to take up the slack.

Don't let the rat bastard run you off.

When she opened her eyes she saw a flashing light indicating a call. She reached for her headphones. Might as well finish the day. She needed the paycheck.

Shay glanced at the clock. It was ten minutes before closing. After fielding half a dozen calls from customers freaking out about their Friday paychecks not showing in their bank accounts, Shay picked up the next call with the numbing hope it was someone who'd forgotten their password.

"I'm lookin' for Shay Appleton."

Shay frowned. She was never asked for by name. "Yes? How can I help you?"

"You can keep your fucking mouth shut to the cops!"

"What?"

"Keep your fuckin' mouth shut, cunt!"

He hung up.

The panic attack came on too fast for her to process, let alone prevent. A sensation like swarming ants ran all over her body. A hard shiver rocked her. She couldn't breathe, couldn't get her diaphragm to draw in a breath. Sensations of being too hot and then too cold hit her, one after the other.

Unable to move, Shay allowed her gaze to sweep frantically back and forth across the main floor of the bank, looking for any sign of who might have made the call. The tellers were all busy. The bank officers with cubicles on this floor were with customers.

Eric. Where was he?

He was emerging from an elevator, in conversation with two men in business suits. They crossed quickly to the main doors and left.

Shay shot to her feet, her head getting yanked by the cord of her headphones. She jerked them off, ignoring the flashing lights of two new calls. She grabbed her purse and shoved a palm against her mouth as she skirted her desk and headed out across the main bank lobby. Her heels made loud clacking sounds as she hurried across the marble floor.

She straight-armed the restroom door open. Thankfully no one else was there. She ran to the first sink, bending low over it. She pushed for the water to come on with one hand, splashing her face with the other.

After a moment, she lifted her head and, eyes closed, drew in a long slow breath.

Breathe. Slowly. In. Out. In. Out.

She curled her hands into fists, digging her nails into her palms until they hurt. Control! She needed to get control! The panic attack would subside with control.

It was only a phone call. I'm not in immediate danger.
She opened her eyes to grab paper towels and dry her face.

She had worked IT in many different companies during the past three years. Dealt with the bug-eyed angry, dithering idiots, the socially inept, and even the occasional prankster or pervert. No one had ever called her that word before . . . except Eric, their final night together.

She stared at her reflection in the mirror. The image staring back looked bloodless, with too big eyes and wet spikes of bangs dripping into her eyes.

Who was the caller? Not Eric. The voice sounded uneducated, husky, burred by too many cigarettes or alcohol, or both.

Had Eric gotten someone else to do his dirty work? Was he expecting her to run to him for protection? Or, was he just trying to mess with her head?

One thing was certain. She'd had enough of Halifax Bank. She was going home. Now. Eric had won this round.

Rage welled up through Shay's anxiety as she reached for the restroom door, shouting, "Bastard!"

Two startled faces met her as she emerged. She ignored them and swept past.

James almost didn't recognize Shay when she burst through the doors of the bank as if someone were chasing her, and headed in the opposite direction. Dressed in a navy blue suit with a hemline his mother would call matronly, she looked middle-aged. "Shay?"

When she swung around he saw that the bangs were the same, as were the changeable tortoiseshell eyes that widened with his approach.

Bogart ran ahead, barking in delight at the sight of the friend who'd emerged from the bank. James gave him enough leash to reach his goal.

A pretty smile lit up Shay's face as Bogart bounded forward, certain of his welcome.

James rubbed a hand over a back pocket of his jeans as he followed. Damn. He was sweating! He would have considered any other man making this miserable move a loser.

Shay bent down to greet Bogart and got a lick in the face with a very wet tongue in response. "What are you doing here, fella?"

"Don't I deserve a welcome, too?"

Her gaze ranged away from the dog to find James standing over her. Her smile faltered. "Officer Cannon."

"The bad penny," he agreed with a small smile.

As their gazes locked, James tried to remember what he'd been telling himself on the drive over to Raleigh. All he could remember now that he was gazing at her was that every time he thought about her his johnson stirred.

The bank doors opened behind them, spilling out several other employees. Two women paused to gaze openly at Shay and the dog she was petting. The youngest woman smiled at James. "That's a really nice dog you got there."

James nodded, gathering up the slack in his leash. "I share him with Shay these days."

Two of the women exchanged glances. "You and Ms. Appleton are acquainted then?" A leading question if there ever was one.

He gave her his best smile. "Oh, we're more than that. Bogart and Shay are in love. Have a nice evening, ladies."

As they moved on Shay came slowly to her feet. James looked good, better than her memories of him. Tall and solid, he was devastatingly virile in ways that models often aren't. Still, he was the very last person she expected to see.

She tried not to sound breathless as she asked, "What are you doing here?"

"Bogart and I have been sent over to a place east of

Raleigh to get some training next week. Seems all your spoiling has ruined him for police work."

He was surprised to see the look of stark dismay that came into her expression. "Joke, maybe?"

"Oh." She smiled but it didn't have much energy. It pained him to think she had been so battered by life that she couldn't take a joke.

Still, James wasn't about to apologize. There'd been too damn much of that already in this relationship.

He handed her Bogart's leash. "I need a burger. You coming?" He turned on his heel and started walking back down the street to where he'd parked his cruiser.

It was a daring move, but he didn't know how else to engage her without starting an argument on a public street.

He was halfway to the corner before Bogart came bounding to his side. A second later Shay was there, too, looking straight ahead. He glanced sideways at her and smiled. So far, so-so.

They paused when the light changed.

"How did you find me?" Shay tried to keep the strain of the last minutes of her day out of her voice but it vibrated there anyway.

First I ran a background check on you and came up empty so I put a professional on it. That didn't sound like the way to start the evening.

He settled for a version of the truth. "I looked you up. Found out you work for Logital Solutions. So I went by there this afternoon."

"I see." Shay ran a mental list of who might have told him what. "You spoke with my boss?"

"No. After I was politely told by your company's HR person that they don't give out information about their employees, a lady named Angie came over and put a note in my hand. It was this bank's address. I hope you don't mind."

Shay shrugged.

"She added her cell number, and said if things didn't work out to give her a call."

That forced a laugh from Shay. That was so Angie.

Conversation met a lull as they waited for the light to change. But it was a strangely comfortable silence.

Shay had almost convinced herself that she had over-reacted to the crank call. More than likely the stupid jerk was someone who had been in the bank this week, noticed her nameplate, and was unhappy with his service. Disgruntled customers often chose anonymous ways to get back at institutions. He must have decided he'd get a live person to dump on if he called IT customer service.

That was a comforting theory, except for one thing. He threatened her very specifically. *Keep your fucking mouth shut around the cops.* Did he mean James?

Out on the street now at twilight, she couldn't shake the feeling of being exposed and vulnerable. That thought chilled her more than the nip of the cold front filtering through the evening air.

When the light changed, she reached out and took James's arm, needing to feel the solid assurance of his presence. He didn't say a word. She was grateful.

"Oh wait."

James turned as Shay dragged him to a halt.

"My car." She pointed in the direction opposite the one they were walking.

James thought about it only a second and then he said. "Right. I'll follow you and you can drop it off at your place before you come with us."

"I'd rather drive myself." Shay held her breath, waiting for his disapproval.

His expression didn't change. "Okay. But first." He caught her about the waist, lifted her chin with his finger and kissed her.

It was such a quick kiss she didn't have time to prepare or respond before he released her.

She stared him. "Why did you do that?"

He stared back. "Seriously?"

She nodded and turned around, not wanting him to see her smile.

She wasn't going to drag James into her problems. But if she went to dinner with him then, for a few hours, she would have protection. Her decision to be with him had nothing to do with the kiss. Absolutely nothing. Except, it had everything to do with it.

CHAPTER FIFTEEN

"I know." Shay mouthed the words and smiled at the pedestrian who had tapped on her passenger-side window
while she waited for the traffic light to change. He was
pointing behind her with eyes wide.

She glanced in her rearview mirror, no longer startled
every time she saw James's cruiser filling up the view. It
must appear to other drivers and pedestrians that she was
being tailed because he made every turn and pause she did.

James didn't know Raleigh so he suggested she choose
where they went. She decided on a place over on Morgan
Street. By the time they'd made their way through rush-
hour traffic, street parking was taken for blocks in all
directions. They ended up in a multitier parking garage
several blocks away.

When James came around his cruiser toward her with
an easy smile, it reminded her she'd spent the entire drive
trying not to think about the fact that he had kissed her.
Which led to thinking about their night together. That
made her body melt yet tighten with the reminder of what
it was like to be under him, over him, with him inside.

Don't go there.

She looked past him. "Aren't you bringing Bogart?"

"No. It's standard procedure to leave K-9s in their crates unless being called upon to work. K-9 vehicles are equipped with a special engine-driven, temperature-controlled environment."

Shay looked in the rear window where Bogart stared back through the glass, ears pricked forward and head slightly to one side. "You be good and we'll bring you a treat."

He answered with a bright bark, as if he understood her.

James took her by the elbow and turned her toward the exit. "Why don't you think about you for a change? It's Friday night. You're out with a pretty decent guy who drove two hours to take you out to dinner."

When put like that, Shay could only nod. Actually, that sounded like heaven.

When he slipped his hand down her arm to take her hand as they walked, she had to resist the temptation to lean in against his arm. This time her reaction had nothing to do with anxiety and everything to do with the most female part of her reacting to the male essence of him.

"Cold?"

He was looking down at her. That's when she realized she was shivering. But it wasn't cold sending little shock waves through her. These were pure sexual vibrations.

She shook her head, afraid if she spoke lust would coat her words with too much meaning.

When he put his arm around her anyway and pulled her in against him, a hurricane couldn't have forced her to move even one inch away from his muscular warmth.

Pushing through the door of the restaurant, they were met by the lights, noise, and crowded warmth of Raleigh TGIFers in full happy-hour mode. Surprisingly, a waitress with menus in hand waved them right in. She led them through the long, narrow establishment with a bar running the full length of the right wall and tables and booths filling the left. The aisle was clogged with patrons who, having spent the day at desks or in cubicles, preferred standing at the bar to sitting, while a thumping bassline filled the air with a heartbeat rhythm. The back room was less crowded only because the bar didn't reach that far.

"What'll it be, folks?"

Shay pointed to the beer menu for James's benefit. "This place carries beer from practically every brewery in North Carolina. Should be something there you'll like."

He shook his head. "Sorry, I'm driving a government vehicle. But you go ahead."

Shay looked up at the waitress. "Two O'Doul's, please." She didn't glance at James for fear of what she might see in his expression, perhaps gratitude she'd chosen to share a nonbeer with him. She wasn't certain she could handle any more positive vibes from him without embarrassing them both in public.

Her phone rang. It was Angie.

"Did he find you?"

"Hi. Yeah. Thanks."

"You sneak. He's gorgeous! Is he really a policeman?"

"That's right." Shay didn't look James's way because she didn't want him to know she was talking about him.

"Where are you? I hear music. And people. Is he taking you out?"

"I'm grabbing a burger."

"Is that safe, taking him out in public? Half the single female population of Raleigh will be on the prowl tonight. You are dressed to impress, right?"

Shay frowned. "Let me call you later."

"I hope you can't call back until tomorrow. And I'll want details."

Shay hung up and glanced around the room. Angie

was right. The crowd was young, and hip, and dressed to mate. By comparison she looked, well, dull.

She stood up. "If you'll excuse me a minute."

James reached for her wrist as she popped up out of her chair. "You are coming back?"

She smiled. "I haven't eaten all day. Order me a burger?"

He let her go with a grin.

Shay pushed into the ladies' room. When she caught a good look at herself in a mirror, she groaned out loud. She looked like a repressed librarian. But it was exactly because she hadn't wanted to attract attention at work, in case Eric did show up, that she'd been dressing down. The only not-ugly thing about her outfit was the sexy camisole she wore underneath her suit to make her feel better about herself.

She took off her jacket and rolled up the waistband of her skirt until four full inches of her legs were visible above the knee. The floating hem of her camisole hung loose, hiding the extra material at her waist. Nothing she could do about her sensible heels. No, wait! She kept a pair of cute flats in her bag. She fished out a pair of silver ballet flats. Okay, where was her makeup?

"Here, try this." The young woman next to her had opened a full bag of makeup. Dressed in frayed denim short shorts, a Mickey Mouse muscle shirt, and western booties, she held out a teal mascara wand. "It goes with everything, trust me."

"Thanks but I found mine." Shay pulled out her old reliable black and began touching up her lashes.

The woman persisted. "I saw your date when you came in. He's hot."

Shay smiled. "Yeah. He is." She reached into her bag for lipstick.

"You so need this." She offered Shay an eyeliner pencil. "I mean that in a good way. You've got amazing eyes but your mascara needs a little help. Here let me show you."

Shay didn't know why she was letting a stranger line her eyes but it was sort of fun to have someone fussing over her. She checked herself in the mirror. "Thanks."

The woman grinned. "Anything to help a girl with a hunk in hand. I'm Carly."

"Shay."

"He's not from around here. I know all the local guys. I'd surely remember him."

"He's from Charlotte." Shay wondered why she was giving away information to this stranger. Except that she'd been really friendly and helpful.

"Known him long?" When Shay hesitated, Carly grinned and laid a hand on her arm. "I know, I'm being nosy but you make such a cute couple. Good luck."

"Thanks."

Shay returned to her reflection. Okay, her hair needed work. She unclipped her bun and pulled a comb through the heavy fall of dark hair, then smoothed out her bangs.

James's eyes widened in interest as Shay came toward him. In place of her business jacket she wore a skimpy little green tank top with a plunging neckline edged in some sort of sparkly beads. And her skirt was definitely shorter, revealing long curvy legs. She'd let down her hair and it fell over her shoulders like a dark shiny waterfall. Her lips were pink, but not shellacked with that gooey kind of gloss that made him feel like his lips were going to slide off a woman's face when he tried to kiss her.

Best of all, a shy little smile tugged her mouth. She wanted him to be pleased. So he wasn't about to admit that, nice as she looked, he preferred her makeupless and in a ponytail, jeans, and scuffed boots. Or, better yet, nothing.

He lifted his mock beer in a little salute. "Nice."

"Thank you." She slid into the chair and picked up her own order. "So, why are you really here?"

James gave his head a little shake. She had a directness that most women he knew wouldn't know how to pull off. At least he was never in doubt about where he stood with her.

He, on the other hand, was feeling downright underhanded. He couldn't keep his mind on his mission when she was offering him an unrestricted view of the cleft between the twin swells of her breasts.

He crossed his legs under the table to cover his need to reposition himself. One glance into her big dark eyes and he knew he was going to lie a little longer about why he was here.

"It's like this. You've stolen my partner's heart. He can't concentrate at work. He's agitated at home. He won't even eat my cooking anymore. You ruined him for anything beyond fried oysters and corn muffins."

"Is that so?" Was that humor sparking in her dark eyes?

"Absolutely. Bogart's a simple sort. He likes a good meal. Hard work. Hard play. A little cuddle. And a nice soft place to put his head at the end of the day."

James would just about swear he saw her struggling to hold back a smile playing at the corners of her mouth.

She leaned back in her chair and folded her arms under her very nice bosom. "Don't you think you're interfering in something that isn't your business?"

"Everything about my partner is my business. He can't speak up for himself so I have to. Are you serious about him? Because if you're not, you need to back off and let the poor boy be."

"Isn't that sweet?"

A waitress neither of them had noticed stood by the table with their orders.

She gave Shay's shoulder a little bump with her elbow.

"You don't find many men who'd go to the trouble of looking out for a friend that way." She looked at James. "What kind of partners are you?"

"We're police, ma'am."

"And your friend is sweet on this young lady?"

"That's how it appears to me." James gave the waitress a by-the-book expression. "She took him in and won his total devotion. Since they parted he just doesn't know what to do with himself."

Shay was biting back laughter now. "You should be ashamed of yourself."

"No, now, hon. He's just being honest." The waitress put a hand on James's shoulder. "I know neither of you are asking, and it certainly isn't my business, but I was married to a police officer for a lot of years. They tend to be moody and men of few words. But that's all right if he loves you and you love him. He'll show his feeling in other ways."

Shay lost the battle with her laughter. "I get great big slobbering kisses every time I see him."

"Hm, maybe you can teach him a little better way to go at it, if that's not something you like. I find most men are eager to please a woman they care about." She looked at James. "Isn't that right?"

"Yes, ma'am." James's gaze remained on Shay, fascinated by her laughter.

"Here you go. Now, I have two orders of bacon cheeseburgers with onion rings." She set the plates before them. "All set?"

Shay nodded at the waitress.

"What about you, Myles Standish?" The waitress winked at Shay.

James looked up. "I'm good."

When the waitress had moved on, James looked at Shay. "What was that about?"

Shay picked up her burger and took a bite. She wasn't

about to tell him. Besides, the waitress had gotten the reference backward.

James reached for his phone. "I'm going to look it up. Miles who?"

"Myles Standish. Pilgrims? What? Did you sleep through American history?"

Shay put down her burger and turned toward him. "Myles Standish and this other guy, John somebody, were in love with the same woman. Only John didn't do anything about it because Myles was his friend. But one day, Myles asks John to go plead his case, because he's too shy to do it himself. The lady hears John out, about what a great guy Myles is and how much he likes her, and then says, 'Speak for yourself, John.'"

"So, what happened next?" James gave her a slow sexy grin that betrayed he knew the answer.

Shay rolled her eyes, not wanting to give him the satisfaction of making her say it. "Can't remember. Probably Myles and John ran off together and lived happily ever after."

James's laughter made the table shake.

Shay joined in, and felt the weight of the week slide away.

Conversation came to a near halt until all that remained on their plates were smears of ketchup, mustard, and crumbs.

Shay looked up from her empty plate and glanced around in search of the source of the live music that was starting up. Instead, she spied the woman who called herself Carly standing at the near end of the bar. She had been staring at their table. Caught in the act, she lifted her beer bottle in salute and then turned her back.

Shay bit her lip as familiar alarm bells jangled in her head. Why was a stranger so interested in how her date was going? Something told her it was more than mere curiosity. She glanced again at the bar. Carly was talking to a guy.

She scanned the room again, this time looking for hints of something not right. Had Eric sent someone to spy on her? Or was he here now, lurking in the crowd? Waiting for . . . for what?

Shay glanced away. Oh God! That sounded totally paranoid, even after the day she'd had. She was losing it. More likely that Carly person was one of those female predator drones who got their kicks from targeting another woman's man. She'd certainly tried to pry personal information about James out of her. Where was he from? How long had they known each other? Now that she thought about it—

"Something wrong?"

Shay was surprised to find James gazing intently at her. "No, just thinking." She leaned in a little, hoping to block his view of the bar. "Sorry."

He reached out and ran a finger over her upper lip. "You have a smear of mustard."

Vibrating from his touch, she reached up and carefully wiped her mouth with her napkin. "Better?"

"The view from here is great."

Right. We're on a date. Not part of some thriller movie.

But the mood was spoiled. Shay could feel herself sliding back into her protective shell. It was a short trip from unease to suspicion before her acutely tuned protective instincts slammed into overdrive. No, no, not tonight.

She looked across at James, using his open honest gaze to shock her heart back into its regular rhythm. Nice guy. No, great guy. He deserved better than her. She didn't doubt he would find that better woman without much effort. "You date a lot?"

He chuckled. "I'm not a horn dog."

"But you're dating someone?"

His expression sobered. "Maybe. I'll know more if she says yes to seeing me tomorrow."

Shay looked away, embarrassed that she didn't have enough experience to successfully flirt with a man who made her want to flee one minute, and jump him the next. Her reactions to him were too strong to control.

She shifted her gaze back to the bar. Carly was gone. That should have made her breathe easier but it didn't. She needed to get out of here.

James had been watching Shay all evening, absorbing details like the fact that for the past few minutes she kept glancing nervously over at the bar. At first, he thought she was on the lookout for someone. Maybe Eric. Then he saw the dirty blonde in Daisy Dukes lift her beer in salute. Shay's reaction had been to go as pale as his tighty whities. That didn't make any sense.

On second inspection the blonde wasn't as young as she first appeared to be. And there was something about her attitude. Then he had it. Cop. It was difficult to shed the posture of a law enforcement officer once it had been learned. This woman was, or had been, on the job. He'd swear to it. That didn't explain Shay's reaction to her.

What are your secrets, Shay?

He reached for her hand, as it lay on the table by her plate. His warm palm slid over the back of her cool hand, covering it entirely. "You want to tell me why you need protection? Is it Eric?"

Shay hesitated. "What do you mean?"

"I've seen him in action. Was he abusive throughout your relationship?"

The warmth in her eyes died, and her whole body visibly tensed. She pulled her hand away. "Are you asking as a friend, or a police officer?"

She had asked him that question once before. His answer was still the same. "Whatever you need to be comfortable."

She stared at him for several seconds, no doubt trying to decide how much to trust him.

"Not here. Okay?" She began looking around as if she couldn't wait to get out of the restaurant.

He stood up. "Then let's get the hell out of here."

CHAPTER SIXTEEN

"Damned if I know."

James ducked out from under the hood of her car. "You say the check engine light was on earlier?"

Shay nodded quickly, her arms wound tightly about herself against the autumn chill. "I guess I should have believed it."

"Well, I can't jump it and you have gas. I'm sorry but you're going to have to get it towed."

He watched her face fall. "I take it you don't have Triple A or something. But your insurance should cover it."

She looked down and didn't reply.

"You don't have insurance?"

She glanced across at him, misery making her eyes appear almost black in the dim light of the parking garage. "Liability and bare-bones collision."

"Okay." He closed her hood. "This is what we're going to do. The car should be okay overnight, but take all your belongings. In the morning, I'll call Raleigh police and get a reputable tow."

"Okay." Shay bit her lip. No point in telling him she couldn't afford a tow, much less a repair bill.

James watched her collect what amounted to very little from her car and then opened the passenger door to his cruiser for her. Her anxiety made him want to tuck her under his arm and promise her that bad things would never again happen to her as long as he was around.

But life wasn't like that. He couldn't stop all the big bad wolves from coming to her door, or anyone else's. But he was feeling the urge to try.

"I'm really sorry about this." Shay sat uneasily in the passenger seat of the cruiser. She had given him directions to her neighborhood.

"No problem. I'm a door-to-door kind of date guy."

Bogart stuck his head through the front hatch between them, tongue lolling out of his mouth, and slurped the side of Shay's face.

She laughed nervously and pushed him away. "The waitress was right. Your kisses need some work."

James glanced at her. "I assume you aren't talking to me."

Shay turned to look out the window so that he wouldn't see her face. She liked him, really liked him.

They drove northwest out of the main part of town. Shay had directed him to avoid the 440 Loop traffic though it took them away from the most direct route to her apartment. Plus, maybe she didn't want to say good night yet, though she was definitely going to leave him at her door.

A little nerve jumped at the corner of her mouth. The problem was, she didn't want to leave him on her doorstep. Or the living room. What would he do about that?

As they left the main part of the city a soft misty rain

began to fall. James turned on the radio. To her surprise, it wasn't country. Pink was singing one of her plaintive songs, something about getting up and trying again.

Suddenly, out near Crabtree Creek, the brake lights of the traffic ahead all leaped into brilliance at the same time. The sound of screeching brakes and squealing tires accompanied them.

"Uh-oh." James stepped on his brake and they rolled to a stop behind a double line of cars. "Did you see anything?"

"No, I wasn't paying attention." Shay craned her head forward to gaze between the pulsing windshield wipers.

Moments later a man came running toward them, arms waving. James let down his windshield an inch.

"You a cop?"

James nodded.

The man pointed back up the line of cars. "Car went off the road up ahead. Blew a tire, I think. Jumped the guardrail and went down the incline. There's a creek down there."

"You call 911?"

"Yeah. I'm a trucker. But we need to get down there, pronto."

"Right. Let me move out of the traffic lanes."

Turning his flashing lights on, James drove his cruiser up over the curb and onto the grassy shoulder and carefully edged forward. He didn't move forward all the way to where the railing was because he knew other law enforcement and emergency vehicles would need the space.

Shay eyed him cautiously. "You're going to help?"

He put the car in park before he turned to her. He'd almost forgotten she was with him. "That's right. I want you to stay in the cruiser with your seat belt on. I'm leaving the lights on but there's the chance of being rear-ended because some driver may come along who isn't expecting a sudden stop."

James got out and rushed forward following the trucker. The lights of the stalled traffic lit up the angled beginning of a guardrail. He noted it was bent and scraped. The car must have catapulted over it. Farther ahead, several passengers had emerged from their cars and were looking over the railing above the creek into the darkness below.

As they reached the rim of the incline that led down to the creek bed, James and the trucker paused.

Two men in business suits carried a half-conscious woman up the grassy incline, her body sagging between them. James winced. Good Samaritans often moved people who should not be moved until they'd been examined. But it was too late to point that out.

The woman came to life as they tried to lay her in the grass.

"My baby! My baby!"

She twisted away from them and began trying to crawl back the way they'd come. One of the men reached to restrain her by the shoulder. "It's okay, ma'am. We're going to send someone back down there in a minute."

"No ! No! No! My baby! Got to get my baby!"

James stepped forward. "How old is your child?"

The woman's eyes darted from one to the other until they came to rest on James. "Mariah. She's six months old. Oh God! Something happened. I just lost control. Oh God! Please! Please! Make her okay!"

James glanced at the two men trying to restrain her without hurting her. "You searched?"

"We checked. It's dark down there." One of the men shook his head. "There's a car seat but there's no child in that car."

"Yes there is! Oh God, Mariah's in there! You've got to believe me!"

James knelt down to bring his face even with hers. "Her name's Mariah. She's six months old. Is that correct?"

"Yes." The woman's eyes widened until the whites showed all around. "Please help her."

"Where was she riding?"

"She's in the backseat. In her seat." She grabbed James's sleeve. "Someone must get her out of there!"

"Yes, ma'am. If she's down there, we'll get her."

Out of breath, the woman sagged back weakly, sobbing.

James looked up at the trucker. "You got traffic cones?" The man nodded. "Okay, make a perimeter. I'm getting my partner to help search for the child."

As he rose to his feet he heard sirens but they sounded a good way off.

As he jogged back toward his cruiser, Shay exited the car. "What can I do?"

James looked back at the frantic mother. "The driver is a woman. She says there was a baby girl in the car but the men who went down to help couldn't find her."

"Oh my God!"

He opened the trunk and took out some things. He put them either in his pocket or tucked them in his belt: a pair of boots, a muzzle, and Bogart's tracking harness. "If there's a baby down there in the dark, Bogart has the best chance of finding her."

"Can he do that without a scent?"

James nodded as he bent to exchange his shoes for heavy tactical boots that zipped on. "It's a search, not a track. As far as we know, the baby is the only one down there."

"Oh." Shay watched him with expanding appreciation for what they did.

Bogart barked, a high excited bark Shay had never

heard before as James strapped on his harness and attached his leash.

"He knows he's about to work, doesn't he?"

"Right. Don't touch him. He's in the zone."

"Is that why you're muzzling him?"

He nodded. "There's a crowd of excited people milling around. I don't want him to bite anyone in the confusion."

Shay backed up, hugging herself as the mist gathered in her eyelashes. "What can I do?"

"You can help see to the mother. Anything to calm her. And don't let anyone move her again until the ambulance gets here."

"Do you have a blanket?"

He nodded. "In the trunk. Roof compartment."

Shay ran to the back and pulled out a lightweight dark gray blanket. As she came around the cruiser, James lifted a hand in salute. "Be careful!"

He then bent over to stroke Bogart, who was visibly excited. "*Gute Hund.* Let's go."

He moved forward quickly, Bogart straining forward as if he already knew what the command would be. James kept him on a short leash to work him past the ever-growing crowd of onlookers. A couple of men had begun voluntarily directing traffic but that was not his concern. There was the possibility of a missing baby out there in the dark.

As he neared the crowd he gave warning. "Stay back!"

His shout made a few young men in lumber jackets and gimme caps look back at him. "There's a kid down there." One man pointed. "We're going to look."

"No!" James flashed his badge. "K-9 police. You'll get in the way. But you can warn local law enforcement police when they arrive that there's a K-9 unit on duty down there."

He glanced at the others. "If any of you have high-beam

flashlights, I could use your help shining some concentrated light down there."

Several of them jumped back toward their vehicles.

James lit his high-performance flashlight to illuminate the darkness below. The misty rain made gauzy globes of the streetlights, dimming their effectiveness. There was no breeze. The heavy dampness, however, might be a help in their search, holding any human scent close to the ground for Bogart to follow. With nothing better to go on they proceeded directly toward the wrecked car.

Bogart, ears and tail high, led the way to the edge of the incline. Only then did his handler give the search command. *"Revier!"*

Bogart scrambled forward and James hustled after him.

The drop-off was fairly steep, more so than he'd expected. Even with his light ranging before them, the gloom of the overcast night plunged the area outside his beam into blackness. The grass was slick from the light mist, making his boots slip and slide as he struggled to maintain balance on the way down. Bogart's pants of excitement were the only sounds for a few seconds. Then the gurgling sound of moving water reached them from below.

He gave silent thanks that it wasn't raining hard or they might have had a flash-flood situation to worry about. However, if the child had been tossed from the car, she could be anywhere, even in the creek.

He shoved that thought from his mind. The mother said the child was in the backseat, in a car seat. He and Bogart would start with that.

Overhead the sounds of emergency vehicles closed in. Red and blue lights flashed in the sky overhead. James didn't pause. Survival often came down to mere seconds.

Finally, his flashlight picked up and gleamed off the rear bumper of the SUV. His spirits went into a nosedive at the sight. Hard to believe the mother had survived. And that a baby might still be trapped in the wreckage. The thought reengaged his focus.

He moved his light back and forth to pick up more details as they approached. The impact had smashed the front of the SUV and it had rolled onto its passenger side on the bank of the creek, its front bumper nosed into the water. The driver's door winged open into the night, like a wounded bird struggling to right itself.

Bogart sprang toward the vehicle. They had tracked and saved accident victims before.

James pulled from his belt a handheld thermal-imaging device. If the baby was alive the device would pick up her body heat as an infrared image amid the twisted metal.

He held his breath for a second, listening alertly for sounds of life as Bogart nosed around. All he heard was the wet swoosh of the water ahead, and the distant sounds of traffic and overhead voices. Nothing remotely like a baby's cry.

A second later, several slats of light forked down around them. A moment after that, a single big klieg light shattered the night, throwing him and the vehicle in stark relief like performers on a stage.

"Hey, fella! Stop where you are. Raleigh police!"

James glanced back over his shoulder into the blindness of white light and held up his badge. "Officer Cannon, Charlotte-Mecklenburg K-9 unit. My partner and I are searching for a missing baby. Permission to continue."

Before he could receive a reply, Bogart jerked hard on the leash, almost toppling James as his feet slipped in the wet mud of the bank. He didn't have to wonder. Bogart was onto something. Bogart didn't lunge toward the vehicle but veered to the right, out of the ring of light made by the overhead beams. James tried once to correct him but Bogart was straining so hard on the harness that James decided to let him lead.

He hurried along behind his dog, moving quickly along the grassy bank to a place where some low-hanging tree branches obscured his view of the ground.

Then James heard it, faint sounds like that of a car radio heard across a parking lot. Bogart was moving toward the brush along the bank, some thirty feet from the wreckage. As James ran behind him, he aimed his infrared device in that direction.

An image appeared on the water's edge. It was a small signature, smaller than Bogart's form as the dog rushed forward to reach his goal. The image could mean the child, even if injured, was at least alive. Or it might be the signature of any of a number of nocturnal creatures that made the riverbank their home. The last thing he needed was for Bogart to get into a scuffle with a nutria or a raccoon.

As if he had read James's thoughts, Bogart slowed suddenly, his steps becoming tentative as he approached his goal. That gave James time to switch out his image scanner for his flashlight, and aim it at the place Bogart signaled.

Dressed in a fluffy pink jumpsuit, baby Mariah lay in a pile of muddy leaves, looking dazed and unhappy.

James's heart did a little squeeze of joy. "Got her! Get the EMTs down here!"

Bogart, for his part, immediately went up to sniff her and then turned to look at James. Mariah chortled in delight when she spied the dog, and leaned forward as if to try to grab for him.

He called Bogart away. *"Fuss. Da. Gute Hund! Platz."* Bogart accepted the praise and then the order to sit and stay. *"Bleib."*

James crouched down next to the baby girl, who immediately began to cry. "Mariah? It's okay, Mariah." He touched her carefully, aware that she might have injuries he might not be able to see. "I'm James. People are coming to take you to your mommy."

Light leaped up over them, capturing them in the glare. He turned to find a group of uniformed officers and two EMTs with gear making their way down the incline toward them.

"You really are a hero."

James gave Shay a doubtful glance as he pulled into traffic that was being diverted away from the accident site. She'd waited very patiently while he'd talked to Raleigh authorities and then changed out of his rain-soaked clothing for the sweatshirt he now wore.

"I mean it. You found a baby in the dark, all by yourself." She was staring at him with eyes wide with admiration. "That's the coolest thing I've ever witnessed."

"Give Bogart a bit of credit."

"Of course." Shay reached up and scratched Bogart between his damp ears. "You two are just like Batman and Robin."

"Maybe Cisco and Pancho." James tried to be offhand about what had just occurred, but he was high on their victory, too.

They would never know exactly how Mariah had been squirted out of her car seat on impact, soared through an opening in the mangled wreckage, and landed in a soft pile of wet leaves twenty feet from the vehicle. All, apparently, without serious injury. He was just happy that chance had been on her side.

"It's why we do the job. Understand now?"

She nodded. "I wish I did something that made a difference like that."

For the first time since they'd met, Shay was looking at

him with the soft eyes of a woman fascinated by the man in front of her.

He recognized that look. She was responding to the successful good-news part of his job. Outsiders never wanted to see the failures, the mistakes, the wrong turns, the grind, the loneliness, the boring shit-filled hours of dealing with the sick, sad, desperate and/or depraved members of the human race that were most often the reason law enforcement was required. But everyone loved a hero.

The hero-worship thing bothered him. No one could live up to it on a daily basis.

After a quick glance in the rearview mirror, he pulled over on the shoulder and brought the cruiser to a stop.

"Something wrong?"

"Maybe." He wiped a hand across his face, clearing it of the trickle of rainwater that had run down from his still-damp hair. He needed to get this right.

"A few days ago, you were completely sure you didn't like me at all. Remember? I'm the guy who burst in on you at gunpoint, called you a liar and a thief. I'm the guy who took your dog away from you. You need to remember that part about me, too."

He saw her straighten up in her seat. "What are you saying? You don't want me to like you?"

"We both have baggage, that's all. My failings run more along the lines of shooting my mouth off before I think. Especially with pretty women. That's who I am sometimes, too, the awkward dumb guy."

She gave him a sidelong glance. "You don't need to worry about your failings. I'm sure women hang all over your gorgeous self all the time."

He angled his body toward her and laid his right arm along the back of her seat, letting his fingers rest lightly on her shoulder. "Gorgeous is not a character trait."

She met his grin with a snarky look. "Pity. It's your best quality."

He brushed the back of his fingers ever so gently along her jawline. "All storm and thunder. That's more like my Shay."

Grinning, he turned back to the wheel and sped off.

CHAPTER SEVENTEEN

"Yeah, it's a dump."

James offered her a teasing smile as he surveyed the sparsely furnished yet immaculately neat living area of Shay's small apartment. She had been making excuses for her place since he pulled up. None of them held up under his scrutiny. In fact, he thought it looked like a minimalist's dream.

"Ha, ha, very funny." Shay looked around, trying to see her home through a stranger's eyes. It gave precious little away, not that anyone came by to see it. Eric had not liked her cramped cell, as he called her one-bedroom apartment. They went to hotels or, occasionally, his place.

She dropped her belongings on the small round pedestal table in the dining area off a tiny kitchen and turned to James.

He toed off his shoes, not wanting to track water in, and then removed his gun to set it out of reach on a nearby shelf. She'd invited him in but he wasn't sure what that involved. She still had time to change her mind before he lost his completely. He unhooked Bogart's leash and turned toward her.

She didn't have many filters. It was all there on her face. Desire, nervousness, indecision, and a flicker of hope that he would take the decision away from her.

He smiled a warm intimate male smile that made her flush. "I hope it's okay to bring Bogart in."

"Of course." She bent down to pat her furry friend on the head. "I forgot to get back the pet deposit I had to put down when I adopted him."

He watched her shoulders rise and fall on a deep breath. And then she was turning back to him. He saw a decision forming in her mind. Her eyes were shining beneath her glossy bangs, drawing in all the light in the room. Her mouth was soft. Yet her words, as always, were meant to deflect any vulnerability.

"We live in different places. So this." She waved a hand around as if to include her apartment and Bogart. "This is just a hookup, like last time."

James heard the question she wasn't asking. It was in the way she'd dipped her chin, looking at him from beneath a thick fan of dark lashes. She wanted confirmation to keep her emotions locked up. He wished he could give it to her.

"Last time, maybe. But I came back."

Her silences were as eloquent as her declarations.

"I don't know what the hell this is. All right?" He brushed a hand over his short haircut, annoyed with himself. All he knew for certain was that he was taking a very big risk. And so was she.

Her smile appeared so slowly he had decided it wasn't going to arrive before it did. Small victory.

He looked over the tiny counter into the kitchen where Bogart was investigating.

"Let me get Bogart some water."

"There's a dog dish under the sink. I couldn't bear to part with it."

James padded in sock feet into her kitchen space and found it. He had enjoyed her company tonight. But he was beginning to feel the effects from the overrun of adrenaline spurred by the night's unexpected call to duty. Usually he and some friends would blow off steam in a bar after hours when the outcome of a situation had a good conclusion. Some men preferred to work off their highs in female company, lots of it. A few got into trouble with too much booze and testosterone-driven high jinks. He couldn't say he wasn't going to be trouble for Shay, but he hoped it was the kind she would welcome.

One thing came through loud and clear. She wasn't the kind of woman who liked to play games or keep things light. He doubted she had ever had a casual relationship. It was all in or all out.

A song his grandmother liked to sing under her breath when she was being positive came to mind. *"Accentuate the Positive"* . . . something, something . . . *about leaving alone Mr. In-Between.*

James let out a chuckle that was strictly aimed at himself. Shay all in? What would that be like?

That thought sobered him as he ran water in the dog dish. Before they did or did not get into each other, they needed to finish the conversation begun at the restaurant.

When he had filled the bowl and set it on the floor, he looked out over the bar to ask her something. Cop instinct stopped him cold.

Shay was standing in the middle of her living room staring at the plank-and-brick bookshelf that held her small TV. Was it his gun that worried her?

"What's wrong?"

She continued to stare, her voice gone flat. "Someone's been here."

He moved quickly over to her. "How do you know?"

She pointed. "I left those books lying flat. Now they're upright on the shelf."

"Okay." He glanced around, noting a small hallway just past her kitchen area. Books out of place seemed like a small thing but he knew from countless patrols that small things often led to larger discoveries. "What's back there?"

"Bathroom and bedroom."

"You stay here. By the door. Don't move."

James raked his weapon from the shelf. He heard Shay draw in a breath of surprise. He held up a finger for quiet.

"Hund. Hier!"

The thirsty lapping stopped. Bogart hurried out of the kitchen. He paused a few feet from James and tilted his head in a questioning manner.

James pointed to the hallway. *"Geh rein!"*

Bogart swung around and headed down the hallway. James followed.

Shay began counting slowly backward in her mind from three hundred to keep herself from jumping out of her skin. She'd felt something the moment she walked in her door. She'd wanted to ignore it. Be with James. But the books could not be ignored.

Two hundred and ninety-two. Two hundred and ninety-one.

Hypervigilance required a lot of coping techniques. Too bad her mind could multitask.

She remembered the books lying prone on the shelf. She was certain.

Almost one hundred percent certain.

Or maybe that was wrong. Her mind was making her squirrely just when she most wanted to be sane and in the moment.

James and Bogart were back in less than two minutes.

He wasn't smiling. "I checked everywhere, the closet, under the bed, the shower. There's no one here. And no windows have been jimmied. But I need you to look the apartment over to see if you can tell if anything else has been disturbed or taken."

Shay shook her head. "I believe you."

"Look anyway."

She did. And when she came back into the living room she felt worse than before.

James read her expression. "Not a thing? Are you sure?"

"You don't believe me?" He saw the stricken look wash over her face.

"It's just a routine question, Shay. Only the books. Down. Up." He emphasized his words with a hand motion. "It's pretty slim evidence of a break-in."

"Break-in?" She glanced at her door to see that all the locks were in place. Had they all been locked when she arrived? She couldn't remember how many keys she'd used to get in. She'd been too busy absorbing the awareness of James at her back, of the desire to just turn around and move into his arms, to touch him, kiss . . .

She could see the question in his gaze. *Why would someone break in on you?*

"It would take someone with real skill to get in here." He pointed out the obvious. "You've got two dead bolts. Does Eric have keys?"

"No." Her voice spiked with irritation. "Anyway, I changed the locks last month."

Right. After the breakup. James definitely needed to know the details that led up to that. In a minute.

"Look, you can never be too sure about these things, especially with an ex who has been stalking you. I should phone this in."

"No, please don't."

"Why not, Shay?"

She didn't have an easy answer. She heaved her shoulders in an exaggerated sigh. "I'm just jumpy. Sorry."

She saw his expression alter, so subtly she doubted she would have noticed if she weren't experiencing the same emotion. It was disappointment. She was wrecking their evening. This time he would walk away, and stay there.

"You want something to drink? I have diet—" She started for the kitchen but James stepped in front of her. His hands came up and landed on her shoulders, his touch warm and firm.

"Shay?" She glanced up at James and this time her expression caught him right between the eyes. "Tell me. What's going on?"

"You." The word sounded almost choked out of her.

Lust engulfed her light irises, her pupils almost fully blown out. The look said she wanted him to jump her. His own body's reaction was no less subtle. It produced a hard-on for her that could drill a hole in a brick wall.

Still, he didn't make a move because behind her full-on lustful glance was the familiar wariness. He could feel it in the tense tremors running through her shoulders where his hands lay and the way she had tucked her lips together. She seemed to be braced for what came next. And then he understood.

She wasn't worried about his but her own control. That was a complicated response to the moment that they shared. Many things needed to be said, questions asked, and depending on the answers, decisions reached. This wasn't the time, probably not the place, but— Fuck it.

His eagerness must have shown in his gaze because her eyes flared and she stepped up against him, slid her arms around his neck and pulled his head down until his lips met hers.

The power of his need blew away any possibility that

he was going to back down now. He reached out to skim the back of his hands down her bare upper arms before cupping her shoulders and drawing her in hard against his chest.

She surged into him, pushing her hips against his groin, directing him backward toward the sofa. And then she was following him down, climbing into his lap before his butt hit the cushions. She pushed back his jacket and began tearing his shirt from his waistband. Her hands were everywhere, giving him no time to enjoy what she was offering. Her mouth engulfed his, wide open and too rough for genuine pleasure.

She made love like a teenage boy, zero to eighty with no shifting. It was as if she were trying to outrun something.

Isn't this what happened last time?

Crap. His brain kicked in. He'd been a cop too long not to weigh the evidence presented to him.

This seduction felt like a distraction. At the moment, sex was a distraction for both of them. They needed to slow down, start over.

He reached up and took her face in his hands and, after a quick hard kiss, held her off. "Hold up, Shay."

She jerked upright in his lap, staring at him with golden-brown eyes blinking in instant wariness. "What's wrong?"

Damned if I know. James sucked in a breath to slow the jackhammering of his heart. It had been a dumb-shit idea to stop. But he had, and she was waiting for an explanation.

He leaned forward to push his forehead to hers. "I like you, Shay. I'd like to screw you, too. But I don't have a plane to catch. We have time."

She leaned away. Caution shone in her eyes. "For what?"

He knew better than to toss Eric's name into the mix at this particular moment. To gain her trust he needed to build back up to that, as any good interrogator would. That thought made him feel like an asshole. Okay, so maybe that's what it took to get some answers. He still needed them.

He kissed her to gain a few precious seconds in which to switch gears. Maybe not the best tactic. Her lips seemed to connect directly to his dick.

Reluctantly, he leaned away from her. "Ah, *hm,* how about we ease into the thing? Slow down. Take time. Try some, some . . ."

"Foreplay?" Her voice was sharp with surprise.

"There you go. Foreplay."

He dropped his hands from her face and reached down to lift her off his lap. Instead he encountered the smooth skin of her thighs. His hands slid up the firm warm flesh until they encountered the edge of her panties. This was not going the way he needed it to go.

Reluctantly he dragged his hands back down the soft plush skin of her thighs. "I must be out of my mind."

"Are you playing hard to get, Mr. Cannon?" She smiled a lot faster than he'd thought she would.

"Hard, yes." He didn't break eye contact until she blinked. Then he looked away, desperate for ideas that would reboot the moment. "TV?"

"Fine."

She slid off him, pulling her skirt down over her very nicely toned thighs and reaching for the remote. The TV sprang to life. An *I Love Lucy* rerun appeared. Okay, that would work.

Under the cover of adjusting his clothing James tried to make an appropriate mental adjustment to calm himself down. It wasn't working. Had he really just backed her off his ready-to-go johnson? He needed his head checked. Yes. Definitely. Maybe if he just . . .

As she sat back down, Bogart jumped up on the sofa

and wedged his hairy body between them, rump toward James and his big head in Shay's lap. The result was a pretty damn effective barrier.

James glared at his partner. Bogart seemed to have an uncanny way of reading his handler's mind and emotions. Spooky, actually.

Shay stroked the big doggy head, the rhythm helping to ease the frustration of wondering how to move on from a moment she had desperately wanted to finish. She noticed James was petting his partner, too.

She didn't have a whole lot of experience with men, besides Eric. He thought she should always be ready for him. Once he was in the mood, nothing stopped him from jumping her and pumping away until he, at least, was satisfied. Foreplay had disappeared long ago. She often felt like a whore. Nothing in that relationship seemed useful when dealing with James Cannon.

She glanced cautiously across at him. He was staring at the TV like he'd never seen one before. He must be weirded out, too. If the silence between them didn't end soon, she knew they would never get back in the mood.

Desperate for the sound of his voice, she said, "Do you always work the night shift?"

He didn't look at her but kept stroking Bogart. "Most K-9 patrols do." He paused to chuckle at something Lucy Ricardo did. "We patrol an area each night, unless there's a special event we need to attend during the day."

Shay cocked her head to one side. "You sound like a night watchman."

That drew a smile from him. It was exactly how his sister Allyson had sized up his career path, night watchman with a pooch. Her spouse was a narc.

"It's a little more complicated than that. I don't just rattle doorknobs. You get to know your areas, the people, the look and smell of places. There's a feeling when something's not quite right. On top of that, we can be called out for any reason on any day, even our days off, for anything from crowd control to tracking a criminal, for a search-and-rescue operation, whatever support we can provide."

"Like finding the baby tonight. That was so cool."

"Yes." The memory gave James a happy buzz. "From the first I prepared to become more than a patrol officer. I got a bachelor's in criminology with a minor in psych and trauma studies before I attended the police academy. How about you? Where'd you go to school?"

She swiveled her head toward him. "Why?"

James kept his expression bland. "I share. You share. It's called conversation."

"North Carolina State." The words sounded as if they'd been mined from somewhere deep. "Community college first. It took me six years because I worked my way through. I don't like owing anybody anything."

"You don't have any debt?"

She glanced at him warily. "No, why?"

He shrugged. "I'll be paying off student loans for a while, especially since I'm enrolled part-time again."

She looked down, shielding her very expressive gaze.

He clicked off the TV. "So, it's time to tell me about Eric."

Shay glanced at him. His voice sounded normal, too normal. Law enforcement calm. Her hands began to tremble with frustrated desire. How could he sit there so proud, so closed, so unemotional? She felt as if she'd been caught up in a class 5 erotic twister that left her bereft, unfinished and unsatisfied.

She snuggled back into the sofa cushions, needing a little more space than she anticipated from him.

Bogart whined and lifted his head, dark molasses eyes staring into hers. Of course he could detect the tension.

The air practically vibrated with it, like the moment before a lightning strike.

"Shay?" James's expression was closed, shutting her out. But his gaze still scorched her skin. She could feel it sizzling under his blue-eyed stare. "You need to tell me about Eric. Why you've let him rough you up and make threats, and yet have never called the police for help."

The accusation stung. "That's not true. I did call the police. Once."

"Want to tell me about that?"

Shay bit her lip and shook her head. If she did tell him, she suspected he would walk out and never come back. Damn it to hell. Eric was still ruining her life. Or maybe she'd done that all by herself a dozen years ago. If James was going to leave, maybe it was better he did so now, before she began to count on his being around.

She turned to him suddenly, her chin cocked in defiance. "Fine. What is it you want to know?"

Everything. Yet. James realized she was moving out of her comfort zone by even offering to talk. He'd take it slow. "Let's start with how you and Eric met."

She took a deep breath. "A little over a year ago I was working a job at Halifax Bank, the main office. I was doing a real IT job, not just answering phones like now. Eric is the area manager for a dozen Halifax Bank branches in the state. We met when he came in to meet with the Operational Risk and Compliance team. He asked me out to lunch with the team. The next time he came through he asked me to dinner, alone."

She quickly went through their get-together time. She'd been flattered by the attention of a senior member of the bank. The fact that he was mature, thirty-four and divorced, and sophisticated made it thrilling for her to flirt back. She was a temp, after all, not a full-time employee who would have to worry about interoffice consequences if the relationship went nowhere or, worse, went bad. Besides, she didn't think he could seriously be interested in a twenty-five-year old still looking for job security.

James waited until she took a breath. "Did you ask any of the other staff about him?"

"Not really. I didn't know them. I wasn't permanent. Besides, I thought he'd stop asking me out when I left."

"Why did you continue to see him?"

She looked away. "He had invited me on a trip." Memory kicked in, reminding her of how charming Eric was in the beginning. Quite charming.

Eric had stopped by her desk at closing her last week on the job.

"You got a passport?"

She did, from a senior trip to Mexico.

"Pack light. Two nights, two days of sun, sand, surf, and me."

She had thought he was teasing. But then he'd laid a plane ticket on her desk. When she opened it she saw it was for the Cayman Islands.

"He said he was supposed to go with someone else. But the person canceled at the last minute so this was my lucky day."

James's voice was calm, nonjudgmental. "So you went."

Shay nodded. "We went on several trips even after I no longer temped there. He was nice, at first."

"Bought you things?"

She glared at him. "Showed me things. Took me places. Let me experience how the wealthy live and play. Stuff I could never have seen or done on my own. He was really kind, at first."

"But there must have been signs. Or were you so grateful you overlooked the other things?" She nodded so slowly that he knew she didn't like his characterization of her motivation. "But that changed."

Shay glanced down. "I feel so stupid. How could I not see what was coming?"

James turned to stare at a spot halfway between the sofa and the TV. "What happened?"

Shay surprised herself by telling him. The many little humiliations. The way Eric could twist her words. How he stopped complimenting her but always found something wrong, however trivial, with her appearance. She even told him about their last trip, about the exhibitionist dancing that ended with his rage. That was the first time he forced her to have sex against her will.

When they got home he became distant. He hardly ever called her or took her anywhere. Then a month ago, he'd invited her to his apartment where he'd set up what he called a special evening for them. That was the night she called the police.

"He had S and M stuff, whips and sex toys and . . . stuff." Shay closed her eyes. "I thought he was joking. He just . . ."

She glanced furtively at James. He was no longer looking at the floor. His eyes were riveted on her. She would have thought telling so intimate a story to this man would be the worst humiliation possible. Yet the way he just sat there, not touching her but watching with an intensity that surrounded her in a cocoon of intimacy, walled off the pain for the moment.

Even so, she was whispering at the end. "When he let me go to the bathroom I palmed my phone and called the police."

James's gaze flickered with curiosity.

Shay shook her head. "It didn't help. Eric had a story ready that made everything sound plausible. It was my idea. I'd been reading those '50 Shades' books and wanted to try something kinky. He was so sorry. He'd never done anything like that before so he didn't realize he was really hurting me. I wasn't beat up or anything, and I could tell the police officers believed him. So I changed my mind about pressing charges."

James was silent for several seconds but his gaze never left hers. "Law enforcement doesn't always get it right. Domestics are hard to sort out. But I'd say they did less than their best by you. You should have asked for a female officer."

Shay looked away, a little shocked by his neutral tone. "It doesn't matter now."

"It matters."

Bogart suddenly got up and left the sofa. He resettled under the TV, his gaze directed at his partner, as if to say, *I've done what I could. You're on your own.*

James watched Shay closely for signs of emotional overload. She had twisted her arms together under her bosom. Did she know how nakedly her emotions shone on her face when she looked at him? He ached to reach for her but that wasn't going to happen until they finished this. Even so, he couldn't resist sliding closer to her until they all but touched as they sat side by side. "When did you break up with Eric?"

"That night. It's been a month."

"And yet Eric's still harassing you. You can go back to the police, have them look up the initial call you made about Eric."

She hunched her shoulders, trying to shrink further into the sofa. "I don't need the hassle."

"Is that the only reason?"

Shay slumped back against the cushions, exhausted and a little sick. "Just leave it, James. I've told you enough."

"I don't think you have." He reached over and placed his hand over hers where it lay on her thigh. "I get it. You're scared. You've been the victim of abuse. Douche bags like Eric wouldn't stand a chance if their true natures were obvious. Now that you know what he's capable of you need to protect yourself."

She gave her head a tight little shake. "I can't."

"Why?"

She made a little sound of misery. "You don't understand. You don't know anything about me. About my past. What I've done."

There was a beat of silence. "Tell me."

Shay twisted away from him, feeling something dark and ugly rip open inside her, something so horrible that she had not been able to face it at the time. "I'm not worth your effort. I'm broken. Screwed up."

"Maybe you need to see—"

"A shrink?" She whipped back around to face him. Here it came, all the things she had hoped to spare herself, and him. She felt her world collapsing inward, the walls of years of effort crumbling beneath her feet as she free-fell into darkness.

"Shay?" Hands framed her face and lifted it. And then she was gazing up from that dreadful bottomless place into the blazing summer blue of James's eyes.

"I stabbed a man."

CHAPTER EIGHTEEN

Shay wondered how long a person could hold her breath and not pass out. James hadn't reacted to her confession. It was as if he, too, were waiting. The only difference was he was breathing slow and even, just as before.

After several heartbeats he said, "Who was he?"

Shay gasped softly before speaking. "A friend of my mother's."

"How old were you?"

"Fourteen."

She felt James shift to angle his body toward hers on the sofa.

"Tell me what happened." His voice was little more than a breath.

"It was a mistake." Even as she said the words Shay gave her head a little shake. She'd started all wrong. This wasn't the way to tell it. But she really didn't know how. She hadn't actually said the words out loud to anyone in a long time. When her world blasted apart, she couldn't. Ever since those years, she hadn't wanted to.

"Does Eric know about this?"

"He guessed something. I have nightmares sometimes. Like the night you were here."

James nodded. "I remember. Go on."

Shay rocked her head in the negative against her palm. She really *really* didn't want to say more. But James was getting close to her very fast. If he was going to bolt, he needed to do it before she started counting on him to always be there for her.

He shifted closer and raised a hand to cup her cheek. "Just say words, Shay. Whatever you're thinking. Just say that."

"I don't remember it. No, I do. Some of it. But then it gets all weird and crazy." She strung the last word out as if it caused her pain.

"Where were you?"

"We lived over a Chinese restaurant in Raleigh." She swallowed. "I've hated Chinese food ever since. Dad had been in the army, a lifer, died in 2000. Nothing heroic. Service copter went down on practice maneuvers out in Arizona."

James let out a rough sound. It caught and perfectly reflected her feelings.

"Mom was an LPN. She brought us back home to live but work wasn't easy to find. She took double shifts at a nursing home. At first, she didn't date much. Then she met Andrew. He was nice to us for a while. But after he moved in, to help with the rent, he would sometimes get drunk and break things. And he looked at me in a way that made me feel funny."

"Yeah."

"Mom said that I was just not used to having a man around the place. But she put a lock on my bedroom door when I asked her to. When she worked night shifts I would lock it and never get out of bed in the middle of the night. Only one night I woke up and had to pee really bad."

Shay swallowed. Things were getting confusing. She could feel a pressure building like two hands clutching her heart. She was opening the door to a horror-movie basement that everyone knew never to go down into. Only, for her, the horror had been all too real.

"I was on the toilet, in the dark, when I heard . . ."

James's arm tightened around her. "You don't have to tell me if you don't want to."

But she did.

The words spilled out over themselves.

The footsteps. Heavy. Andrew's. The shadow of his feet under the bathroom door from the light he'd turned on in the hallway.

She was washing her hands when the doorknob began to turn.

She'd yelled she was inside. But he only shouted back for her to open up. He was drunk. Nowhere to hide.

That's when she remembered the scissors in the drawer, the long narrow-bladed pair her mother used to trim her bangs. She grabbed them and hid them behind her back.

The door opened.

Then she was on the floor, his breath in her face as he groped her under her pajamas.

Shay sat forward suddenly, gasping for breath.

"I can't remember! I can't remember!"

James touched her lightly on the shoulder. "Shay?"

She jerked away from his touch. "Don't touch me! Just don't."

He twisted away and reached for the lamp beside the sofa. It flared to life.

Shay sat hunched over, gasping as if she'd been punched in the stomach.

He leaned close but didn't touch her again. "You need something? Water?"

She shook her head tightly. "The scissors just missed his heart. They said I could have killed him."

"Serves the asshole right." James didn't sound in the least bit doubtful about that opinion.

She turned her head toward him, a deep crease between her brows.

"You were being attacked. You defended yourself. Should have been an airtight legal defense."

Shay shook her head, years of therapy unspooling in her thoughts. "No. It wasn't like that. Andrew admitted he was drunk when he went to take a leak. He said he didn't know I was in there. I just went berserk when he opened the door."

James frowned. "People who are afraid sometimes overreact but you were defending yourself, Shay."

"Not everybody would have stabbed someone."

Shay turned away from him. It was easier than watching his expression of sympathy. "Mom said the police found me in the middle of the street screaming and screaming, with blood all over me. They thought I was injured. By the time the EMTs got there, I'd shut down. Everything. Couldn't even speak. They took me to emergency and then checked me into a psych ward. The doctor said the traumatic event of the stabbing caused me to have a nervous breakdown."

"Christ!" James made a fist to keep from touching her. "How long were you there?"

"Thirty days. Court ordered. I was evaluated with a dissociative anxiety disorder and as a possible endangerment to myself and others."

"None of that has anything to do with attempted rape. The authorities would still have to take into account your statement of what happened."

"They didn't get my statement." Shay swallowed, the

rest of the story coming a little easier. "I couldn't defend myself. When I could talk again, after twenty-four hours or so, I couldn't remember what happened. I didn't for weeks. By then Andrew had pressed charges. He was out of the hospital and said I needed to pay for what I'd done."

"Screw that! You had every right to defend yourself."

This time James reached out for her and tried to draw her back against him but she resisted. "Don't do that."

"Do what?"

"Try to make me sound . . . normal."

"You were normal. It's the situation that was bat-shit crazy. Andrew tried to molest you. You did finally remember that."

She flinched as if his compassion were just another burden. "Not soon enough. My mother had pushed me to accept a plea bargain of temporary insanity. I was tried as a juvenile. I didn't have to do jail time. But there was court-ordered therapy."

"Aw shit, Shay." Her words grabbed him by the throat, choking off the life's blood of his professional detachment until he was just a man aching over the pain of someone he cared about deeply.

Shay sat with her fingers twisted together, gulping in uneven breaths. Shouldering the unfamiliar feeling of helplessness, he watched her silently wrestle with her old demons. He knew that he couldn't simply talk or argue her out of her feelings. She'd lived too long with this for him to change years of thinking in a single conversation. But the story made him want to break a few heads, specifically ones belonging to Andrew and Eric. Andrew's vicious actions had screwed up her sense of self and of justice at a tender age. Eric, though he did not know why, had taken advantage of her need to keep all aspects of her life secret.

Yet, somehow, she had survived. That grit had to be admired. "What happened next?"

"By the time I remembered enough details for my doctors to believe my story, the courts said it was too late to change the plea bargain. But my records would be sealed after five years if there were no additional misconduct charges."

"Anything else?" There was always more in cases like this.

She heaved in a big breath. "The story made the papers. 'Fourteen-year-old Stabs Mother's Boyfriend.' It was big news. I was famous."

"That shouldn't have happened. Juveniles are not named in reports."

Shay's mouth jerked but it was not in a smile. "There were enough people who saw me that night to tell their friends, who told their friends, that the girl without a name in the news was me."

He tried to absorb the implications. None of them good.

She glanced at him from under her bangs. "Yeah. Who wants a homicidal loony, fresh-sprung from the nuthouse, in the classroom with their precious children?"

James sighed. "What did you do?"

"My mother left her jobs and took me up to the lake cabin. It belongs to my dad's uncle and wife. We lived there a year while she did homeschooling, as best she could. Waitressing and cleaning other cabins to make ends meet." Her voice began to wobble. "I was a total burden. I ruined her life." Shay slumped into an even tighter huddle.

James reached in and found a calm tone completely at odds with his emotions. "Did your mom think so?"

She twisted the hem of her skirt in her hands, not speaking for several seconds. When she did there was a new bitter tone in her emotion-ravaged voice. "She felt guilty about bringing Andrew into our lives. Now she had a freak for a daughter. She was stuck."

Mistakes. Guilt. Being trapped. A triple whammy of emotional disaster.

He had heard tougher stories, and ones with sadder endings. Some survivors didn't make it through the trauma. Others were human husks, or living like bombed-out buildings that were still standing but damaged beyond repair. It was a wonder she wasn't strung out on drugs, or worse. Yet here Shay sat, in her own place, with a job, whole but hurting.

Some of his thoughts must have been playing across his features because when she looked over at him a little of her temper flared through the haunted shadows in her eyes. "Don't you dare feel sorry for me."

"I was thinking about how strong you are. It wasn't your fault. None of it. The courts and society got it wrong."

She stared at him, looking strained and vulnerable after her confession.

"What did you and your mother do after a year?"

"We moved to Durham. She got a job, a good one, and I went to public school."

"So, things got better?"

She shrugged. "There were records the school required. Things got leaked. Teachers. Counselors. They were always looking for signs that I would freak out again. When I didn't, some kids started . . . doing things."

To make her react. Damn. He did feel sorry for her.

"How bad did it get?" '

She stared at him in that familiar walled-off way. He understood now how her defiance had sustained her. "They pushed. I fought back. A lot."

It didn't require much imagination to guess what her

high school years must have been like. But he sensed a change in her tone. She wasn't asking for understanding any longer. She was now fighting back, testing him.

He gave her a sly look. "You never went all 'Carrie' on them, did you?"

She almost smiled. "I thought about it. Especially after they nicknamed me 'Psycho Shay.' But then if I'd done something really badass I'd have been put back in that hospital."

Jesus. Her world had been too full of assholes, creeps, and failures.

Yet she had rejected his sympathy so he wasn't about to dish any more up. "Smart thinking. You didn't want your past to follow you. Is that why you changed your name at eighteen?"

Shay stilled and then her gaze went supernova. "You knew!" She sprang from the sofa. "You son of a bitch! You already knew all this."

He wasn't going to lie to her but he spoke slowly and calmly, trying not to accelerate her anger. "When I got back to Charlotte, I realized I didn't even have your address or phone number, or have any way to get in touch with you. I needed to file a report about Bogart's abduction. So I did some investigating."

"You put a tail on me?" She sounded horrified.

"No. Nothing like that. It's the age of digital pursuit."

"I don't have much of a digital imprint."

"Tell me about it. I had to put a department professional on it. He's better and has more resources. He discovered what I needed, and other things."

"Other things." He clocked every emotion as Shay's face reflected her thinking processes. The final result of hurt and outrage was tough to take. "If you already knew everything, why did you make me tell you?"

"I didn't know jack, Shay. I had only a few scattered

facts. Your juvie record is sealed, as you said. Now that I understand what you've been through I'm totally on your side. If this is what's been keeping you from filing charges against Eric you can stop worrying. I'll help see to it that the system works for you this time."

She jerked as if he had slapped her. "Don't you understand anything? If I filed charges Eric would hire an expensive attorney who would dig into my past to try to discredit me. That's the last thing I want. I have a record for violence. I cried rape and was institutionalized." She waved her hands around, as if trying to chase away her thoughts. "It would be all over the news. No jury would believe anything I have to say. And everyone who knows me would learn about my past. I won't allow that. Nothing can make me go through that again!"

Then she looked at him. Her face went slack. "Get out!"

It was a raw moment. He had torn open old wounds and she was suffering. He hurt for her. But this wasn't about him. James knew he couldn't make another mistake or she would rip him out of her life as she had tried to do earlier. Not this time. He couldn't just leave a card and walk away.

He stood up. "Just hear me out, Shay."

"Are you deaf? You can't be here. Not after you lied to me. I trusted you!"

She came at him so unexpectedly, for once, he was caught off guard. She struck, hard. His lip burst where it was ground against his teeth by her slap and he tasted blood.

At the corner of his vision he saw Bogart rise, two concerned eyes shining with clearer vision than his own. His partner had just been attacked, and Bogart was trained to take sides.

James reacted quickly. *"Nein! Geh raus!"*

Bogart hovered a moment, made a whining sound of disapproval through his nose, then settled back.

James watched him a moment longer, noticing his tail swooshing in agitation. He needed to calm Shay down, fast.

It turned out not to be necessary. She was gasping for breath and began to sob as she collapsed like a rag doll onto the carpet.

James knelt down beside her, as close as he could get without actually touching her. She had covered her face with both hands. Choking sobs lifted her shoulders with every breath. "I'm so sorry. I hate violence! I didn't mean it. I'm so sorry."

"It's okay, Shay. I think I'll survive."

When she didn't respond, he placed a hand on her shoulder.

Her hands fell away from her face. Her eyes were an angry red, her mouth wet and blurred. He saw pain served up raw and unfiltered in her expression. Her eyes widened suddenly.

"You're bleeding!"

James put a hand to his mouth. It came away with a bright smear of blood. He smirked. "I've had worse."

Shay looked stunned by the evidence of what she'd done. She lunged at him and grabbed him about the neck. "I'm so sorry. I'm didn't mean it. Don't hate me!"

"I don't hate you, Shay." He enfolded her, absorbing the shock of her. Her skin was chill from the night air and her extreme emotional state.

He reached a hand toward the sofa and grabbed the throw flung across the back. He wrapped her in it and then adjusted his embrace to bring her tighter against himself to share his warmth.

Fitting her head more snugly into the curve between his shoulder and jaw, he kissed her hair and waited until she stopped sobbing, this time in remorse.

Finally, she stilled against him, all the fight and fear ebbed away on her tears.

He continued to hold her tight in one arm while his free hand stroked down her back. "It's okay, Shay. It's really going to be okay. We'll figure something out."

She didn't say anything, just pushed her arms up through the covers until her hands were framing his face. And then she smothered his words with kisses. It stung a bit and he wondered fleetingly if she realized he was still bleeding.

Finally, she moved a little away from him. But not by much. Her sorrow-soaked gaze bored into his. "You can stay."

He tilted his head back to better see her. "You've been through a lot tonight."

She slid a thumb over his split lip. "You can stay."

He hesitated to act on her invitation. So much had gone down between them tonight. Much as he wanted to, and as easy as passion was between them, she was exhausted. And enough people had taken advantage of her in her life.

"We've got time."

He stood and then picked her up with surprising ease. She hooked a hand over his shoulder and rocked her head against his neck as he carried her to the bedroom. When he bent to place her on the mattress, she wrapped her arm tighter to hold on to him. "Please stay."

He made a purely masculine sound of distress. She couldn't see his face in the darkness but she knew he was trying to do the honorable thing.

"Stay here." She pointed to the bed. "All night."

"Okay." It sounded nothing like surrender. "I've got to walk Bogart then I'll be back. Promise."

Shay nodded, letting her body relax against the bedding.

* * *

James was as grateful as he'd ever been in his life for the fact that Shay was asleep when he returned from walking Bogart. That didn't stop him from staring.

She had undressed while he was out. Sprawled on her tummy, she slept in a lacy tank and a tiny pair of pink briefs with a single black sheep printed on the rear. That black sheep boldly hugged the generous swells of her butt. Her long legs were tangled in the bedding she'd half pulled back before collapsing, his guess, onto the bed. Her dark hair spilled across the pillow. Every soft womanly curve spoke directly to his libido. He'd never had a better silent invitation. Or a tougher test of his morals.

Shifting his duffel from his shoulder, he tried not to make a sound that would awaken her as he stripped down to his skivvies. Then he carefully worked the bedding down her legs to free them and re-covered her up to her neck. Only then did he stretch out beside her, on top of the bedding. He was a decent man but he wasn't a saint.

He knew it would be a while before he could relax. Instead, he went over in his mind with an officer's precision all that she had told him. She still felt responsible for things that had been out of her control. It was not unusual for victims of violence to blame themselves. But it tore him up to know that the very people who were supposed to protect her had heaped blame on her, as well. He had felt a lot of things while she talked, mostly he'd wanted to grab and hold her until he had absorbed all her pain and anguish. It was more than sympathy. It cut right through to his core. Shay Appleton had been messing with his head since the moment he first saw her. Now she had burrowed into something else a foot lower and to the left, which shoook him more.

He turned toward her. She was facing him, her lashes

dark smudges on her upper cheeks. Her lips were parted, moist and soft.

He looked away. If Shay were a sheep, then he was here to be her sheepdog guardian. But his dick kept twitching like the tail of a fox. It was going to be a long night.

CHAPTER NINETEEN

Her body throbbed in protest that they weren't done yet. Mercy, not nearly done!

Shay scrambled through the drag of dream-filled desire to consciousness. Where was James? They'd been talking. No, she'd been talking. Too much. She'd told him all the terrible truths about her life. And yet, underneath it all, she could not shake the need swamping her every time she glanced his way. She wanted him bad. But it was a lost cause. He had left. This time, she was sure, for good.

Blinking away tears in the darkness, she watched the familiar surroundings of her bedroom, dimly lit by the tiny bulb from the fire alarm in the ceiling, gradually come into focus.

The dream had left her damp and shaky with desire. For James. Who wasn't here and wasn't coming back.

Sighing in regret, she slid fingers across the sheet and came up against a firm hairy thigh. She turned her head on the pillow. James was lying there beside her, sound asleep.

She almost burst out with laughter in relief. She had

long ago stopped believing in miracles. They didn't happen for her. Yet here he was.

Her hand moved up over the top of his thigh, feeling his heat against her palm. The delicious sensation forced her eyes closed. He was here. With her. That must mean something. She didn't dare put a name to it.

Smiling at the thoughts floating through her mind, she opened her eyes and felt a zing of surprise. James had turned his head and was staring straight at her.

"Hi." His voice was husky but it wasn't with sleep.

"Hi." Hers trembled with desire. Since there was nothing else to say, she walked her fingers up the warm hard surface of his thigh until she encountered the edge of his briefs.

James felt his entire body clench in response to her light touch.

Don't hurt her more than she's already been hurt.

Thoughts such as that usually came with a voice attached. His mother's for manners. His grandmother's for common sense. His dad's for duty. This one came straight from his own heart, directed at his libido.

He grasped her fingers and squeezed them, hard. "You don't owe me anything."

His rough whisper told Shay all she needed to know about how to proceed. He wasn't going to take advantage of her. He was worried that she might be damaged or too fragile after her confession to withstand his brand of lovemaking.

He had forgotten how tough she could be. Or determined, when she wanted something very badly. She needed to remind him.

She owed this to herself. This would be something good and positive to hold on to during the next dark night in her life.

She rose up on an elbow, close enough to see the light

from the ceiling reflected like twin stars in his eyes. "What if we owe each other?"

James reached for her hand and pulled it toward his crotch. "This?"

Her fingers flexed in anticipation of the feel of him. Instead he released her just short of the goal.

Luckily, it was only one short inch.

She touched him, sliding two fingers lightly down the placket of his briefs. The caress made his breath escape in a swoosh.

She didn't look up, more fascinated by the interesting mound to the left of the row of stitching. Should she just . . . ?

She stroked the bulge and found his cock hard as a lead pipe. A shudder passed through him. He was trying so hard to be noble. But he wasn't that noble. She knew what she'd uncover if she lowered his shorts. She'd already seen and touched. Thick and impressively long, his shaft would jut proudly from the nest of tight curls.

She sucked in a quick breath as her womb contracted at the image she'd conjured. Her hand reflexively closed over the cloth covering his erection and he sucked in a more ragged breath in response.

He'd said earlier he wanted foreplay. She'd never been asked to take the lead, not in any way that gave her full control. It wasn't that she'd never thought of it. But she had never been with a man who made her want to lose her natural inhibitions. James made her want to turn herself inside out for his pleasure.

Could she lead in the game of seduction? It felt thrilling and empowering to think about, and it was making her damn horny.

She sat up and reached for the bottom edge of her top and pulled it over her head before she could think too much about what she was doing.

She saw his eyes gleaming in the dark as he looked at her. But he couldn't really see much. She leaned over and switched on the bedside lamp. He blinked and then his gaze went wide as he looked at her. She held it for only a fraction of a second before hers darted away. What did the girls in the videos do?

She closed her eyes and reached up and rubbed her hand over first one mound and then the other, taking pleasure in the feel of her own flesh. Her hands scooped under and around until she cupped the full weight of each breast in her hands. Her nipples were firm and pebbly as they pressed into her palms. If he touched her like this, she would moan in rapture.

"Shay?"

Her eyes popped open. He was frowning at her, as if something else was called for. She just didn't know what. Was she making a fool of herself? Probably. Confused, she shifted away from him, turning her back.

She felt him moving on the bed. Almost immediately, she felt a touch on her back, one finger tracing up her spine from waist to the back of her neck.

"You don't have to try so hard to please me, Shay. Just being with you does that."

The heat of his slightly abrasive fingers skimmed the back of her neck, shifting the curtain of her hair aside. He leaned in and placed a kiss behind her right ear. The shudder of delight that passed through her body startled her. Just the touch of his lips anywhere was seismic.

His finger went roaming down her back again until it came up against the waistband of her bikini panties. It skimmed from side to side then paused at the top of her cleft, bared by the low waistband. Shay held her breath as his finger slid slowly down over the swatch of fabric concealing her butt and then cupped her.

He leaned in again, this time catching her earlobe in

his teeth. "Always been partial to black sheep. Just how *baaaad* can we be?"

He was trying to lighten the moment but her heart was too full to respond. She had awakened ready for him. Could not handle anything less.

"Shay?"

She shook her head, afraid she was going to do something dumb like cry.

"This is for you," he whispered into her ear. "All you want, as much as you want, as long as you want it. Change your mind, just say no."

His hands slipped slowly up her arms before cupping her shoulders and drawing her back against the hard-muscled planes of his chest, cocooning her with the heat of his body. The skin-to-skin contract was devastating to her sanity, overriding her with sensations she'd never felt before. His heart beat behind her left shoulder blade, a little fast but solid. He scooted in until his erection pressed against her. But his hands were gentle. Nothing said he had lost control, would not yield to her command. She didn't know how to handle that. He felt strong and capable, and his tenderness was taking apart every defense she'd ever built.

Then his hands slipped past her sides and his fingers worked up under hers to cup her breasts.

He nuzzled her neck. "You're so soft. And sexy, Shay."

He took his time, playing with each nipple separately, as if each were a little present not to be missed. It was an excruciating tease, shifting her excitement into a higher gear.

Finally he dropped his hands from her breasts and scooted back. She felt cool air move in between them. Then the shock of his tongue, warm and sinuous between her shoulder blades, made her gasp. After a few more licks, he pushed her to the edge of the bed and lifted her to her feet. He slid up behind her and pulled her back between his spread legs. "This is for you, Shay."

His warm wet tongue found the indentation of the small of her back, using long licking strokes to trace her spine. Both hands slid into her waistband, pushing her bikini bottoms down. His tongue followed the exposed indentation of her spine downward, each lick moving a little closer to her cleft.

He reached around to the front with both hands. One splayed across her lower belly to hold her while the other moved down to cup her mound. Forced so tightly against him, Shay had to bend forward slightly to keep her balance as his fingers delved deep into the vee of her body. Then his rasping tongue slipped into the shallow dimple at the base of her spine.

Shay whimpered in pleasure laced with embarrassment. She couldn't help herself. She pushed her hips against his probing fingers, opening for him so that he could find her melting wet center.

He took his time, fingers moving in a slow pulsing rhythm between the slick wet folds of her body. No man had ever touched her so gently and with such assurance. His tongue and teeth licked and nipped up and down her spine in time to the friction of his fingers as he made love to her with everything but his cock.

It was wicked and so strange, and so good!

When he finally lifted his head, his voice was deeper than she'd ever heard it. "This is all for you, Shay. You deserve to be appreciated. To feel every good thing a man can give you."

Dry-mouthed but weeping below from his stroking, Shay couldn't deny it. Yet some protective corner of her female brain told her not to surrender completely.

"*Hm,* it's better when you fully participate." Damn. She sounded as breathless as Marilyn Monroe.

He chuckled but it sounded half strangled by desire.

He withdrew from her slowly and then his hands on her bare hips were turning her to face him. He kissed her navel, darting his tongue into it before lifting his head and smiling at her. His fingers peeled her panties down her hips. "You want more." He kissed her below her navel. "You'll get more." His kiss moved lower still.

And then he made love to her with his tongue.

She held on to him for dear life, fingers digging into the muscles of his shoulders for support because her knees had gone weak. He cupped her butt in both hands, bracing and holding her in place for his tongue fucking. The term had always sounded, well, dirty to her before. But with James it was the most delicious torture. When she flew apart, little cries of ecstasy breaking from her, he held on, loving her with his tongue and teeth until she collapsed against him.

He gathered her to him, kissed her navel and pressed his face into her lower abdomen. "Enough?"

Shay caught her breath, her eyes flying open in outrage. He couldn't be serious. "More."

He lifted his head, lips glistening with the essence of her. "Then come here and I'll give you more." He pulled her down onto the bed.

Lying spread on her bed with her legs hooked over James's shoulders, Shay thought her bliss couldn't be any greater. He was moving inside her, his chest arched high and away from her as he flexed his hips to plunge deeper with each stroke. He worked her slowly, deliberately, pushing her up but not over the edge. With each stroke he gave his hips a little wiggle that made her gasp with pulse-pounding delight.

"Please. Just . . . *Ooooh*. James!"

James gritted his teeth. He'd been holding himself a little apart, prepared this entire time for her to suddenly change her mind. She'd been through so much. Suffered too much. He didn't want her to think he was another user, out for what he could get from a woman. He had been prepared right up to the very second her cries of fulfillment filled his head to pull back, if that's what she suddenly needed.

Now he didn't have to. The pent-up frustration of balancing on that knife's edge, for her sake, was released. Her cries turned him inside out and upside down. And stoked his lust to a level he'd never known. And then he lost control, moving high, hard and fast to her sweet little cries of pleasure.

Her body still quivering with little aftershocks of pleasure, Shay lay staring at him through her lashes for a long time before she spoke. "Where did all that come from?"

A tiny smile tugged his mouth as he reached out to brush strands of her hair from her cheek. His eyes still radiated the heat they'd generated. "I don't know. I just went for it. Too much?"

"I never— No. Just . . . wow."

A little after six A.M. Bogart pushed through the mostly closed bedroom door and padded over to James's side of the bed. He didn't bark but he did move in until his nose was within inches of James's face. The perfume of warm doggy breath woke him.

Golden eyes stared intently into his.

"Right." He tossed off the covers and reached for his jeans.

"Where are you going?"

He looked back over his shoulder. Shay was looking at him with a big grin on her face. That was a new and welcome sight.

He grinned back. "Taking Bogart for a walk."

She rolled over, dragging the covers with her. "I'll do it."

"It's chilly. I won't be long."

She gave him the porcupine look. "You forget. For a whole month he was my dog. I miss taking care of him. Please?"

James hesitated. He didn't want to spoil what would be a normal moment between them. An easy couples moment. "Okay, but don't go far."

He looked at Bogart, who was giving him that lolling-tongue doggy grin. "Do you see what you've done? I even have to share my girl with you."

Bogart barked brightly and padded over to Shay's side of the bed.

CHAPTER TWENTY

Shay sat behind the wheel of her car, trying to get up the courage to drive into work. It was Monday morning. James had already left to report for retraining, but the look on his face as he kissed her good-bye was anything but happy.

"Get a restraining order against Coates. Today."

Balloons? Harmless.

After she'd walked Bogart early Saturday morning, James had walked in on her popping the balloons in the kitchen. The sexy sleepy-eyed man of early morning vanished. Pissed-off Officer Cannon was a force to be reckoned with.

Shay thought about lying. But there was a note tied to the bouquet of balloons she found on her doorstep that read "First Anniversary. Think of me." No name. No need.

James looked at the note a long time before saying in a flat voice that this was the last time he was going to hear Eric Coates's name without doing something about it.

Then he had gotten dressed and taken care of her car problem.

Someone had yanked out her spark plug wires. The

Raleigh police officer who'd volunteered to help them out after he heard about James's and Bogart's rescue of the baby on Friday night spotted the problem immediately. The officer said vandalism was not unusual for a car left in an unmonitored car park. The two officers got her towed and then her car fixed in a matter of hours. Free. Professional courtesy, James told her. She suspected he had paid without letting her know.

Shay smiled to herself as she started her engine. She'd always shouldered her own world. Trust hadn't been part of her vocabulary. She didn't know what to do with gratitude, either. Thanks to James, the new emotions coming to life inside her were far more than thankfulness. Dangerous, because she didn't know what to do with that new feeling of *more*. James was more than she ever expected in her life, better, kinder, a good man. But even a good man could only take so much. Their relationship was barely a week old. Already, he knew more about her than anyone else in her life. They needed time.

That's why she hadn't told him about the obscene phone call. She couldn't afford to dump everything on him, even if her heart wanted to. If it didn't work out, her world would shatter. To have him for now, that was more than enough. Right now, enough felt damn good.

She pulled out of her apartment complex and turned toward downtown and work. Three days ago she had been ready to grab what little she owned and run. Now she was going in to face down her fears. That was because of James. She felt her karma changing over the weekend. It wasn't just the terrific sex. It had to do with every other moment.

There was the spur-of-the-moment Saturday afternoon picnic drowned out by a sudden shower that had left them scrambling for cover with soggy fast-food fried chicken, and an eat-everything-in-sight dog. Who knew Bogart would gobble up a carton of wet coleslaw? And sofa pillows! Fair enough, she'd offered them to him as a substitute for his bed, which she'd tossed out in a fit of self-pity after losing him. What he did with them was his business. And her mess to clean up.

Shay felt her mouth tugging upward as happy images of the weekend cascaded through her thoughts. No frown could last long when confronted with the memory of James with a skimpy towel wrapped around his hips as he made pancakes Sunday morning. Not wonderful pancakes. But who cared when a half-dressed male was in her kitchen?

She had not known it was possible to have so much easy happiness in her life. Now, more than ever, she wanted to clear away the ugliness she had let rule her life for the past year.

Her cell phone rang. It was James. She put it on speaker to keep both hands on the wheel.

"I made a call to the main office of Halifax Bank this morning, asking for a meeting with Eric Coates."

"You shouldn't—"

"I'm talking here, Shay. It's polite to listen." He was still in officer mode. "I was told he's out of the office at a bank conference until Thursday. Looks like I'll have to wait for a little chat with the asshole until I get back. I just thought you should know you have some breathing room. Meanwhile, you need to get a restraining order."

Shay frowned as the light turned red ahead. "I've already told you why I won't do that. If my past is revealed—"

"A restraining order wouldn't cause anyone to check into your past. I'm a cop. I know how this goes. He won't stop until you stop him."

Shay sighed. "I know you mean well but I'll have to think about it. It's my life."

James couldn't argue with that. He knew how to back

people into corners and make them say and do things they didn't want to. Yet Shay was the last person with whom he wanted to use that kind of manipulative bullshit. As worried as he was for her, he wouldn't undermine her just when he was winning back her trust. But he didn't have to be happy about it. At least Eric was gone for the week.

"I'll be back in Raleigh on Friday. Meanwhile, you think hard. If there's any problem, anything at all, you call me. Okay?" His colleagues would shit their pants with laughter if they could hear him backing down like this. The things we do for . . . like?

"Okay." She sounded relieved. "See you Friday."

"Right. And, Shay? Be careful."

Not even the sight of the façade of Halifax Bank could ruin Shay's mood. She wasn't wrong. Something was shifting in her life. Something better than this temporary pain-in-the-butt job. She could feel it like the touch of the sun on her face as it emerged from behind the last wisps of morning fog. Best news of all, Eric would be absent all week.

She paused to let a car pass by before crossing the street. It slowed as it came even with her to allow another pedestrian to cross a little farther along. A little boy in the backseat waved. She waved back. And then he put a metal handgun to the glass of the window and aimed it at her.

It's a toy, her brain said. But her heart leaped and her feet propelled her backward in recoil even before common sense could register. She saw him laughing wildly as the car moved on.

"Kids!"

She looked to her right to find a male bank employee she only knew by sight standing next to her.

"It—it looked so real!" She was stammering.

"Yeah. I could tell you thought so." He shrugged. "Who can be sure these days, right?"

Shay swallowed and gripped the strap of her bag tightly as she crossed the street. Her flawless day now had a ding in it.

An hour later, she glanced up at the clock. Even for a Monday the calls were coming thick and fast. It was the last full week before Thanksgiving. People were double-checking their balances and moving money from account to account as they made plans to travel and Christmas shop. She didn't have reason to do either. Angie had invited her to her family's house, as usual, but she was getting a bit weary of spending holidays with people who thought turkey should be served by noon so that it didn't interfere with football. Angie claimed she only watched for the close-up shots of all those tight ends.

What would James's Thanksgiving be like? Not that she would get a chance to find out. He had lots of family to celebrate with. Must be nice. But too intense for her taste. Maybe she would volunteer to serve the holiday dinner at a soup kitchen.

She was only half listening to the next caller when she suddenly frowned.

"Excuse me, ma'am. Did you say you need to move fifty thousand dollars from your account?" Her gaze shifted to the guideline sheet she kept close by for backup. It stated that large sums were to be run by a superior if there was any hint of a possible problem. The caller, who sounded elderly, couldn't remember her password.

She glanced at the name on the account. "Just one moment, Mrs. Leggett. I will need to put you through to a personal banker. This might take a minute but don't hang up. I promise someone will answer. Thank you for your patience."

Shay's finger punched a key that would put her in touch

with a superior. The instant she heard a pickup, she launched into her request. "This is Customer IT. I need verification on a customer's withdrawal. It's—"

"Shay Appleton." Eric's voice was practically a snarl.

Shay felt herself flush, her heart rate accelerating. "It's for a fifty-thousand-dollar transfer. And the customer doesn't have her password."

She heard him swear under his breath. "Haven't you learned anything while you've been here? Stick to bank policy. Call a personal banker."

"Transferring call now." Shay had connected Eric with Mrs. Leggett. The click echoed so loudly in her earphones she flinched.

Oh God. Shay had stared at the keypad and realized she had punched the wrong extension. Even so, Eric wasn't supposed to be here. Now he knew she was here, too.

Follow bank policy. That was what he'd told her.

She glanced around the bank lobby. Two personal bankers were with customers. The third was nowhere to be seen. When the personal bankers were busy, bank policy said she was to move up the ladder. She'd done just that. Even if it was by mistake.

Doing my job. As much as she wanted to grab her purse and walk out, a new sense of self held her back. She was working. Whatever craziness Eric might come up with after hours, he wouldn't dare do anything here, in his place of business.

She adjusted her headphones and punched up the next customer.

A few minutes later she was back in full efficiency mode, hanging up from one call to field the next without a hitch. "Halifax Bank IT Customer Service. How may I help you?"

"I seen you talking to the police." The gruff voice ignited every synapse in her brain. "Told you, keep your mouth shut!"

"About what? Who are you—"

"You're gonna pay!"

Shay stabbed the end call button and jerked the earphones from her head. Yet she didn't feel as panicky as she had the first time. The jittery sensation tingling her nerve endings was more like the revulsion she'd felt that time a boy at school had dropped a slug down the back of her tee. It disgusted her but she wasn't actually hurt.

Sliding her chair back from her desk, she ignored for the moment the two new calls rolling onto the waiting list. She smoothed her hands up and down her sweater-clad arms, feeling a chill at odds with the bank's overzealous heating.

The caller had made a new threat. Don't talk about what? Eric? Too late.

Only Eric wouldn't know that.

She was certain Eric had hired some lowlife to track her moves. It was the only explanation. This way, he wouldn't be directly connected to the harassment. So like Eric to do things from on high.

He wanted her to submit.

Or she could run away.

Running away. She'd been doing that half her life. Hiding, staying small, not wanting to draw too much scrutiny for fear people would learn her secrets and pull away.

Only James hadn't. He'd listened and not judged so much as let her be. He was urging her to fight back. And maybe she would, when he came back.

Shay sat up straight in her chair and reached for her earphones. Eric Coates could go straight to Hell without passing Go.

* * *

"There she is."

Shay paused just inside the bank's entrance. She'd been out having her lunch.

Eric stood on the main floor with two female bank employees.

"Come here, Ms. Appleton!" Her name echoed in the bank's cavernous space, drawing every eye in the lobby.

Shay clenched her jaw, refusing to even try to smile as she approached. "Yes, Mr. Coates?"

Eric held his head at an angle that allowed him to glare down at her. "Did you answer an IT customer call this morning from Mrs. Elsa Leggett?"

"Yes. I—"

"Your actions reflected poor judgment and an indifferent attitude concerning this bank's policies."

"What are you—"

"Not here." He actually used his hand in a slashing motion to cut her off. His face was cold, the muscles locked in an emotion she recognized as anger, if not the reason for it. "Come with me."

The curt words were spoken with such viciousness Shay couldn't quite believe it. Usually he hid his contempt behind an amiable façade. Unless he'd been drinking. The two employees he'd been chatting with darted speculative glances at her as they moved rapidly away.

The ride up one floor was more than long enough for Shay to feel her fried egg sandwich begin to go rancid in the nervous gush of acid flooding her stomach. She didn't look at Eric but stared at the dully gleaming panels of brushed metal before her. She used the tense silence to try to calm her nerves and prepare for a fight.

Something had gone wrong. But she had followed bank policy. He might be angry but whatever happened as a result of that call was not her fault.

The elevator didn't stop on two but continued. She didn't glance Eric's way but kept her eyes on the numbers until they reached the top floor, where the top bank brass had offices. How had she not noticed that he had put a key in the elevator pad that would allow them to take it to the top floor?

Once off the elevator, with Eric in the lead, they bypassed several empty offices. Senior management must still be at lunch, she thought absently, and followed him straight toward the president's boardroom. Had he convened a meeting to deal with her supposed bank policy infraction, whatever it might be? She squared her shoulders, readying to defend herself.

Eric used a key to unlock the door. He pushed it open and indicated that she should enter. She was in the room before she realized they were alone. She turned around, but he was there, blocking the door.

"Have a seat, Shay. No one will bother us here."

Shay watched him lock the door, her heart starting to pound. She hadn't seen this coming. She was so certain Eric would not make a move on her at work.

"Lunch hour's almost over." She was glad to hear her voice was steady. "People will be returning to the floor soon."

His mouth sketched a smile. "You think you know everything. There's a banking convention in town. The keynote speech should be under way. No one wanted to miss it. I'm supposed to be there, with other senior staff. However, I volunteered to hold down the fort today. So for at least another hour, it's just you and me."

That shark grin. She felt the ground shifting beneath her feet. But he mustn't know how rattled she was.

"What do you want?" She stared right back at him until he looked away.

"Have a seat, Shay. You're always in a hurry. Except when it counts." He was staring at her with a strange look of triumph that tugged at his mouth.

"I'll stand." She moved to put more of the length of the expensive mahogany inlaid board table between them. Behind the table, the skyline of Raleigh stretched out like an IMAX theater screen. The long wall of glass was a little dizzying for anyone afraid of heights. She wasn't. She scooted to the far side of the table.

Eric moved more slowly, slipping out of his suit coat and hanging it on a chair back. His fingers slipped over either shoulder, smoothing out phantom wrinkles.

"You said this was about that call and following bank policy. That's what I did."

He waved off her words with a hand. "What am I to do about you, Shay Appleton? You no longer answer my calls or show any respect for my feelings." He slanted a dark look her way. "You prefer your new blue-collar boyfriend. What should I do about that?"

"Forget about me. You have someone else." For once, Shay swallowed the defiant words that flowed through her thoughts. Maybe if she pandered to his ego, he'd be satisfied. "You're going to marry a senator's daughter. You're handsome, wealthy. Any woman—" She ground to a halt, choking on the insincere words.

"Any woman but you? That wasn't always true. There was a time when all I had to do was call and you came trotting after me like the little bitch you are."

Shay lifted her chin. "Open the door, Eric. You've made your point. I'll leave Halifax Bank today and you'll never see me again."

"Yes. That's exactly what you're going to do. But not until we settle up."

He was moving toward her and she was backing up. Nowhere to go, of course. The only way out was through locked doors. The more she backpedaled the more frightened she became. *Mouse in a maze.*

"I've tried to reason with you. Tried to be nice and charming. Tried to please you. But there's no pleasing some bitches."

Shay moved to a corner of the window and glanced out, not knowing what she expected to see. There was no escape that way.

"There's only one thing I want from you. One last fuck. You can relax and enjoy it, or you can just take it. It's up to you."

Shay stopped. His words didn't shock her. They focused her. "Is that what this is about? You want to get in my pants one more time. Not. Going. To happen."

She didn't move away as he came toward her. She let all her anger burn through the fear. When he touched her face, she knocked his hand away. With an expletive, he grabbed her breast and twisted it painfully.

Gasping in pain, she turned into him and brought her knee up quick and hard.

She heard him grunt in agony but she was jerking free of his grasp and racing to where he'd left his jacket hanging. She'd seen him drop the key into a pocket. She snagged it, searching madly for it as she headed for the door.

She was shocked that he staggered up as she stuck the key in the lock. He grasped her by the hair and pulled so hard she saw stars. But the key had turned. She was almost free.

She shoved an elbow into his ribs but he caught her and spun her around, twisting his hand in her hair.

She gasped from the pain but made herself look up and hold his gaze. "I will fight you, Eric. I never did that before but I *will* now. I swear I'll scratch and bloody you, make you bruise and bloody me. And then I'll go downstairs and stand in the middle of the lobby and scream the place down around your ears. Rape. Rape!" She shouted the word the second time, loud and harsh.

His expression turned so ugly she thought for a second he was going to hurt her anyway. Then he suddenly swung away, freeing her.

He leaned back against the wall, his tie askew and his face mottled with rage. "You won't win, you little bitch. I still have many ways of ruining you. So run along. Back to your temporary life. I'm going to make it perfectly clear to your boss that, due to your ill-handling of certain matters today, Halifax Banking Corporation and all of its subsidiaries will no longer hire Logital Solutions employees in any capacity in the future."

Shay swung around. "I did nothing wrong."

"Are you sure your employer will believe that when we've pulled our business?"

His threat didn't shock her. It focused her. *Get away. Then fight back.*

She ran.

Moments later, she was alone in the elevator, headed back downstairs. She stared at the geometric design on the rug until her eyes began to burn. James was right. Eric wasn't going to go away. This would never be over, until she did something about him. Even if it cost her everything.

"Seriously, that shit is unreal. Sorry."

Shay didn't even look up. The sight before her was so awful she couldn't look away from the reason for the passerby's comment.

Etched into the paint of the driver's door of her car in crude capital lettering were the words DIE CUNT.

Under the parking lot's lighting the jagged words gleamed silvery where the blue paint had been scrapped down to the door's metal.

It was too much. Tears welled in her eyes, blurring the insult. All she could think of was that her car had been violated, again, and that she could not afford to erase the damage this time.

She could not drive home like this.

On legs that felt wooden, she stiff-walked her way to the trunk of her car and pulled out the roll of duct tape she kept for emergencies, along with an old map. Within minutes, she had covered the scrawl. Yet it seemed to her as if the hideous words might burn through for all to see.

She sat behind the wheel, staring out at the darkness. Night had fallen with the suddenness of late autumn. It didn't matter. She was blind with rage.

Pick on someone your own size, dickface!

Bullies never chose the strong. They had a mean hunger that could only be fed by taunting the weak. Even after she had forced herself to finish her job, sitting in plain sight all afternoon as if nothing had happened, did she still look like a victim?

The long-ago day came tumbling back into her mind with a clarity that ripped through her blind rage.

When she'd mentioned the skit to James, she hadn't felt a thing. But now her heart accelerated. She closed her eyes. Her hands flexed over the steering wheel as she held on for dear life. She was no longer remembering the past. She had dropped into it.

It was a skit for homecoming weekend. Her junior year. New school. New town. New life. Nine weeks into the semester, she was doing okay. At least, she was not being looked at weirdly, as she had at her former school. She didn't worry about friends yet. The only person who talked to her regularly was the junior varsity team captain, Ned Jackson, who was failing precalculus. Because she wasn't, he'd been paired with her to do in-class practice assignments. Boys made her nervous but Ned didn't seem to notice that she was a girl, so it seemed to be working.

The only time he'd said a personal thing to her was the day before the homecoming game. The school always held a pep rally, he told her, and he was going to be in one of the skits. She should come and see it.

So she went and sat in the bleachers, ignored by anyone who thought enough to even look in her direction.

Midway through the rah-rah speeches and drill-team-led cheers, the skits began. Finally, there was Ned in his football uniform, sitting at a desk before a blackboard. A chill slipped up Shay's skirt as a girl student joined him. She wore jeans and a big baggy sweater, and a fake ponytail hiked so high it look like a horse's tail growing out of the crown of her head.

The snickering began in the audience but Shay didn't really pay much attention to it. Her gaze was glued to the stage. The girl wrote a math problem on the board then stopped to listen as Ned made lame attempts to solve it. Each time he got the answer wrong, the girl got twitchier.

Shay began to fold up inside. They were making fun of her. But that wasn't right. She thought Ned was becoming her friend. How could he betray her like this?

The girl wrote another, easier problem. Ned hammed up the dummy role. As he voiced more wrong answers the girl started to writhe in frustration. When he finally got even 2 plus 2 wrong, the girl suddenly screamed in primal rage, whipped out a giant pair of scissors from behind the chalkboard, and began stabbing the team captain. On cue, the band began to play. It was the music from the shower scene in *Psycho,* shrieking clarinets punctuating the stabs.

Paralyzed by shock, Shay sat there, her heart pumping so hard her body shook with every beat.

When Ned was sprawled on the floor, the girl stepped forward and cried, "Don't mess with Psycho Shay!"

A blur of faces had turned toward her, many laughing, others staring at her in doubtful surprise or horrified recognition of what the skit meant.

In that instant, shame burned her to the ground. All her mother's efforts and planning and secrecy had come to nothing. Everyone knew!

Someone rapped on her car window.

Shay nearly jumped out of her skin.

Doris Butler was peering in at her, her gaze sharp and mouth primmed. "Are you okay, Ms. Appleton?"

"Yes. Of course." Her words sounded awkward, as if the muscles no longer knew how to work together to form words.

"Very well. Good evening."

Shay watched as Doris moved on toward her own car. She was sweating. Her blouse beneath her jacket was sticking to her back. Her face was damp and her hands were slippery on the wheel. Yet in her core, she felt ice-cold.

She had not gone back to that school. But word always got around. Another school, another revelation. When she begged to leave, her mother lost it. For the first time in two years she had a really good job paying wages that put a decent roof over their heads. She had sacrificed so much. No, everything for her daughter. Shay would just have to find a way to live with what she'd done, to both of them.

After that, the crack that had been there between mother and daughter since the night of the stabbing widened a little more each day.

At eighteen Shay moved out and changed her name legally to one that she hoped would allow her, and her mother, to outrun the past.

Only she hadn't. The past was still ruling her life.

Shay leaned her forehead against the wheel. The joy of the morning had dried up and blown away. She wanted back that rare and precious feeling of happiness in the worst way. The impulse to reach for her phone and call James was strong. He'd given her his number in case of emergency. Didn't this qualify?

Her reach stuttered to a stop just short of her purse. James was new in her life. This might be the one thing too many, even for him. Or perhaps he would come back to Raleigh and confront Eric. He was a police officer. If he assaulted a civilian he'd be in more trouble than the average person. It could ruin his career, his life.

Shay felt the familiar glowing coals of rage kindle to life inside her. It wasn't a new feeling. Yet this time the fury felt more focused. She wasn't a helpless fourteen-year-old. She'd come through that, and a lot more since. She knew exactly who her enemy was, and why.

She'd let Eric's rat-bastard bullying and abuse go on for too long. She'd told him it was over but he refused to accept that.

Eric had made it clear he thought he was calling the shots. The phone calls, now the damage to her car. He was playing mind games with her. And it was escalating. Only a fool would think he would stop now.

But this time she wasn't going to ask for help. She wasn't going to be the cause of any more destroyed lives, except maybe her own. She just needed to think through the plan forming in her mind.

CHAPTER TWENTY-ONE

Shay let out a long breath as the elevator doors closed on the top floor of Halifax Bank. She had just lit a match to her reputation, and possibly her job future. Shay smiled at her metallic reflection in the doors. It felt glorious.

She'd been waiting in his outer office when. Cadwallader Jones, president of the bank, arrived this morning. She had expected to wait hours to see him but he ushered her right in.

"What can I do for you, Ms. Appleton?"

Shay lifted her chin, her cheeks burning as she made eye contact with the man into whose hands she was about to place her future. "I'm here to report systemic sexual harassment by one of your employees. And, I suspect, misuse of Halifax Bank funds."

Cadwallader Jones blinked behind his glasses. "You should take a seat, Ms. Appleton. Do you mind if I record our conversation?"

Shay hesitated only a second. She was about to tell the truth. It couldn't hurt her more than the lies Eric meant to spread.

He called in his secretary.

In the beginning, Cadwallader Jones listened to her with a neutral expression, neither commenting nor reacting. But she noticed a slight tightening of his mouth as she told him about Eric courting her a year ago. There was a banking policy against interpersonal relations between upper management and employees who reported to them. The story of their illicit trip to the Caymans on the company's dime briefly widened his eyes. As she ticked off their other travels, financed by the bank or bank customers, his eyes narrowed to slits. Then she moved on to the sexual harassment charge.

She stopped far short of her explicit confession to James, but offered some telling details of Eric's harassment that finally led her to call the police the night of their breakup. She told him of Eric's refusal to accept their breakup, including his attempts to bring her back into his control by finagling a job here at the bank a second time.

As she talked, she glimpsed a sheen of sweat rising beneath the pale strands of Cadwallader Jones's thinning hair.

By the time she finished with Eric's attempt to rape her in the conference room down the hall the day before, the secretary was no longer taking notes but simply staring at her. Finally, she reported the threats Eric had made against her employer if she told anyone about his actions yesterday.

When she was done, Cadwallader Jones steepled his fingers, elbows locked by his sides, and asked her three questions.

"Can you corroborate your statements?"

"Do you understand the seriousness of what you have revealed, because some of it could be considered criminal?"

"What do you expect in return for your reportage?"

She answered without hesitation.

Yes, she pulled from her purse itineraries of their trips, with ticket information for the flights with Eric, and even receipts for some of the gifts he'd bought. But he need not take only her word for it. "Ask Doris Butler. I overheard her say last week that I'm not the first woman Mr. Coates has taken on his trips.

"And yes, I understand I have implicated Mr. Coates, and possibly myself, in what could be criminal offenses. But I did not understand that what Eric was doing was illegal until recently. He always said the trips were our little secret, so other employees wouldn't be jealous. But last night when I pulled out the paperwork I'd kept I noticed Eric never paid for a single thing. It was always charged to this bank, or a customer. I never handled or took any funds from the bank, or Eric.

"Finally, I don't want Logital Solutions to suffer for my actions. I take full responsibility. I do want the harassment to stop and for everyone to know what an asshole Eric Coates is. And, though you didn't ask, it's important for me to say it. I didn't know Mr. Coates had a fiancée. Poor woman."

"Amen," the secretary murmured under her breath.

The elevator doors whooshed open onto the main floor. Ahead of Shay three men were trying to wedge a twenty-foot live Christmas tree through the double doors of the lobby. There was already a stand erected for it in the center of the marble floor. It smelled heavenly of deep woods growth and the tarry turpentine that reminded her of the holidays. It would be lit Thanksgiving week, she had been informed in the Monday-morning bulletin. She wouldn't be around to see it.

She took her seat and picked up her earphones. Only then did she glance at the clock. It was 10:17 A.M. Cadwallader Jones had directed her to resume her job until further notice. How long would it take until others knew what she'd done?

It did not take long.

At twenty minutes to eleven, Doris Butler, Eric's executive assistant, came up to Shay's desk, clutching a cardboard box of belongings. Her face bore a hectic complexion of anger barely contained. "Spreading lies that cost me my job. How dare you!"

Shay looked up slowly in answer to the angry whisper. "You covered for your boss, didn't you? You made all his arrangements. Knew what was going on. I only told the truth."

"Shut up! You, you just shut your vicious mouth!" Doris raised her hand as if to deliver a blow.

Shay stood up, narrowing her eyes. "You touch me and I'll take you to the floor."

The older woman's eyes widened and she began to back away. She turned, her shoulders hunched as if expecting a blow from behind, and hurried toward the exit.

Laughter gurgled up out of her that Shay couldn't completely still with the hand she pressed to her lips. She was close to seriously losing it. There was nothing remotely funny about what she'd done, or what might happen to her as a result.

You won't get away with this. Eric will see to that.

Shay sat down, fear trickling in behind her amusement. What had she set in motion?

Exactly nineteen minutes later, Eric burst out of the elevator.

He came straight toward her, nearly knocking over one of the men who was gauging whether the Christmas tree was straight in its stand.

"Excuse me. I need to put you on hold for a moment." Not waiting for a reply from her customer, Shay pushed the hold button and rose to her feet just as Eric reached her.

His eyes were half crazy with rage. His lips were bloodless. He came right up to her, skirting the desk until they were a foot apart.

"You calculating little slut!" His voice was low but his eyes were bloodshot with the strain of containing his rage. "You're trying to fuck me over. I won't let that happen."

Shay flinched with every word. It was as awful as if she had not tried to prepare herself for his reaction. She grabbed the edge of the desk with both hands to steady herself.

"You should have listened to me when I said we were over. You gave me no choice."

His eyes widened way past pissed off. For a second she thought he would, unlike Doris, actually try to strike her. But then he seemed to realize where he was. He was a senior bank official. Customers were watching, even if they couldn't hear the exchange.

"You think you've won? You have no idea of the size of the shitstorm that's about to dump on you. Cadwallader Jones and my father are fraternity brothers. I fucked up bad, but that isn't how it's going to end. I won't be bested by a little bitch with a GED and secrets that make her cry at night. I will find a way to destroy you."

Shay blinked back the insult. "Fuck off, Eric."

He leaned in but Shay refused to back up. "This isn't over," he breathed in her ear. And then he swung away and left through the main doors.

Shay sat down hard, her breath coming in little gasps.

Doris's threat hadn't moved her. But the anger in Eric's voice had chilled her in a way no sweater could insulate against.

DIE CUNT.

The crude, ugly words carved into her car door seemed etched in her mind.

Did his latest threat mean he would ratchet up the harassment? No, he couldn't afford to be caught doing that now that she'd gone public with his treatment of her. Even if he didn't totally believe her side of it, Cadwallader Jones would be bound to look into the story she'd told him this morning. She only had to ride out the storm. The lightning and thunder couldn't touch her now because she'd taken shelter in the truth.

It took a few more seconds for the stares of the customers in the lobby to penetrate her awareness. Eric was gone, blown through the exit like an expensively clothed tornado. Every person in the lobby was staring at her.

For an instant the world swooped down to pinpoint size, a prick of light in a black field.

She was sixteen, in the bleachers. Everyone was laughing . . .

And then the scope of her vision widened again, the room brighter than before.

She was twenty-six years old. In a bank building where she worked. Everyone who wanted to judge her for standing up for herself could go straight to hell.

Shay sat back down, picked up her earphones, and pushed the answer button on the next call.

Ten minutes later, Cadwallader Jones came into the lobby with one of the bank's security personnel. Together they watched as she gathered her things, picked up her purse, and then escorted her to the door.

"I don't know what to say, Shay."

Perry Deshezer stared at his employee as if a whole new being had emerged through her skin.

"I don't expect you to forgive me. What I did was unprofessional and unethical. But Eric put me through hell this last year. I couldn't let him get away with it anymore."

Perry rubbed his bald head absently. "I've known for

some time you weren't happy but I, none of us, ever guessed the cause. Why didn't you say something?"

She shrugged. "At first I thought it was all my fault. Later, I didn't think anyone would believe me."

"What will you do now? Do you think Mr. Cadwallader Jones will press the issue with you?"

"The last thing he said to me was that my services, professional and otherwise, were no longer required. And that he hoped I would find other opportunities for employment soon. I hope that means he plans to take care of things himself."

Perry raised his brows. "In that case, it's my turn."

Shay bit her lip. She knew what was coming. That's why she'd come here instead of going home to sulk. "I'm fired."

"That's not even remotely on my mind. I think what you did was a brave thing. I wish you had told me what was going on sooner. I'd have backed you up, Shay."

That snapped her head up.

Perry was smiling. "You're one of my most reliable people. That phrase should sound familiar to you. I respect your opinion and your word. Sexual harassment is covered in our agreement with our customers. I'll have something to say if Halifax Bank tries to screw us out of business, or talks against us to any of their business partners. To my way of thinking, they can't afford the bad publicity associated with a problem like Eric Coates. They may cover this up, to keep feathers from being ruffled among their investors. But Eric's future there is gone. And I don't mind going to the mat for a good cause. If they don't take appropriate action, Logital Solutions will go public with our side."

Shay tilted her head, gratitude warring with anxiety over that word "public." "You don't have to do that for me. Eric will leave me alone now. He's got problems of his own to deal with."

Perry wagged his finger. "I'm very disappointed in you. I'd do that for any of my employees. I just happen to like you particularly well. A customer tried to extort sexual favors from one of my employees. I can't allow that. But, quite frankly, I think you need to stay in-house until we know what's going to happen. I need a person to work the Logital Solution's reception desk. It's a full-time position, and the pay is about the same."

"Thank you."

"Go home, get some rest. Then we'll see you in the morning."

Shay nodded.

Perry's reaction was better than she could possibly have hoped for. He believed her. Just as James had. Maybe after being so accustomed to hard knocks, she had been missing the thumbs-up and helping hands around her. All she had had to do was stand up for herself.

When she reached the parking lot she saw that the wind had torn an edge of the map away from the tape. It flapped back, revealing the scratched *D* and *I* and part of the *E*. She retaped it before driving away.

CHAPTER TWENTY-TWO

On day four of his retraining, James had decoy duty. After three intense days of class work and technique workshops, he and Bogart had already passed the agility, area-search, and building-search tests. This morning Bogart got to rest while his handler did some of the work. After dark, they would be tested on the night obstacle course.

Dressed in a well-padded bite suit that made him look like the Pillsbury Doughboy's blue brother, James lumbered across the grass to get ready for the next attack.

The dog, a bitch, came at him at full speed from thirty feet away.

A spurt of adrenaline gave James suspect-alert status as he turned to run.

The dog's lunge knocked him back a step and he turned with the impact to deflect the direct force of the hit.

He took the full-mouth bite high on the inside of the upper arm, shouting, "Fuck! Fuck this shit!" He hit at the dog but without a lot of force.

The shouts and slaps were intended to intimidate, the kind of frightened, angry responses the dog could expect

from a real suspect high on drugs. If the dog flinched and
released then there was a problem.

The dog growled deep in her throat but did not relax
her bite.

He dragged her along in the grass, hind legs on the
ground as she tugged hard to try to bring him down. Then
suddenly he planted his feet and used his arm to swing the
dog up off the ground, the bite the only thing holding her
to the suit. He grabbed her under the belly and heaved her
hind legs first over his shoulder as he continued to slowly
spin around. Well trained, she growled louder, escalating
as her prey did, fully engaged in getting and maintaining
control.

Officer Matt Spurlock came up to claim his dog. When
he had attached the leash, he gave the command to release.

James nodded in approval. "Good work. She's tenacious."

Matt grinned. "Yeah. My wife says I tend to bring that
out in females."

James leaned forward, placing his hands on his thighs
as he caught his breath.

Fully protected by a bite suit, he wasn't getting beat up
or abused, but he was getting exhausted. The incredible
force of a K-9's grab-and-hold was nothing to take for
granted. His shoulders and thighs ached from taking the
repeated attacks from sixty-five- to ninety-five-pound dogs.
He needed his full concentration or, even in his cushioned
bite suit, he could be injured.

To truly understand the power and commitment to
purpose of a K-9 there was no better way than to suit up
and experience it firsthand. He didn't do it often but each
time he came away with a new respect and admiration for
these wonderful creatures.

A hand landed hard on his shoulder. "Good work,

Cannon. You're done for the day. Anyway, there's someone looking for you."

James straightened and looked back in the direction his trainer pointed. Near the entrance to the training hut a deputy sheriff stood waiting. His first thought was *Shay*. He took off at a sprint toward the visitor. Well, a lumber. Sprinting was impossible in his suit.

James held out his hand when he got close. "I'm James Cannon. What's up, Deputy?"

"Howdy, Mr. Cannon." After he shook James's hand, he pulled out an envelope. "I got something with your name on it. Looks important."

James recognized a summons when he saw one. "Shit."

The deputy smiled. "Have a nice day."

"What the hell do you think you're playing at, Jaylynn?" James palmed his cell as he eyed the locker room where he'd gone to change out of his decoy suit to make certain he was not being overheard.

"Hello, Jimmy." Jaylynn's voice was all cane-sugar sweet. "I'm hanging up now. My attorney says I'm not supposed to talk to you."

"You can talk to me over the phone or you can talk to me in person. You decide."

There was a pause. "What do you want?"

"What are you trying to do by suing Shay Appleton?"

"I'm trying to keep my career from being derailed."

"You did that all by yourself."

He thought he heard her yawn. "Did you really think I was going to stand by and let you ruin my career? Over a dog? I'm not stupid, James. I sought legal counsel. My attorney advised me to not wait for charges to be filed against me but to take an aggressive approach."

"He can't change the fact that you stole Bogart and lied about it to the police. That's going to stick."

"I don't know about that. My attorney says there were miti—minta—er, extenuating circumstances which led to my actions."

"Like what?"

"Like, I was ashamed your dog got away from me. And I thought the police would act faster if I said he was stolen. And that nobody would care about how he got away when he turned up again."

James gritted his teeth. Her way of thinking had become self-delusional. Whatever she wanted to be true suddenly was, in her mind. "You were seen with Bogart at a Raleigh shelter. You can be identified."

"So you keep saying. My attorney says that woman's testimony has been tainted. That could have been anybody bringing in your dog. You found the witness. Only you have talked to her. Only you are saying she can identify me. And you wrote up the report. You aren't unbiased by a long shot, mister!"

"Is that all you've got?"

"You wish, you bastard! I know you were over in Raleigh this past weekend. I know you're seeing her, probably fucking her."

James made a quick calculation. "You hired a private investigator."

"Two. My attorney said I needed to get information quickly. One to find her and one to watch you. Funny how they met last Friday in Raleigh. I hear one PI gave your little slut makeup lessons in the ladies' room. God knows, she needs the help. We've got pictures of you two together. I hit the jackpot, didn't I? Now that I know you two know each other I can see that I was framed. You set me up!"

Every muscle in James's body tensed as the minefield of Jaylynn's thinking opened up before him. The woman at the bar, the one he'd pegged as police. PI. He swallowed his anger. He needed to know just how elaborate her negative spin had become. "Why would I set you up?"

"Because I'm a celebrity. You're trying to ruin me because I dumped you. You've been feeding that little slut information about me. My attorney says that amounts to co—cohesion."

"I think you mean collusion." *And extortion.* But why help her out?

"Whatever. Once the judge sees pictures of you with that slut, who's going to think you chose her over me?"

"Nothing you've said changes the fact that you went to the police with the story that Bogart was stolen from your car, Jaylynn."

"That's right. I lost him, like I said the first time." She sounded so confident. "For all I know, you hired your slut to steal him so you could have an excuse to go after me because you knew I was moving on. I'm the victim here."

James shifted quickly through her argument. Someone was coaching her, and doing a damn good job of burying the truth with innuendo. While he was certain she hadn't thought up any of this herself, Jaylynn was a pro at delivering someone else's script. She would be believable in front of a judge. He needed to crack her story in order to refute it.

"Have you moved on, Jaylynn?"

"Wouldn't you like to know?"

"Bet I can find out who he is by reading a few copies of the society pages."

There was a long pause. He knew he'd hit a nerve, and a thread to follow up. "Is that who's footing the attorney bills? And hired the two detectives? I'm impressed."

"How I conduct my life is none of your business."

He needed to put her back on the defensive. "You must be more generous in bed with him than you were with me."

She didn't answer for so long he thought she'd hung up.

"I'll bet trailer-park Barbie doesn't know how little you make as a doggy cop. Or maybe she thinks that being with you is trading up from the bubbas she's known. We're digging into her background. Who knows what else will turn up?"

James went cold inside. "What do you want to make this go away, Jaylynn?"

"Oh no! You started this. You're the one accusing me of stealing your damn dog. Now you'll have to deal with my payback. Tell your bitch I'll see her in court!" She hung up.

James palmed his forehead, trying to concentrate on every word spoken as he played their conversation back in his head. Jaylynn's attorney sounded like one of those grandstanding types who'd do anything for a client, providing it made the papers and enhanced his career profile.

He needed to put in a call to his sergeant about what the department was going to do about Bogart's disappearance. He doubted it was top priority. He'd wanted to scare Jaylynn, shake her up for all the worry and pain she'd put him and Bogart through. For trying to kill Bogart.

James could have kicked himself for not seeing something like this coming. He knew Jaylynn was arrogant and self-involved, and ruthless. He had counted on her pride forcing her to make a strategic retreat out of town before she was charged. Or if she had turned on him, he thought he was prepared.

But Jaylynn had seen through his tough stance and found a vulnerable spot. She wasn't going after him. She'd chosen to focus on the one innocent party in the whole screwed-up business. Shay.

James swore colorfully enough to turn a few heads but he didn't even acknowledge the men he passed as he headed back to the field.

He should have told Shay about Jaylynn being a possible threat. But so much was going on when he found her in Raleigh that that concern was wiped right out of his mind.

Strange as it seemed, the moment he met Shay, Jaylynn had gone from being his ex to someone he once knew way back when. He could take care of himself. But dammit, Shay didn't deserve another stone in her road.

He wasn't arrogant or foolish enough to think he could just swoop in and make Shay's life all better, or even that she'd want him to, in the long run. Their relationship was too new for that kind of thinking.

James's steps slowed. But he was thinking about it. He just hadn't realized it until this second.

Shay'd had so much grief in her life. She had paid too heavy a price for an incident that left her unjustly accused, tried, and convicted in the public eye. All she'd ever wanted to do was outrun her past. How could he tell her he was responsible for the shitstorm that was about to drag her into public view again? And worst of all, that it was his fault?

"Damn it!" He slammed a fist against the closest wall. In trying to set the record straight about Bogart's disappearance, he'd royally screwed the woman who'd saved Bogart's life.

"You ready?"

James looked up. Matt Reed stood before him in full gear for the next test. Had he seen the punch James had thrown? Possibly. It didn't show on the lawman's face.

"Yeah. Ready. Wait." James sent Matt a direct look. "I need to go into Raleigh this evening. After the testing."

His trainer frowned. "You know the drill."

James did. It would be twenty-four hours more before he was done with his retraining. K-9 boot camp was a lot like regular boot camp. He hated asking for favors. He locked his jaw against doing so.

Matt stared at him. "Somebody dead or dying?"

James wagged his head though he suspected his relationship with Shay might be on life support after she received her summons.

"Then it can wait. Let's get 'er done."

James glanced at his phone. Shay would still be working. She hadn't called him so it might be safe to assume she had not yet been served. He really didn't want to drop this bomb on her in the middle of the day and have to hang up.

He could text her a warning. No, that would only scare her. And without an explanation, she would freak—and who could blame her?

He needed to be able to reassure her that he would figure out a way to protect her. And be right about that. But first he'd have to explain all about Jaylynn. Couldn't really text that, either.

He punched a few words into his phone. *We need to talk. I'll call late. Love you.*

He stared at the words then punched the key to back up and erase "love you." Too soon. And not even remotely relevant at the moment. Considering what he had to confess.

He was getting soft between the ears.

CHAPTER TWENTY-THREE

Shay ached all over. Her head throbbed. Her eyes itched and burned as she read her monitor. Her knuckles ached where she gripped her mouse. Maybe she was coming down with the flu.

"That's all I need." She rubbed two fingers between her brows to smooth out the tightness. The flu. Final insult after a roller-coaster week.

"You up for pizza and a beer?"

Shay made the effort to smile at Angie and Henry who had come up to her at the receptionist's desk. They were dressed similarly in jeans, tees, and leather jackets. Of course, Angie's jacket looked like a zippered version of a fifteenth-century gentleman's doublet, tightly fitted with puffed sleeves and a ruffle on each upper arm: Charles VII meets Steampunk.

She glanced at the wall clock. "I've got six minutes to put in."

Her friends exchanged glances. "Perry is making you punch a clock?"

When not out working a temp job, Logital Solutions's

employees had a lot of freedom. Many still came in and often stayed late, because it allowed them access to some of the fastest computers around. Because much of it wasn't paid work, Perry didn't keep track of hours.

"I'm not temping. I'm staff. We clock in and out."

"All the more reason for us to spirit you away, lowly drudge," Angie intoned in her best snotty English accent.

"I don't think so, guys. Have you heard if anyone in the building has come down with the flu?"

They both backed up a foot.

"You do look sort of illin'," Henry said, sliding a hank of long black hair back from his face.

"No, you should come. Beer is a natural viral deterrent."

Henry turned to Angie. "Seriously?"

"Absolutely. Don't you remember *The Andromeda Strain*? The drunk guy didn't get the virus. Something about acid levels in his blood. Shay needs isoalpha acids to fight her plague." Angie said it with such conviction Henry nodded.

He glanced at the clock. "That settles it. Beer therapy for Shay in T minus five minutes and counting."

Shay didn't say no a second time, though the last thing she felt like doing was sitting in a too warm, too loud overcrowded bar. She wanted to go home and curl up in bed clutching a pillow that still smelled a tiny bit like James. How dorky did that sound?

"Okay, but only one. It's Thursday. I have work tomorrow."

"We'll be over here." Henry pointed to the waiting room chairs where they went to sit. Each whipped out the video device of their choice, instantly engrossed.

When their boss came by a minute later, on his way to a late meeting, Shay gave him a half smile. "Good night, Perry."

He gave her a smile but didn't break his stride. As

far as she knew, Halifax hadn't called to dump on her record of model employee nor to address her claims about Eric.

Or was Perry keeping that to himself?

Shay tucked her head down to finish the job before her, and pushed the anxiety away. It scooted four inches and then settled back to peer over her shoulder. Something was wrong. She couldn't put it into words or even explain it. Yet she still felt *watched*. Sometimes when she was on the street and, most often, when she was arriving and leaving places. Hypervigilance turning to paranoia?

Shay sucked in a breath. She needed to distract herself. *Think of James.*

She had gotten his text earlier. And while there was nothing even remotely romantic about it, he had promised to call tonight. She had been waiting to tell him about her week, and what she had done. Maybe she'd tell him when he called, and have it out of the way. Then tomorrow he'd be back, in Raleigh, in her apartment, in her bed.

When she thought of James everything else faded. Nothing seemed to matter when she conjured up memories of him. In his arms, kissing him, loving him, the world stopped. She could breathe freely.

"All ready?" Angie flashed five fingers, a fist, and then five fingers at her. It was 5:05.

Twenty minutes later, they had wedged themselves into a corner booth of a local brewery, a different microbrew in front of each of them.

"Is James coming over to Raleigh this weekend? Or are you going down to Charlotte to crawl all over his gorgeous co—" She glanced at Henry and blushed. "Body."

"Neither." Shay hadn't missed the glance Angie flung Henry's way. Usually, Angie was unflappable. She said things just to see how outrageous she could be. But with Henry . . . hm.

"So, you got a guy?" Henry reached for one of the nachos piled on a plate in front of Shay.

"Sort of."

"He's a cop." Angie reached for one, too.

Shay surged forward, circling her arms moatlike around her plate. "Hey! Order your own food. This is lunch and dinner for me."

"Let's see. You got your dairy, your protein and vegetable, and your starch." Henry bobbed his head. "I guess that constitutes a meal."

"There's no green vegetable there." Angie wagged a finger at the platter. "Without something green that doesn't constitute a full meal."

Shay reached out and dumped her side order of jalapeños over the top of the stack. "Green vegetable. *Ta-da.*"

"Damn. That was just mean, Shay." Angie didn't do jalapeños.

"Serves you right, criticizing my food." She slipped a chip piled with beans and trailing hot cheese from her plate and leaned forward to bite into it. Maybe she wasn't fluish, after all. Maybe she was just weak-kitten hungry.

By the time she stopped chewing, Angie's and Henry's orders had arrived.

For the next couple of minutes all that happened at their table was chewing and swallowing and more chewing.

Shay watched as each of them slanted speculative gazes at the other when the other wasn't watching. Something up here. Time to test her hypothesis.

"So, Henry, you still seeing that girl from Durham?"

Henry darted a glance at Angie. "Ah, no."

"She was so not his type," Angie chimed in. "She claimed to be an old-school video-game nerd. But she didn't know Samus Aran from Metroid. Can you even believe that?"

Shay grinned. That answered one question. "So, who are you seeing, Henry?"

He ducked his head. "Not really anyone, at the moment." He half glanced at Angie again. "Just hanging with Angie."

O-I-C. Shay formed the letters for the words "oh I see" with her right hand and then laughed. One really slow week at the office, they had had a contest to see who could communicate most effectively without actually resorting to speech. Nerd entertainment.

"It's not like that." Angie put down her fork. "Well, it's not."

Shay aimed raised brows at her. "Why not?"

"Because, well, because . . ." Angie glanced at Henry who had paused in chomping his burger to glance over at her.

Shay decided to push. "Why not?"

Henry dropped his burger onto his plate. "Yeah, why not?"

Angie went deer-in-the-headlights. "I didn't think—you never said. I don't know." She glared down at her plate of Buffalo wings as if daring them to take flight.

Henry picked up his glass of beer, grinning. "I guess that's settled then."

Angie looked up. "How is it settled?" Her sweet face went all evil cherub. "You don't just get to nod and smile, fella. Are we seeing each other or not?"

Henry choked, spewing beer out his nose.

Shay handed him a napkin, trying not to laugh too hard.

"Ah sure. You and me. I'd like that," he finally gasped out between beery sneezes.

Angel-face Angie returned with a smile to put Cupid to shame. "That's settled then."

Shay smiled. Her two favorite people were now officially seeing one another. Maybe when James got back to town the four of them could double-date. Like normal people. Like friends, even.

Unless she decided to keep James locked away all weekend in her apartment.

That possessive thought brought a sudden jolt of emotion with it. She wanted James all to herself.

It was a new feeling. *Waaaay* too soon for that emotion to be taken seriously.

Yet it felt good just knowing she was capable of it.

She'd never met a man and thought, yes, please, that one. On loan. Possibly permanently. The feeling was more than enough for now.

Glad she hadn't turned down her friends' offer of company, Shay turned to order another beer for Henry. From the corner of her eye she saw a familiar face. Well, not exactly familiar. The woman from a week ago, the one who'd called herself Carol? Carrie?

Before she could think why she was doing it, Shay was out of her seat. "Be right back," she told her puzzled companions.

Every sense tingled as she neared the bar. She took in the woman's long lean body. This time she wore jeans so tight they seemed painted on, much to the appreciation of the males nearest her. Dirty blond hair stuck up under a battered cowboy hat, she leaned on the bar, one hip jutted out while one booted foot rested on the rail. Something about that pose struck Shay wrong. She seemed like a caricature of a hot Southern college girl. Like Angie in costume. A great face and bod, but she wasn't an undergrad sporting a false ID and a big thirst. She was older.

Shay came up beside her before the woman looked her way. "Carly, right?"

"Right. And you're ah, *shoot*. I never was good with names." Shay didn't help. The woman blinked but her smile stayed wide. "How are you, girl?"

"Why are you here?"

Carly's smile stiffened at Shay's tone. "Like I told you, I'm a regular barfly." She made a big production of looking past Shay, leaning out into the path of customers. "Where's that hot stud boyfriend of yours?"

Shay's gaze never left her face. Definitely closer to thirty, with those squint lines. "Why?"

Carly's attention snapped back to Shay's. "Ah, look. You're getting all protective." She put out a hand to touch Shay's arm but Shay drew back, halting the gesture.

Ignoring the rebuff, Carly continued grinning. "I'm just admiring, honey. He's all yours."

"Right." Shay let her gaze remain on the woman a moment longer.

When she turned away, she felt as if a hummingbird were trapped inside her chest. She'd just stared down a woman who was thinking about poaching her boyfriend.

Oh my God! She really had officially reached "my man" status.

Shay saw the doors to the bar kitchen swing open on her right and a huge tray of food emerge. She heard a waiter behind her call, "Coming through— Aw, fuck!" Then things went sideways.

Shay was bumped from behind and stumbled against a customer's chair as an icy cascade of beer and glassware came flowing over her left shoulder. It soaked her hair, her blouse, the man whose chair she'd fallen against, and splashed every other diner at that table.

"I'm sure whatever beer is left will come out in the wash."

Angie was holding Shay's shirt under the hand dryer in the restroom while Shay tried to rinse the beer out of her hair at the sink. "Who was that woman at the bar?"

Shay grabbed for a handful of paper towels to squeeze the water out of her hair. "Someone I met last week."

"Dry enough." Angie shook out Shay's shirt. "She certainly is pushy."

Shay straightened up. "What do you mean?"

"She came into the office Monday. Said she needed a job and would Perry consider hiring her because you had recommended her."

Shay went still inside. "What did he say?"

"That's all I heard. I know he didn't hire her."

Anxiety bounded in and leaped on Shay, leaving her staggering around in her thoughts. She was still being followed.

Shay glanced back at the empty stalls to be sure they were alone. "Is she still out there?"

"No, she left as soon as you took that suds bath." Angie handed Shay her shirt. "You ready for a second beer?"

Shay shook her head stiffly. "My headache's back. I need to go home." She pulled her shirt over her wet head. "But you and Henry stay."

"If you're sure?"

Shay nodded absently, wondering what that woman could possibly want. Was Carly trying to get information about her for Eric? Was she the stalker he'd hired? Wait, no. That was a man's voice.

Her headache kicked up a notch as anxiety dug deep claws into her. "I—I need to go home and—"

Angie leaned in. "Say, you don't look so good. Want me to drive you?"

"No. You guys need a little together time. It's your first official date." She was surprised she managed a smile. "I'm really happy for you both."

Angie beamed. "I know. I've liked him for like forever, but did he notice?"

"He has now."

* * *

Every nerve was on full alert by the time Shay turned into her apartment complex. Why would Eric have anyone stalking her after she had confessed everything to Cadwallader Jones?

Her head hurt, worse than before. She'd checked her rearview mirror so many times her eyes had whiplash. Not that she'd know if anyone was following her. It was dark. The cars in her rear-view were shadowy blurs behind their headlights. All she wanted was to get to the safety of her locked door so she could wait for James's call.

She passed several lanes within the large complex of apartments and town houses. She lived toward the back. As she turned into her lane she thought she saw someone standing in the shadow of the stairwell that led to a block of upstairs apartments. There were always people coming and going, she reminded herself. Nothing extraordinary.

But her anxious mind kicked into high gear and wouldn't let go of the sight.

Never wavering from gauging the man's movements, she moved slowly down the lane to find her designated parking space. As she did so, the man reached the sidewalk right in front of her. He was wearing a jacket with the hood pulled up against the chill. And he carried a bundle under one arm.

As she turned into her spot, he suddenly stopped, pivoted, and ran past her, tossing something at her rear passenger wheel.

Shay slammed on the brake but it was too late. She heard the terrible screech of an animal in pain and then silence.

She scrambled out of her car. What had she run over? It made an awful sound. It must be—

"Oh . . . *no!*" A long-haired cat lay crushed beneath her

rear wheel. She recognized it as belonging to a neighbor, though it was rarely allowed out.

A neighbor came up beside her. "I heard a noise. What happened? *Ohhh*. That's the Sanderses' cat."

Shay straightened up. "There was a man." She swung around straining in the dark for a glimpse of the figure but he had disappeared.

"What are you talking about?"

She turned back. "There was a man. Standing there." She pointed to the sidewalk. "I saw him as I turned into my space. He threw the cat under my car."

"I see." The woman backed up a step. "I'll just go ring the Sanderses' bell."

"Yes." Shay turned and pushed her hips against the rear passenger door, as if to defend her back as she searched the dark. Who would do—no, why would anyone do such a thing?

The Sanderses' father came running, with his daughter right behind him.

When he reached Shay, his face was a mix of trepidation and anger. "What happened?"

Shay heaved a shaky breath. "There was a man. He was on the sidewalk as I turned into my space. He ran past and threw the cat under my wheel."

"Oh, Daddy! Gandalf!" The girl's shriek of pain stabbed through Shay's thoughts.

Gandalf. The wise wizard. Shay felt even worse.

The father turned and grabbed her to his middle, pressing her face away from the sight. "It's okay, sugar. It's okay." His voice was tender for his daughter but the expression on his face when he turned his head to Shay was anything but.

Shay shook her head, her hands rising in protest of the rage on his face. "There was a man."

"Who would do something like that?"

"I don't— Someone." It was a hollow finish.

"Come on, lady. You killed my daughter's pet. You obviously weren't looking where you were going. At least show her how a grown-up owns up to something that's her fault."

Shay glanced at the crying girl. The bottom dropped out of her stomach. "I'm so sorry. I really am. I couldn't stop. It all happened so fast."

The father ignored her and picked up his crying child.

"But there really was someone. He caused me to do it."

"Do I smell beer?" He took a step toward Shay and she instinctively backed up. "You've been drinking!"

"Just one. That smell, a waiter spilled a tray of beers on me."

"You're drunk!" The expression on his face changed. It was worse than anger. Contempt. Disgust. Fury. "You're lucky I don't call the police. Driving drunk. Killing children's pets. You're disgusting!"

"I'm not drunk."

He adjusted his child higher in his embrace. "Come on, sweetheart. I'll come back and get Gandalf later."

"I'm not drunk!" Shay took a step toward them. "And I didn't—I couldn't . . ."

He stiff-armed her out of his path. "Keep away from us or I'll call the cops!"

"The nerve of some people." The do-gooder neighbor followed him back toward his door. "Wouldn't even take responsibility. I saw it. Saw it all."

Shay stopped herself from following, biting her lip in frustration as she met the eyes of the few curious residents who had approached to see what the argument was about. They dispersed quickly.

There was no use in continuing to protest that it wasn't her fault. She'd seen the look on Mr. Sanders's face. If she pursued it, he would call the police. And they would not believe her, either.

She'd had a beer. She smelled of beer. Her car ran over the cat. The fact that it didn't happen the way it sounded wasn't going to bring the kitty back.

Accused, tried, and found guilty, again. The situation was ugly and familiar. No one knew or wanted to know the truth.

Yet she did. That man had deliberately made her kill that poor cat. And he was still out there in the dark.

Hugging an arm to her queasy middle, Shay swung around, panic seizing and holding her in place as her eyes searched every shadow for the sight of the man who had done this. Was he watching her from behind some bush? Had he heard every word? Was that what he wanted, to start trouble with her neighbors? Why?

Shay captured a sob before it could escape. Whatever the reason, she'd given him a bonus by having been the victim of a beer shampoo.

A new thought struck her, one that unglued her shoes from the pavement and sent her running like a frightened child for her door.

The man and Carly from the bar might be working together.

Maybe they weren't done yet.

She needed help. She needed James.

As she approached her apartment she spotted something on her door, a note. The note simply said "YOU."

CHAPTER TWENTY-FOUR

The sight of a sheriff at her door an hour later mustered only mild surprise. The owner of the cat must have called them about the death of Gandalf, after all.

Shay took her time unlocking her locks. She had showered, brushed and gargled, put on fresh clothes, washed her beer-soaked ones. She opened her door a crack with the chain still on, her gaze unwelcoming. "Yes?"

"Are you—" He paused to glance at the envelope in his hand. "Ms. Shayla Denise Appleton?"

Shay blinked. Very few people knew her full legal name. "Why?"

He pushed his hat back with a hand, his expression still bland. "Are you Ms. Appleton?"

"Yes."

"This is for you." He inserted a manila envelope through the narrow space of the open door.

Shay didn't reach for it. "What is that?"

He didn't answer, just held it there.

When she took it, he touched his hat in salute and

backed off. "You have been served a summons. Good evening, Ms. Appleton."

Shay held the envelope in two fingers. Every sense was telling her it wasn't good news. She carried it over to the table where the paper with the word "YOU" had been dropped. It didn't take her long to figure out that the sign referred to the crushed cat. It was an ugly threat and more direct than any of the others.

She went back to her sofa and picked up her phone, then reread James's text for the tenth time.

We need to talk. I'll call late.

She desperately needed to hear a friendly voice.

She had texted him two hours ago, after the cat incident, but there'd been no reply.

She hadn't expected him to stay in touch during the week. She'd even told him not to bother to call, because she didn't want to be disappointed if he forgot. Yet he'd texted *Good night* each evening about ten P.M. It was ten-fifteen.

She dropped the phone in her lap and let her gaze stray back to the table. A summons. She wasn't certain what a summons was. Something to do with Halifax Bank, probably. Or Eric.

Possibilities shot through her like an electric current. What if Eric was suing her for slander? She'd need to hire a lawyer to defend herself. She didn't have that kind of money. Couldn't even afford to get her car door painted. Still, she should know what she was facing.

She opened the envelope, unfolded the sheets, and read a few lines. It was a copy of a complaint and the summons. It stated that she was listed as the defendant in a civil suit. She was being sued for false accusations and for defamation of character.

Of course she was. That was all there was left to happen in her life. The only amazing thing was how quickly

Eric, or Halifax Bank, had filed a petition with the court. There must be a VIP lane in court for bankers like Mr. Cadwallader Jones.

She flipped through the rest of the paperwork without any real curiosity, yet mild surprise bubbled through her when at the bottom of the final page she saw the plaintiff's name. *Jaylynn Marjorie Turner*. Who was that?

She went to her desk and opened her computer and typed in the name.

Shay sat down with a thump as the images appeared. Images of Jaylynn Turner turned out to be plentiful. And in every one the face of the woman who had brought Bogart in to be put down was staring back at her.

Stunned, Shay switched to reading articles.

Jaylynn Turner was a TV personality in Charlotte. She had plenty of other titles. Miss North Carolina Petite, Junior Miss Charlotte, winner in the North Carolina Perfect Pageant, and runner-up of Miss North Carolina.

None of those titles were as impressive as the fact that Shay recognized her as the woman who had brought Bogart in to be destroyed.

She skimmed a few more articles, including the most recent one, less than a week old, where Ms. Turner claimed to have been a victim of a cruel hoax by parties yet to be determined.

Shay glanced over at the summons in disbelief.

"But that's crazy!" She had done nothing, didn't know the woman from Adam, except for the fact that she walked in on a day when Shay had been volunteering at the local animal shelter.

Shay read through that last article again, looking for clues to the hoax Jaylynn claimed had been played on her. There were none. In fact, there was a very noticeable absence of details. Leading a cohost at a competing network to comment in print, "Let's hope this isn't one of those attention-grabbing stunts. We are, after all, in the midst of November sweeps."

"I can't believe this," Shay murmured. How had Jaylynn found her? She wasn't easy to find. Even James said— Of course! James had filed a report. That report would be public record, and that's how Jaylynn knew how to find her.

Shay searched the Web for the Charlotte-Mecklenburg police blotter. It took her nearly five minutes to read through all the public records of crimes in the Charlotte newspapers for the past two weeks. There was nothing about Bogart, or his return, or actions filed against Jaylynn Turner.

Shay sat back and hugged her arms to her body. Maybe this was a mistake. It would all just go away.

The bump of relief lasted no longer than it took her gaze to settle on the summons again. She was being sued. That was very real.

"That's crazy." Shay said the words aloud to make them real.

What made Jaylynn think she could accuse her of anything? Being a finger-pointer was the very last thing she needed in her life these days. Not after her accusations against Eric. No way would she agree to be a witness in another case. In fact, no one in Charlotte knew who she was.

Except James.

Something cold and heavy and ugly sank down through her.

James had told her he'd had her investigated for details he needed to complete the police report on Bogart's return. Why hadn't he warned her about Jaylynn's intentions? Or, was he using her information to get back at his ex?

Other dark thoughts swarmed through her head like a colony of bats leaving their cave. For several dark minutes she let that sense of betrayal and anguish snatch her up and carry her along in a flurry of self-pity and desolation. The dark flight was familiar.

But at the end of that very long, scary flight, Shay wasn't decimated. She wasn't soul-scorched. She was angry.

Maybe James didn't know about the civil suit. No, of course he knew. This didn't just materialize overnight. He must have known what Jaylynn Turner was up to before he left Charlotte. It was in all the news accounts she just read online. Why hadn't he warned her?

Shay grabbed her phone and dialed James. This time he answered. She didn't give him time to say hello.

"You lowdown, lying rat bastard!"

"You got the summons." He didn't even sound surprised by her anger. "I'm sorry. I wanted to call sooner—" His voice sounded muffled. "Hold on."

Shay closed her eyes, her heart beating as quickly as if she'd run a mile. She'd trusted him with so much—no, everything. How could he do this?

"Okay. This is better." His voice sounded normal, happy even. "I was in the kennel putting Bogart up. We just finished a night course. You'll be really happy to hear that he took first place overall."

"Don't! Just don't!" She didn't want to hear happy news. She was too furious for any kind of happy to leak through. "You lied to me! You said you'd take care of things. You did that, didn't you? Only you took care of them in a way that's going to humiliate me and drag my life out before every news agency in the state."

"I got a summons today, too."

There was a beat while she took a breath. "What?"

"I'm named as a coconspirator or something, for collusion with you to extort— Hell, I didn't finish reading the thing."

Shay swallowed. That took a bite out of her anger. "Did you know about this before today?"

His turn to pause. "I thought Jaylynn was bluffing about the claim she'd been defamed. At the time I hadn't even filed my report. Once I did, I thought it would all go away."

"Well, it didn't." Shay was pacing, needing the activity to work off the extra energy. "I've been on the Internet. I know who she is now. Why didn't you warn me that she's a celebrity? In court it will be my word against that of a TV personality. It doesn't take a lot of imagination to see how the testimony of a 'nobody' is going to stack up against the words of 'Charlotte's Sweetheart.' Oh my God, and once they find out about my past—"

"They won't. Shay, listen to me. This is my mess. I'll figure out how to clean it up. I'm going to fight her. I already told her that."

Shay took a breath in surprise. "You've already talked to her?"

"It's not like that, Shay."

Shay shook her head though he couldn't see her. "You can't help me. You've no idea what you've done!"

Her head was pounding with thoughts moving too fast to put into words.

The suit would make all the papers. With a prominent person like Jaylynn Turner involved, it would be front-page news. Everyone in the state would know about it. About her. About her past. And then Eric would pile it on. Perfect excuse. He'd love this shit. Oh dear Lord! He'd make his claims about her public, too. Once more she'd be painted as a crazy, vindictive bitch. She would never escape.

"Shay?"

The sound of her name coming from so far away badly startled her. And then she realized she hadn't disconnected. James was still on the line. She lifted the phone to her ear.

"Leave me alone, James. You should have just left me alone."

"Not a chance." He took a breath. "You're angry. You've got every right. I messed up. But we can fix this. Not now. Not over the phone. I can't get away until tomorrow. But I'll be there, Shay, by two P.M. I'll come straight to you and we'll figure this out. We're in this together and we're worth fighting for."

He's using his calm, authoritative police officer's voice, Shay thought absently. She must sound genuinely shaken. Like the mother at the accident scene. He was good at handling crises. That was his job.

She had been in one emotional traffic wreck after another during the two short weeks since they'd met. She didn't doubt he would try to help her. He might even succeed. But she didn't need a trained professional to clean up behind her. She wanted to be his friend and lover. Not some lost cause he'd taken on out of pity.

"Don't come here, James. Just leave me alone."

She did hang up this time.

When would she learn? She could never rely on anyone but herself.

She turned off her phone as it began to ring again and stuffed it in the sofa cushions. This time she did feel as if her heart were shriveling up and dying. James wanted to help but she knew better than he did what was about to happen.

She had wanted to be someone different. Her job at Logital Solutions and her friends were less than eighteen months old. She'd wanted to be normal. Just that. And she had almost succeeded.

Shay drew in a shuddery breath. She had been determined not to make any more mistakes, to build her life into something worthwhile. But what was the point when it all was about to explode in lurid headlines she wouldn't be able to live down this time?

She went and curled up on her bed, sobbing until there was nothing left.

* * *

Just before her alarm went off, lying dry-eyed in the dark, Shay had a thought. Something didn't make sense. Not all the things that had occurred since James barged through her door were necessarily connected. Eric. Stalker. James. Carly. Now Jaylynn. Her life these days wasn't making sense. She was missing something. But she wasn't going to get it straight as long as she was darting at shadows. She needed to get out of town.

But first she would go in to work and talk to Perry. Because if she left Logital Solutions in the lurch she would lose her last connection to what had been her life. If that happened, she might just retreat into a feral being that people avoided on the street.

As for James, well, she was in no emotional state to hold him at arm's length if he came near her. She needed to hide from him, too, until she had sorted out her feelings. As it was, those feelings were swamping her highly tuned protective instincts. When he was too close, her brain turned to mush. So she needed to get away, even from him.

She ignored the little sinkhole that hollowed out in her middle when she thought of James leaving her life.

She needed to think. She needed to get to the one place of solace in her life. A safe place away from everything and everyone trying to ruin her life.

The cabin.

CHAPTER TWENTY-FIVE

The dawn was a frosted glass of beer, chill and opaque with an amber glow. Fog hugged the lowland clearing then lifted where the woods began, branches holding it tented at treetop height.

James's feet made very little sound as he jogged along the dirt road in back of the K-9 kennel site. Bogart bounded along beside him, putting in less effort to keep up. They had run several miles before James's breath became labored and his energy began to flag. So he pushed harder.

Anger was sometimes a useful motivator. Right now it was the prime reason he was up with the sun, beacons flashing on his cap and armbands, and on Bogart's collar. He'd fucked up. Bad.

Shay had every right to be furious. Hell, he was furious. But she wasn't going to get away that easily. As soon as the awards ceremonies were over, he was heading to Raleigh to face the pissed-off woman in his life.

After another mile, he paused and dropped down at the base of a loblolly pine, resting his back against the thick rough bark. Bogart settled in beside him, pressing in close to his side as he panted from his exertions. He stretched out one leg, bent the other at the knee and rested an arm on his partner's back.

"We're just a couple of simple guys. We like things simple." He glanced down at Bogart. "Okay, I got a bug up my butt about a beauty queen. But that was just my dick thinking. Now I'm in real trouble. But for the first time in my life I feel good about that. This making any sense to you?"

Bogart watched him with quiet eyes and then licked the sweat off his handler's chin.

"Yeah." James nodded. "Shay's tough. She's not simple. But there's a good heart inside all that barbed wire. She doesn't complain or ask anyone to take on her stuff. Hell, I'm still not even sure that I know all her stuff. But there's something about the way she looks at me. Like I was everything a woman could want. Like I'm enough."

James gazed up at the new morning sky growing mauve at the edges. That's how Shay made love. Like it was the first and the last time and every ounce of her, body and soul, was in it because it had to be enough. She did everything that way, come to think of it. She had been totally in for Bogart. She'd been ready to face down Eric all on her own. That counted for a lot. Maybe everything.

Bogart nudged his nose up under the hand dangling over his head. James grabbed him by the muzzle and wagged it playfully. "Yeah, she likes you. I notice she didn't kick you off the sofa the other night."

Bogart made a funny noise low in his throat.

"You're right. That was me. But I got dibs on her in the sack. And the shower. And the front seat. Hell, I got dibs, period."

James climbed to his feet. All he had to do was make Shay understand that he wasn't going anywhere. He would stand by her, fix what he could for her, and have her back when she stepped out to fight her own battles. He just hoped she'd let him fit all that into their next conversation before she tossed him out.

James was devouring his final lunch plate of fried catfish, hush puppies, and coleslaw when his cell buzzed. He set down his fork and surreptitiously pulled it out of his pocket. They were in the middle of the awards luncheon.

Jaylynn. What could she possibly want? Whatever it was, he wasn't going to find out until he had talked with Shay.

Twenty seconds later a text came through. He peeped at it.

A man broke in. Tried to rape me. Please come.

It was a testament to his feelings about Jaylynn, James decided, that it took him a whole five seconds to decide that it might be true.

"Shit!" He grabbed a piping hot fillet of fish and stood up.

"Woman getting restless because you been gone too long?"

James winked at his chuckling tablemate. "You know it."

He retreated to the hallway, wolfing down his catch before calling her.

"Jimmy! Oh my God, Jimmy. Where are you? I need you! Come to my place now!"

"Sure, Jaylynn. And why would I want to do that?"

"A man broke in and robbed me!"

"Call 911."

"You know I can't do that." He noticed her voice lost some of its fear to irritation. "Not after—well, you owe me. This is your fault!"

"I don't owe you. And just to prove what a great guy I am, I'll call it in for you."

"No! Oh God, Jim—James. You don't understand. He—threatened me. And your new girlfriend."

"Right. Good try."

"No! Please. Don't hang up."

He'd heard Jaylynn in a lot of different moods, from lusty to pissed off. He'd never heard this note in her voice before. It sounded like genuine fear. Oh, she was definitely trying to get into his head.

"Sorry. No. Call the cops."

"I don't trust anyone else." He heard her swallow. "I need you."

She was trained in emotional vocal delivery but he knew she wasn't that good an actress. He heard weakness in her tone. She was really scared.

Or did he just need to get his head checked?

"I'm more than two hours away. If this is some kind of trick—"

"Swear to God it's not!"

"Did you go to church on Sunday, Jaylynn? Because all hell's going to break loose on you if you're lying to me."

"Tell me that again."

"What part?"

"Start at the beginning." James sat on the white sofa in Jaylynn's apartment, the one she had never let Bogart near because he shed. Still dressed in his police uniform from the K-9 ceremony, he was in full law enforcement mode. Nothing about her story of forced entry and robbery added up. "Why would a man think you'd have a lot of money in your apartment? You never carry cash."

She made a helpless gesture with her hands. She looked small, huddled in a nearby chair with her legs pulled up under a short pink kimono. Her hair was back in a messy ponytail and her makeup was smeared from crying. But there was no bruising, no cuts or abrasions on any part of her that he could see. She looked vulnerable and adorable, and he wasn't buying any of it.

"You know this guy?"

"No!" She looked horrified by the suggestion.

"Checked the locks coming in, Jaylynn." He glanced over to where Bogart lay calmly on the rug before the front door. "There isn't even a suggestion of a shoulder smudge or a scuffle on the door or frame. Of course, forensics will check for prints."

"Why?" Her brow furrowed.

"You're wondering who else's prints might turn up when we run them?" James had the rare satisfaction of watching her try not to squirm. "Let me guess. The new guy is married."

"Not technically."

"Will his wife verify that?" He shook his head. "Why am I here? And it better be a better lie than the first one you've told me."

She straightened up under his stare. Long legs came untucked. Funny how he hadn't noticed she was wearing next to nothing in November until now. "Okay, Ji—James. Here's the truth. I'm being blackmailed by a man who said he was trying to help me track down the person who's been spreading rumors about me."

That was probably a lie, too, but he'd set that aside for the moment. "Why would he do that?"

She offered him a double wrist roll signifying "I don't know." "I have fans. Lots of loyal fans. When I went on TV to say I was the victim of a cruel hoax, they got really upset for me. I've gotten e-mails and tweets of support like you wouldn't believe. My agent is fielding all of it. I simply wanted to get my version of the story out first but my agent says it's been a huge PR boost. I couldn't have bought publicity like . . . this."

His expression must have prompted her faltering on the last word. Now he knew a bit more. "Why didn't he field this guy?"

She frowned, clearly unhappy he was calling the shots. "He called my cell number. He said he knew I wouldn't want anyone else to know about him."

"Because?"

She leaned forward suddenly, one hand landing lightly on his knee. Her attempt at seduction was as subtle as a baseball bat to the groin. "You've got to understand, a celebrity isn't responsible for who becomes a fan. After I made my announcement on the morning show last Friday I got a call from a really loyal fan. He said he knew people who could help me track down my unknown detractor."

"In addition to the private eye you hired to tail Shay?"

"And you." She smiled and squeezed his knee.

He pushed her hand away and checked his watch. Two fifty-five. He'd promised Shay he would be in Raleigh by two P.M. He was at least two hours away. "You had this fan hire someone. Who is he?"

Jaylynn sat back, her investigative reporter face slipping into place. "You really are falling for her, aren't you?"

"You really are about to watch me walk out of here with that guy still loose."

"Okay." But then she didn't say anything for so long, James made to rise. "Okay. There is this guy at the state prison who said he had friends on the outside who'd see to it that your girlfriend changed her mind about testifying against me."

James felt like a rock slide had hit him. "A criminal, you mean. You let loose an ex-con on an innocent woman?"

He must have looked as wrathful as he felt because she leaned back and pulled in her legs to wrap her arms about them. "I didn't say that. In any case, I don't think he meant to have her harmed."

"What exactly did you think he meant to do?"

"I don't know. Scare her. Oh, for pity's sake. I didn't ask. Okay? I didn't want to know, or get involved."

"But you didn't tell this scumbag *not* to bother her?"

"I didn't know for sure there was even anyone doing anything until this guy called me yesterday." She looked away. "He said some things."

"What things?"

She wouldn't look at him.

James got up but he didn't head for the door. He moved to stand over her. He bent over and placed a hand on either side of the back of her chair, bringing his face down to within inches of hers. "I'm a cop, Jaylynn. You keep forgetting that. Talk to me or I'm calling the station to send over an on-duty officer, and you can explain your connections to criminal activity to him."

Her eyes grew big in defiance, then her mouth went crooked in defeat.

"He said he was doing a job for Big Bog—that's the nickname of the con I've been corresponding with. He said he was doing it for free because he owed Bog. But that it had occurred to him that he didn't owe me a thing. And how about I show him some respect by paying for his work from now on."

"What kind of work?"

"How should I know? I told him I didn't know who he was or what he was talking about, and to leave me alone."

James levered away from her, afraid he might throttle her if he stayed too close. And he needed to know everything. "Go on."

"So then he says he could go to a source he has with the police and they might be interested in what he had to say about being asked by a mutual friend on the inside to take an interest in my case. That's when I knew who he was."

"And?"

Jaylynn folded her arms, expression going pouty. "So, I told him I would meet him in a public place. We met at the Reedy Creek Park, by the dog park yesterday."

James stared down at her. "Describe him."

"He was ugly. Big. Not tall but thick like a brick. Black hair, scruffy, like a street person." She wrinkled her nose. "He smelled."

She glanced up at James. What she saw was enough to keep her talking. "He said he wanted ten thousand dollars to keep quiet and keep scaring her. I told him I didn't have that kind of money. He said in that case, he wanted five thousand not to—to hurt the person. That's when I got scared."

"Only then? What do you think he's been doing to Shay up till now?"

She shook her head. "I don't know. I tell you, I didn't authorize any of this."

"But you didn't say no to the idea."

"I guess I thought, what if the little bit—woman decides it's not a good idea to testify against me? Then I can go back to my career, which I worked very hard for, and get on with my life." She looked up at James, peeking through her false eyelashes. "I didn't do anything to her. But she could ruin me. She brought this on herself by interfering."

"Bullshit, Jaylynn. You deserve what's happened to you because of what you've done."

She looked at him with incomprehension. "You think I deserve this?" She pulled back her kimono top and he saw bruises on her neck and shoulders. "I told him I'd give him some money to just go away. I'd bring it to the park today at noon. But he came to my door this morning just as I was leaving and forced his way past me. I only gave him five hundred dollars. I told him that's all I could get together overnight. So then he . . ."

James licked his lips, his mouth having gone dry. "Did he rape you?"

"He tried to." She flinched. "But I then remembered

about Big Bog. I said Big Bog would not be happy if he heard that he'd done anything to hurt me."

"That stopped him?"

She nodded. "I guess he owes the guy big-time."

"Or Big Bog knows people deadlier than him." James tried to think like a policeman. But his brain was working like a boyfriend now. Shay was in trouble! All he knew was that he was too far away. He needed to get closer fast.

He looked down at Jaylynn. "You didn't deserve to be attacked. But you started a shitball of trouble rolling downhill. You're to blame for that."

"I didn't mean for any of this to happen. I was just protecting myself."

"You were protecting your image. Who you really are sent a criminal after an innocent, unsuspecting woman."

Bogart bounded to his feet as James reached the door.

"Be careful, James. He knows where she lives and has been threatening her with phone calls and other stuff for a week."

James flinched as her words hit home. Shay hadn't said a word about any threats from any source but Eric. But then, would she? She was too accustomed to taking care of things herself. That hurt him more than he expected.

"James? If you can handle this, and get my money back, I swear I'll withdraw my civil suit against Shay."

James looked back from the door.

She nodded. "It would ruin me if it got out I knew anything about her being harassed by an ex-con."

"You're still thinking of yourself." That much he believed.

"Fuck!" James punched "end call" on his screen. Of all the times for Shay to pull mad girlfriend on him. She wasn't answering her phone. He doubted she had listened to his messages since she hadn't responded. He would pull over and text her again but he didn't want to waste the time.

As he left Jaylynn's drive, he had called in to his department in Charlotte. He wanted them to get Jaylynn on record while she was still scared. But he had an even more important reason for calling. "Get me someone in the Raleigh police department. I have reason to believe a woman there is in imminent danger."

He used his emergency lights and a very heavy foot from Charlotte all the way to the city limits of Raleigh.

All he'd been able to think about on the drive was that he was responsible for the mess Shay was in, and that she had no idea how bad it was.

Worse yet, she couldn't protect against what she couldn't see coming.

CHAPTER TWENTY-SIX

Shay pulled up the hood of her heavy sweatshirt as she slipped out from behind the wheel. Being on the lake dropped the normal November evening temperature of the surroundings by several degrees. A damp breeze chafed her cheeks. Her cowboy boots made crunchy sounds on the gravel as she walked around to the rear of her car.

She gathered her grocery bags by their handles to haul them out of the trunk. Four bags' worth was probably too much for a weekend. But she couldn't decide what she wanted to cook for James. There were T-bone steaks, a fillet of salmon, sweet potatoes, greens for salad, fruit, eggs and bacon because she was pretty sure James was the kind of man who would want meat with his homemade waffles. On top were a couple of big doggy bones that the butcher had promised wouldn't splinter and harm Bogart.

Yes, she'd spent too much of her final Halifax check on food but she didn't care. Next week, probably, would be a different story.

She slammed the trunk and turned toward the cabin, still preoccupied with menus. How funny was that? She'd never thought of herself as the domestic type. She could cook, sure, yet longing to impress a man with her kitchen skills seemed so old-fashioned and subservient, until now. Now, she wanted all the schlocky moonlight and madness of a real romance. Go figure.

She was still mad as hell at James, sure. But after storming around the cabin for an hour, she had realized that he had been fighting back when she told him to get lost. He said he wanted this relationship. He said they were in this together.

That was a part of the argument that she hadn't considered the first hundred times she refought their phone call in her thoughts. He thought there was a "them."

She might not have a lot of experience with men in relationships but she had instincts. Her intuition told her that James was willing to fight for her, and that was worth something.

That didn't mean she was going to let him off easy. She wasn't going to text him or tell him where she was. He'd have to figure that out. He'd have to go into Raleigh, realize that she wasn't home, and then figure out where she went to shelter when her world collapsed, as it seemed to be doing on a regular basis these days.

Shay smiled to herself as she climbed the two shallow stairs to the porch. With all her problems unsolved, and worried as she was about the rent, at the moment there was only one thing on her mind. She expected to be pursued.

James would pursue her. She had no doubt. He wouldn't expect her to make it easy. That's why she had taken Perry's offer to leave at lunchtime, citing a lack of work for her. James might be furious that she was making him jump through hoops to prove his interest. But she needed him to make this final jump so that she'd know he meant what he'd said. They were worth fighting for.

When he arrived, and they had fought it out all over again, she would reward him with smiles and food, and love.

Shay bit her lip. Too soon to use that word. She didn't want to come off all needy. It was another of those milestones in her life she had never before reached: the possibility of loving.

Maybe she was being foolish. Or maybe she was suffering from a new form of dissociative behavior. Whatever. The feelings inside her were a welcome alternative to fear and anxiety.

As she put down her bags to search for her key, light from the NightWatcher on the post near the front door fell across the bag nearest her. There was microwave popcorn and salsa and chips, and chocolate-covered raisins in that one. All the things she could think of that she liked but would never buy to eat alone. It was single-girl loser food. But not when shared with a boyfriend.

It took her a while to turn three keys in three locks but the knob turned easily enough. She picked up her bags. One shove and she was through.

Standing by her cozy chair near the fireplace with her only bottle of liquor, a cheap tequila, gripped in his fist was a man. He was big. Not tall but solid. Built like a cement block on end, balanced on a pair of hams.

She saw how he'd gotten in. Through the entrance to the kitchen she could see the battered back door leaning open and off one hinge. So much for locks and keys.

Her gaze came back very unwillingly to him. Homeless? Druggie?

He must have seen her gaze slip sideways or her right foot begin an instinctive back step because he raised the barrel of a gun he'd been holding at his side until it came to a stop aimed at her midsection. "Get the fuck in here."

Shay froze. That voice. She knew it from the phone calls.

Her stalker. The man who'd carved that ugly word into her car door. The man who'd tossed a cat under her wheels. The man Eric had sent here to—what?

A fist of fear closed over her stomach. She moved backward automatically.

"Stop!"

Her feet stopped their backward motion.

Grinning, he waved her in with the barrel. "I said get in here."

She thought of running anyway, but she knew the instant she saw him that this man would use his gun.

"Who are you and what are you doing here?" Useless questions but they were all that came to mind.

He looked at her as if she'd spoken to him in a language he didn't understand. Finally he shrugged and set the tequila bottle down by the chair. "Stupid bitch."

This time he beckoned to her with his free hand. "And shut the door," he added as she hesitated.

Shay pushed it to with her foot, wondering what time James would show up. She had no doubt now. He and Bogart would show up. They had to. *Tonight.* She just had to stay alive until then.

She walked over to the living room table on legs that had gone stiff as a pair of chopsticks, and placed her canvas grocery bags down. She had reached for the lemon sorbet ice cream to put it away, buying a moment to collect herself, before she realized she was testing the patience of a man with a gun. She turned around slowly.

He was still there, only he was no longer by the easy chair. He was much closer.

Fear set fire to her senses. Unlike when James had burst in on her, and she could see nothing but gun, this time her senses bombarded her with vivid detail. The red-

and-black plaid shirt over a greasy tee, the jeans, the sneakers that were much more expensive than anything else he wore and, finally, his face. It was big and round and red with a fringe of black stubble, like a beet that had just been dug up. Black hair sprouted from his scalp like monkey grass. Eyes black and intense as a hawk's sat above a squashed nose. And then there was the gun.

She didn't know guns but she thought fleetingly that this one had had a hard life. Compared to those on TV, so shiny they vibrate with light. The one he fisted was dull and grazed with use. It seemed deadlier.

She chased around in her head looking for an attitude to adopt. Because it was all she really had, she chose pissed off. "You're making a mistake. I know who sent you."

"You don't know shit." He moved toward her, but not too close. "I been watching you all week. You didn't know that, did you? Stupid bitch! Watched you go to work and come home. Lucky thing I showed up in time to follow you out here. Saved me trying to snatch you."

Several responses whip-snaked through her thoughts but only one seemed pertinent. "If you've been stalking me then you know my boyfriend is a cop."

He grinned. It revealed a shantytown of bad teeth. "You like to fuck?"

She didn't shrink back in revulsion but beneath her sweatshirt her muscles contracted, ready to fight for her life. Her phone was in her purse. Impossible inches away.

She strained to keep her gaze from shifting toward it. Even so, he seemed to know what she was thinking. He waved her away from the table. "Over there, by the chair."

She moved in a half-circle around him to reach the oversized stuffed chair he pointed to.

As she moved, her overstimulated gaze raked every

inch of their surroundings for weapons. Logs stacked by the fireplace. The poker leaning against the hearth. The kerosene lamp on the mantel. The tequila bottle by the chair. She would have to be fast to grab any one of them. And then what? None of them were more dangerous than a loaded gun.

When she reached the chair it suddenly seemed like a trap, something that would restrict her ability to move. Instead, she perched on one arm, her body tensed for flight though where or how seemed to face insurmountable obstacles at the moment.

Buy time. Keep the assailant talking. Learn something. Anything. She'd watched crime shows. That's what all law enforcement professionals told hostages to do.

A shudder rolled through her. "Did Eric send you?"

He snorted, as if she'd said something funny. "Who the fuck is Eric?"

She glanced away in confusion. She had been so cocky, so certain she knew who her enemy was. Had she missed all the signs that it might have been someone else? No, it was Eric. It had to be. Maybe this man didn't know who'd hired him.

One thought chased another through her overloaded brain. Eric was a dick. But he was no fool. He had hired this man to torment her, to embarrass and frighten her. But he wouldn't send anyone to kill her. So then, her life was safe. Although she wouldn't feel safe until James and Bogart arrived. They would come. They had to come.

She looked up and swallowed the burn of acid at the back of her throat. "Why were you hired?"

"You think I'm stupid, don't you? I ain't stupid!" He took two steps toward her, staring hard as if he were trying to gauge where to place a shot.

She breathed in through her nose, fighting off panic.

Her stomach cramped hard. Angry Shay had deserted her. Whoever was still home was talking.

"What do you want?"

"That, for sure, is a better question." He did a curious side jerk with his head, like a parrot trying to size up a stranger.

She tensed as his gaze moved from the hood still covering her hair down over her torso. She could feel his eyes pause, greedy for the feminine contours of her breasts. She crossed her arms over them. He continued to ogle her in a familiar way, as if he had done it before and often.

I been watching you all week. Oh God! What had he seen?

"You got any money? And don't lie. I can tell when I'm being lied to. I don't like liars."

Shay looked away, because she couldn't speak while staring into the abyss of those black eyes. "I wish I did."

"Then I guess you can pay me another way."

She felt her face go red as she met his leer. No need to guess what had entered his mind. Keep him talking. "What do you want money for?"

"For me not to kill you, for starters."

He was looking at her with the blank stare of complete indifference. She was looking into the face of a stone-cold killer.

"You thought I was here to mow your grass for cash?" He grinned for a second then it vanished.

He moved in so close that she could smell the rank pig sweat of a man who hadn't bothered to change his clothes in days. She looked away as he reached out and jerked back her hood, wincing when he caught some of the hair beneath in his fist. He grabbed her chin and jerked her face up to his.

"Look hard, slut. And think."

The gun loomed up before her. The most hypnotizing thing on the planet, she realized, was the barrel of a gun.

She kept swallowing, again and again, as he bruised her chin with the clamp of his fingers.

"I figure someone owes me. So here's what we're going to do. You can either get me some money or—"

The "or" did it.

She threw up on his expensive sneakers.

"Fucking shit!" He danced out of range in a delicate two-step. "Goddamn it!"

Shay merely shook her head and let the heaves continue, helpless to stop and yet gaining hope that he'd be so grossed out he'd walk away.

Shay stayed doubled over until the heaves subsided and let the awful acid burn in her throat remind her that at least she was still alive and untouched. Then she carefully wiped her mouth and chin with her sleeve. The feeling of relative safety didn't last long.

He slapped her hard, his palm connecting with the side of her head with shocking force. She bit her tongue and tasted blood. "Don't do that again."

He grabbed her by the arm and pulled her upright. "I don't like hurting women. I like women." The tenement row flashed between his lips. "But I got needs. And needs require money. So you can do me and you a favor and give me some."

Shay risked everything by looking directly into his empty eyes. "All I have is in my purse."

She held his gaze a long time, longer than she thought possible, as her knees loosened and threatened to buckle. She understood that what he did next would be entirely beyond her control.

He dropped her arm. "Might as well check."

He moved backward until he reached the table where

he dumped the contents of her purse. Gaze darting back and forth between her and the things on the table, he quickly sorted them. Finally, he tore four singles from her billfold.

"There's nothing here!" His face went dark with anger as he came toward her. "You trying to punk me?"

"No! I swear." She grabbed her middle and faked a couple of heaves. Not surprisingly, he stopped short. Maybe sex in a puddle of vomit didn't appeal to him. Good.

Shay let out a shaky breath, nothing faked in that.

Her cell rang.

He glanced back at the table. "Who's that? You expecting the cop?"

Lie! She shook her head ever so slightly. "Probably my girlfriend. She's coming to spend the weekend with me." She pointed a very shaky finger at the groceries. "That's dinner."

His eyes became slits, narrowed between little pillows of reddened flesh. After a moment he backed up and rifled through the mess he'd made until he found her cell phone. She knew who had called by the way his expression changed when he saw the caller ID. "Fucking bitch!"

She jumped to her feet.

He aimed the gun at her. "You lied to me."

She looked away, her insides tweaking her even though there was nothing left to come up but her boots.

The sound of an incoming text chimed. He glanced at her phone again. This time he smiled. "Boyfriend says he's on his way. Twenty minutes."

He put the phone in his pocket. "You all excited about that? It's got me excited." He grabbed his crotch with his free hand. "I won't need twenty minutes to get you all juicy for him. Move over here and take off all your shit."

But as he waved her toward him, Shay found her legs wouldn't work anymore. "I—I can't."

He pointed at her left knee with the barrel of his gun. "You can strip or I'll shoot you and strip you. Nicer if you do it."

She nodded and reached for the edge of her sweatshirt. If she got a chance to run she wouldn't care if she was cold. Cold was better than . . . so many things.

It was no striptease. Between numbing fear and weakness from nausea, she moved in slow jerky movements. It took her forever to wrestle out of her sweatshirt. Her Henley shirt clung to her arms damp from flop sweat as she peeled it off.

She didn't look at him. She would have lost the last of her nerve. What next? Not her bra. Her jeans? *Keep the boots on!* If she got the chance to run she would need her boots.

He is going to kill me. Now. Or later.

The thought struck through her brain like the brilliance of a spotlight. He was on the clock. James was coming. She would be able to identify him. He would not allow that.

Now or later.

She had a choice.

"Fuck this! You're taking too long!"

He grabbed her by the arm and shoved the small coffee table aside with one foot. It struck the tequila bottle and knocked it over, spilling it on the floor. He jerked her to the center of the rug.

He let her go and then, using the same hand that had dragged her along, he backhanded her across the face.

She wasn't prepared for the violence. It caught her full force, snapping her chin toward her shoulder as pain ignited from her eye to her jawline. Too shocked to cry out, she reeled backward.

He caught her by her ponytail and jerked her head back against his cinder-block chest. He bent his head toward her. She smelled tequila on his rancid breath.

He tried to kiss her but she opened her mouth and breathed hard into his face.

He recoiled from her vomit breath. "Disgusting!"

She might have smiled if she hadn't been so scared.

He jerked her hair again, this time pulling some of it out by the roots. She cried out in pain, which seemed to satisfy him.

"Get down!"

She went down on her knees to escape the possibility of another blow that might make her too weak to think. Her thoughts scurried in a frantic circle. Oh please, oh please! Think of something. Anything.

As she slid past his hips she saw the log lighter. It lay on the hearthstone a few feet away.

He grabbed her by the back of her head and jerked her toward the crotch of his jeans. He jammed her face against his groin. She felt his hard-on and the scrape of his zipper as he ground his hips against her cheek. "Show me how the cop likes it."

Shay stiffened. She felt her gut cramp as it all went watery. "I—I can't."

"Useless cunt." He shrugged and lifted the barrel to her forehead.

She gritted her teeth and shut her eyes. Now. Not later. Her choice.

The pain blinded her but the blow from the barrel sent her sprawling on her back. She let herself fall in the direction of the hearth. Her choice.

He was on her so quickly the force of his body knocked the breath out of her. Gasping for air she knew a panicky moment when her grasping hand met only hard slate. She had lost. She couldn't fight him and win. If he hit her again she would pass out and all the choices after that, even to the end of her life, would be his.

She went limp beneath him.

Chuckling with satisfaction that he had bested her resistance, he grabbed the front of her bra and yanked it up over her breasts. With a grunt of animal lust he grabbed one breast and squeezed it so hard she moaned in pain.

This seemed to excite him even more. He reared back to reach for her jeans zipper.

Shay turned her face away, as if she could not bear to look at the foul man straddling her, and opened her eyes. She saw it. The log lighter. *Too far away.*

He was pulling at her jeans but he couldn't get them down. "Raise up!"

"I can't. You're too heavy. Get off."

He pointed his gun at her. "Nothing funny."

She nodded and, coming up on her elbows, scooted backward out from under him when he rose up on his knees.

He watched with greedy eyes as she slipped her jeans down to the top of her hips. But then she couldn't do it. Couldn't let him think she'd wanted this, no matter if he killed her. She had been a victim too often in her life, at the whim of circumstances beyond her control. Not this time.

She screamed, levering her torso off the floor with hands curled into talons.

He didn't hit her with the barrel this time, simply struck her in the solar plexus, the blow knocking her back to the floor.

He was on her, this time not taking any time to enjoy the unique features of the woman beneath him. He even laid his gun down behind his right knee, impossible for her to reach.

Shay grunted in pain as he tore at her clothing, and turned her head. Not everything was out of reach.

He didn't notice her arm snake out, or the soft click. He had her jeans to her knees but her boots prevented him from tugging them further. He tried to flip her over, and she knew what he was planning to do. This time, she fought back, keeping his attention just long enough.

A lovely blue flame had leaped up by the hearth slate. It ran quickly along the top of the tequila spill line that ran under the chair and into the braided floor rug. The rug caught first. He didn't notice. He only knew she was losing the fight.

In the end Shay found herself crying out, "Fire!"

"What the fuck?"

"Fire! Get off me!" Shay pushed at him with all her might. The flames were only inches from her face.

His eyes went wide as he scrambled off her. He reached for his gun even as the undercarriage of the chair began to smoke. He backed off and got to his feet. Seemingly confused by the fire, he aimed his pistol at the carpet first and then at the chair, as if the flames would surrender to his firepower.

Shay didn't wait to see who would win. She rolled away from him and onto her feet. Even as she grabbed her jeans to pull them up over her hips, she headed for the door.

"You bitch!"

She ran. She didn't look back. She didn't even cower from the shot she knew was coming. Her choice.

The report was louder than she expected. She stumbled at the threshold as every muscle in her body contracted for impact. The fiery burn of the bullet still surprised her.

From the room behind her, her phone began playing Katy Perry's "Wide Awake." It was like music wafting in from another world, a world where there were boyfriends, and dinners to be cooked, and a fire to cozy up next to.

And then she was through the door.

Her world was filled with November darkness, the chill thrill of a damp north wind whipping in from the lake, and the insistent throb of a burning wound.

CHAPTER TWENTY-SEVEN

Go right!

She didn't spare a second to wonder why her brain was directing her there. Right would take her into the woods. Harder to find. Harder to track. Yet Bogart would know to look for her.

She heard it, perhaps because she had been praying so hard for it, the sounds of a truck. Was it James's truck turning off the main road? She stopped running at the edge of the woods. Maybe if she could just double back to the road, meet him— She looked back toward the cabin that stood in the way.

The metallic gun barrel shone under the radiance of the NightWatcher light as her assailant paused in the doorway of the cabin. He was coughing and cursing and then he was off the porch at a dead run. She waited to be certain he wasn't coming her way. She decided he was headed for the campground parking lot on the other side of this strip of woods where she supposed he had parked his vehicle. But maybe not. Maybe he was still looking for her. And if she risked going back into the open too soon . . .

Survival impulse took over the decision. She turned away and took off at a run, the moist ground sucking at her boot heels as she fled into the underbrush. But within seconds she came nearly to a halt. She ached in every part of her body. It was impossible to catalogue all the pain. She put a hand to her head and it came away with a wet smear. Must be blood. Her legs were rubbery and her stomach burned with a hollow fire. Her arm—no. Couldn't think about the arm.

The autumn-stripped trees kept the woods from the pitch-black darkness of a summer-night canopy. Overhead the sky glowed faintly with the Milky Way. If she didn't find shelter her stalker might find her before James. She had to move!

She was familiar with this section of wilderness, and during the day she would not have been afraid to cross it alone. But in the dark, with the wind whipping her hair into her face, she might as well have been in another country. Nothing was familiar, or comforting, or tinged with the presence of another human being.

She thought she heard the moment a vehicle turned off the road into the hundred yards of gravel path that led to her door. The man behind her would have heard it, too. She moved on.

Tired, running on adrenaline and fear, she was acting purely on instinct. And instinct told every hunted animal to go to ground, to hide.

She fretted because her boots made swishing sounds as she passed through the leaves that were knee-high in places. If there was anyone to listen. *Bogart!*

She almost closed her eyes to pray that Bogart would hear those *shussh shussh* sounds and know she was in trouble. She'd never needed a Prince Charming more.

After several minutes of running and stumbling, she reached a clearing where a new road was being laid over a narrow stream. Winded and shaking from nerves, she paused again. And squinted.

The starlight was brighter now that she had reached the other side of the tree belt. Ten feet away, gleaming darkly as if they were oiled with tar, long PVC pipes lay stacked like firewood against an embankment. They had been brought in to form a culvert for the stream that ran under new road construction.

Shay closed her streaming eyes. Shelter, if only she had the guts to use it.

She had a fear of tight places. Of tunneling into the ground, a cave getting the farther along she went until she was unable to back up. It was a nightmare she'd had many times.

Behind her she heard sirens and shouts. And then, from somewhere much closer, the sound of pounding footsteps. James? Or him? She couldn't risk being wrong.

She ran the short distance and dove for the opening of the middle pipe in the stack.

As she scrambled into the opening, she tried to stuff the fear aside. What would she tell a child who needed to take shelter from a—a thunderstorm, or a bear? Yes, a bear. Big bear. It was November. All the creepy-crawlies should be hibernating by now. Snakes would have gone to ground under stumps where it would be warmer than the inside of the cold PVC piping she was being forced to crawl into. It was safe in here.

She paused a couple of feet in, the throbbing from her injured arm making her dizzy with pain. No. Mustn't think of that. *Think only of survival.*

Though the faintest light glowed at the far end, it was much too dim to see her surroundings. She felt the walls. The space was maybe thirty inches in diameter. High enough for her to be on hands and knees and still not quite touch the top. It wasn't so bad.

Shay crawled a little farther into the pipe. It was corrugated and rainwater must have gathered over time, making the bottom feel slimy.

I'm not dead. I'm not dead. I'm not dead. The litany pulsed through her mind, growing louder and faster with every heartbeat. Shay closed her eyes and made herself breathe. She was safe.

But this time the feeling wouldn't gel. She'd started a fire. Probably burned down her uncle and aunt's cabin. Her assailant had gotten away. No one else had seen him. Her words against a phantom. No one would believe her. Why should they? And what about the cat? No way she could prove he did that. No way to prove that she was innocent of Jaylynn Turner's accusations. She should have gotten proof that her attacker was still out there.

She moaned like a wounded animal as other images pressed in to drown out the first.

Headfirst into a hole. No light at the end of this tunnel. Why wasn't there night and starlight at the other end?

She couldn't breathe. Couldn't see. Couldn't be sure her assailant wasn't still looking for her. Suddenly she realized it didn't matter, she couldn't stay here. Had to get out.

She began back crawling backward, whimpering as her hands touched unspeakably wet and smelly debris lining the bottom of the pipe.

Her panicked jerky movements were uncoordinated. The curved surface beneath her hands began to tremble. Her palm slipped in something slick and wet and she lost her balance and fell hard against the concave wall.

She felt something shift beneath her, a slight roll, and then a thud struck above her head, jarring the pipe in which she was encased.

She held her breath in fright as the movement reverberated beneath her palms. Strange squeaky squealing sounds came from deep below her. More slippage. Then the bottom fell out.

She was rolling over and over, bouncing and bumping, unable to control her body or brace herself. There was nothing to hold on to. There were only the sounds of her cries and the low rumbling like a herd of buffalo crossing a plain.

The stop was more abrupt than the free fall. The pipe she was in slammed into something hard.

Shay's head whiplashed, hitting both sides of the curved wall. Then she was spiraling down a black hole.

CHAPTER TWENTY-EIGHT

The pickup truck that roared past James on the county road that led to Lake Gaston sported a flashing dash-mounted emergency light. He noticed the sticker in the rear window said: WARREN COUNTY VOLUNTEER FIRE DEPARTMENT. It made his heart rate tick up a beat with impatience. Not even the traffic was cooperating. Nothing he could see was on fire. Most likely they were just out joyriding on a Friday night.

"Bastards," he muttered under his breath, allowing a trace of anger to keep him focused and alert. Every minute delayed was eating at his control. He knew when he found the man who had been stalking Shay he was going to need it, every damned ounce.

He'd called the Warren County sheriff's office from Raleigh. The dispatcher said the sheriff and his deputies were out, part of an investigation over a hunting accident. She'd have someone check on the cabin as soon as they could shake loose. So far, he'd heard nothing back. Shay still wasn't answering, either.

Eyes locked on the road ahead, he blocked the feeling

eating him up inside whenever Shay drifted into his mind. He had wasted more than two hours going all the way to Raleigh. He should have known better.

Raleigh police had been by Shay's place of work only to be told she no longer worked at Halifax Bank. Nor was she at Logital Solutions when they checked. Finally, as James was entering the city limits, a final call came in that turned him north, toward the cabin.

Shay wasn't at home. But one of her neighbors had come over when she saw a police officer at Shay's door. She told the Raleigh officer he was the second law enforcement officer at Shay's door in two days. She also told him that she had seen Shay packing her car earlier in the afternoon. And then she related the incident about the run-over cat the night before, and that Shay had been drunk when she did it.

Driving drunk. That didn't sound like Shay. Going to ground for the weekend at the lake cabin did. Shay probably thought she was running from the threat of a civil suit. If only he could warn her that she was running from something much more dangerous. An ex-con with an open-ended authorization to take care of her.

He hit the steering wheel with the flat of his palm. Why the hell didn't she call back? Was what he had done, or not done, so unforgivable?

He had a suspicion that it was.

He pressed the gas pedal harder.

From the rearview mirror he saw a second vehicle coming up fast behind him in the darkness with flashing lights and an earsplitting siren. This was a fire department vehicle, a pumper.

Cursing under his breath, he pulled over, his cruiser's tires kicking up gravel and red dirt as he hit the unpaved shoulder. He yanked the wheel to bring him back on to the tarmac and floored it, gaining speed until he was almost on the bumper of the truck.

Okay, so there was a fire somewhere. It wasn't much farther to the lake itself. The vehicles would have to turn soon.

A few moments later he saw through a thinned-out line of trees a small orange glow off to the right ahead. The hair lifted on his nape. That was the direction of Shay's cabin.

Something raw and wrathful swept through him. If the bastard had hurt Shay—

Bogart pushed his muzzle into the opening, and began to vocalize softly. James took a breath. His partner was feeding off his heightened emotions.

"It's okay, boy."

Sucking air until it whistled between his teeth, James struggled to rein in his most savage emotions. This was not the time to lose control. This was the time to think and act like a lawman. He and Bogart would get the ass-hole. But they'd do it the right way.

He had to brake hard when the fire truck swung off the tarmac onto the gravel lane that led to the cabin. When it pulled over near a red fire hydrant, he shot past it.

There were already people in the yard, neighbors who had left their homes to come and help. What filled his vision was the cabin. Smoke poured through the open door-way while flames danced behind the glass of the windows.

Dear God, don't let Shay be in there.

He slammed on his brakes, halfway out of the cruiser before he skidded to a stop.

His heart was pounding so loudly he couldn't make out any individual voices, but he swept the face of every-one he passed looking for Shay. Not here. Somehow he knew that. She wasn't in the yard. The only place she could be was inside.

He didn't hesitate. He broke into a trot, heading straight for the door.

Someone checked him, throwing him off balance, and then a gloved hand pressed hard into his chest, forcing him to a stop.

He turned to shove the intruder off and saw a man maybe twenty years his senior in seventy-five pounds of firefighting gear. Their gazes met, an older unyielding purpose matching younger single-minded determination.

The fireman dropped his hand and pointed at his comrades from the pickup, geared up and ready to go in. "This is our job. Let us do it."

"There may be a woman in there."

The man looked at James only a second longer, then shouted to his companions, "Possible woman inside!" He turned back to James. "We were told it was empty."

James noticed the firemen didn't head for the front door where smoke billowed. They headed for the back of the house where there were no flames or smoke visible. James followed. The man who'd stopped him stayed by his side.

He'd heard other firemen say, "We fight from the unburned to the burned." That meant getting behind a fire to keep it from spreading through the structure, saving, if possible, what remained.

The kitchen was relatively free of smoke. Two firemen went in with hoses while James spent the longest five minutes of his life waiting in the yard for one of them to return.

When he did, the man made a motion with his hands that said they had not found anyone inside.

James moved forward, about to ask if they'd looked everywhere, but the fireman beside him intervened again and met him eye to eye. "They looked. Everywhere."

James nodded, shivering against the adrenaline rush of relief. Shay wasn't in the fire. But where the hell was she?

He waited a few long minutes, just to be certain, as the hoses did their job.

Finally one of the first to go in came out and walked up to James.

"No one in there. But there is evidence that someone was here recently. There're groceries still in bags. Maybe she ran when the fire started."

That should have made James feel better but it didn't. If she'd run from the fire, she would have called it in or gone to the nearest house for help.

He turned and looked, and sure enough her car was still in the yard. Had Shay been surprised by the ex-con? Had he kidnapped her and set the fire to leave no trace? No scenario running through his thoughts was a good one.

Something began to ache deep in his chest. It grew so quickly that a groan escaped him.

A hand fell on his shoulder. "You okay?"

He glanced at the older fireman who was still watching him.

"Yeah." And just like that James shut down. Time for emotion later. He was a lawman and needed to do his job. He walked around to the rear of the cabin.

"Did your people do this?" He pointed to the kitchen door, all but off its hinges.

The guy shook his head. "Someone did that for us."

"Right." James turned back to his vehicle to get Bogart. Shay and her attacker must be somewhere out there in the darkness, shielded by the surrounding woods. The thought that her stalker might have driven off with her to God-only-knew-where was too much to contemplate.

As he neared his cruiser he saw a sheriff's vehicle pulling into the yard. It was Deputy Ward. He met the man at his door.

"I have reason to believe Shay's been abducted." James

went through the key points quickly in an unemotional voice.

The deputy looked past him at the house, his face serious under the light of the NightWatcher light. The firemen were winning. The fire seemed to be all but out. "One of the neighbors from down the road just made a 911. There's been a break-in. On the other side of these woods, over by the parking lot of the public pier about three miles from here if you drive around. Witness says the guy's armed. Could be unrelated."

James didn't think so. "That's got to be our man."

Deputy Ward hitched up his pants. "Shay wasn't with him."

"Then he'll know where to find her." James locked out any other possibility. "I want to come with you. Bogart and I can be very useful."

The deputy looked at Bogart, who was barking and circling inside his cage, eager to be let loose, and then nodded. "I deputize you right now."

"He ran that way." Two young men in gimme caps and hunting jackets who flagged them down in the street pointed toward a wood-and-metal-frame building in the distance. "We were camping in the woods when this guy comes running in out of nowhere. Nearly knocked the tent over. He shot at us and then kept going. We followed him here."

"Okay. I appreciate your help. Now you fellas step over there across the street. I wouldn't want either of you to get hurt." They moved so quickly the deputy had to call after them, "Don't go too far. I'm gonna need statements after we get this situation sorted out."

When they had pulled in and parked a safe distance away, James and the deputy studied their surroundings behind the safety of their vehicles. Little detail could be seen beyond the ring of light cast by a lone bulb posted in the parking lot, but the shuttered building appeared to be abandoned. The door had clearly been kicked in and only halfway reclosed.

"Why do you suppose he's hiding instead of just taking off?" Deputy Ward looked at James.

"Maybe Shay got away from him and he realized that if he left her behind she could later identify him. Or maybe he thought he'd stick around to find out how much trouble he's in."

"Hell of a thing." The deputy sounded almost wistful but when James glanced at him, the lawman's face was a solid wall of pissed off.

James gave a chin-up motion to indicate the structure. "What is that?"

"Bait shop during the high season. This ain't the season."

James waited impatiently while the deputy radioed in for backup that would include the state police. He needed to find Shay. To do that, he needed to capture her assailant. Or did he?

He glanced around, taking in details of everything within view. He was pretty sure Shay was out here somewhere in the dark alone, afraid, maybe hurt. He didn't let his mind speculate on what could have happened to her before she got away from her attacker. He could only handle ideas with actions attached at the moment. For instance, he could let the deputy keep the fugitive pinned until help came while he went to look for Shay.

He shoved that thought aside. Her attacker was inside, armed and willing to use that weapon on anyone who got in his way. No way he could leave here knowing that someone might die if he did. It wasn't so much a hard choice as no choice. Shay was tough. She'd gotten away. He had to believe that. After he took down her assailant, he'd find her. She had to know he would do that. Whatever stupid argument was between them, she would remember that he had promised to come to her. The reasons why didn't change that promise.

He turned to the deputy. "Tell me about the layout."

As the deputy talked, James watched the building, measuring out his and Bogart's plan of attack. It was a simple building with one large room, and a smaller storage room and unisex restroom. Unless the suspect was stupid he wouldn't blockade himself in a room without an escape. More than likely he was hunkered down behind a counter or display case in the main space, or trying to get out the back door.

When he was done, James moved to the back of his vehicle where he opened the trunk.

"What you got there?"

"Night-vision goggles, infrared scanner, and a vest for my dog."

"That's some nice equipment."

"It'll do the job."

He indicated a rifle case to the deputy. "Need anything?"

Deputy Ward just smiled and backed up toward his own car. He opened his truck and pulled out a rifle. "Pretty, ain't she?"

James eyed the weapon, thinking of Shay. "I'd like to take him alive."

The deputy shrugged. "That will be his option."

"Bogart and I get to work the scene first. Agreed?"

"Sure. Never got to see a K-9 team in action before. However, you flush him this way, he's mine."

James nodded. "I'll check the rear." He and Bogart had a job to do.

He harnessed his partner into a bulletproof vest. It wouldn't protect much. If the suspect aimed for the mouthful of sharp teeth, Bogart would go down. But Bogart associated armor with man work and gunfire exposure. Their prey was armed. It was their job to scare the man into surrender rather than fight.

James stroked his thick coarse pelt, readying them both for action. "*Gute Hund!* We're going hunting, Bogart. Just like last night."

He picked his dog up and set him down on the drive. They had made a near-perfect score in a dark-building search last night. They were fresh and ready. But each search had its own unknowns. And this time their target was armed with real ammunition.

Bogart stood with his tail held high and the muscles beneath his coat bunched, reacting, James knew, to his handler's adrenaline rush feeding down the leash. Yet he waited for James's command.

James gave a thumbs-up to the deputy and then moved out.

Walking carefully, James circled the building with Bogart. They moved as quietly and cautiously as possible, listening for sounds of movement within. The only sound other than distant background noise of the night was that of Bogart's panting.

James pressed himself against the side wall and then peered cautiously around the corner. There was no way to tell if the suspect had bolted out the back. That was the greatest concern, that the SOB had gotten away. He pulled his FLIR and scanned the wooded area behind the building. He didn't see anything moving.

Giving Bogart a bit of lead, they moved to the back of the building and inched toward the back door. It was still closed. He was glad to see that it wasn't very sturdy or paneled with glass that might allow him to be seen by the suspect inside. It would be their best way of entry. But first he needed to focus the suspect's attention on the front door.

They retreated to the front of the building. James signaled to the deputy that as far as he could tell, the man was still inside.

From a protected position beside the sheriff, James lifted his head and shouted, "Police K-9 Unit! Surrender or I will send the dog in and you will be bitten."

James gave the alert for Bogart to bark. *"Gib laut!"*

Bogart responded enthusiastically. Straining against his collar, he barked loud and piercing, enough to send shivers up the most hardened criminal's back.

After ten seconds James called him off. *"Ruhig. Platz."*

Bogart dropped back into position beside his handler, shivering with energy but silent.

James leaned forward, listening for any sound. This time all he heard was the distant wail of a police siren. That would be the state police. He wanted the satisfaction of this takedown himself. They needed to move out.

"You keep him entertained. We're going in from the rear."

Deputy Ward smiled. "My pleasure." He reared up and shouted, "Sheriff's department. Put down your weapon and come out. You hear them sirens? State patrol's on the way, son. You're done!"

Moving quickly, James and Bogart took up a tactical position at the rear of the building by a dumpster. He hunkered down and stroked his partner. "We just did this yesterday. Textbook. We got this."

He unleashed Bogart, gave him a good hard pat, took in a quick breath and drew his weapon. When they came even with the back door he placed a strategic kick by the knob.

The crack of wood was as loud as a gunshot as the door flew open. *"Revier! Fass!"*

Bogart shot through the doorway, barking like a four-footed fanged avenger. James heard a man's cry of alarm and then the sound of scurrying footfalls as he entered through the door behind his partner. Night goggles revealed a man in silhouette. He heard a shot and saw a flame of report.

His heart stopped. And then he saw Bogart leaping at the man with tremendous ferocity and they went down. The man screamed as James rushed them.

"Put the gun down! Gun down now!"

The man was kicking and thrashing, trying to throw Bogart off, but he was locked on tight. The dog fought back, thrashing and jerking as he held the man down. The man screamed again and again until, finally, James heard him release the gun with a clatter on the floor.

Flipping his night-vision goggles up, he scooped the weapon up out of the way.

Deputy Ward burst through the front door, gun in one hand and a high-beam flashlight in the other. What he saw brought a smile to his face. "Well, lookie there."

Bogart was still locked into place, all four paws firmly braced along the man's chest as he clamped the man's shoulder between his teeth.

"Bogart! *Aus.*" Bogart released his prey instantly.

James reached into his pocket and withdrew a ball. As it bounced away, Bogart leaped after it like a puppy at play.

The deputy whistled. "Well, what do you know?" It never failed to impress civilians how quickly a well-trained dog could go from vicious attacker to playful pup.

With the deputy standing guard, James rolled the man over and cuffed him. Then he dragged him up to his knees by the back of his shirt and thrust his face into the man's. "Where is she? Where is Shay Appleton?"

The man sneered at him. "Fuck you!"

James looked up. "Bogart! *Fuss!*" His partner came running.

The man's eyes got big. "Okay! Okay! She ran away.

Into the woods." He cowered away from James's grasp of his collar as Bogart growled. "Don't let him bite me again!"

James wouldn't do that but he wasn't about to let this man know that. He tightened his grip, pressing his knee into the man's back. "You don't want to fuck with me right now. Is she hurt?"

The man glanced fearfully from James to Bogart. "I don't know. She set fire to the place. She's a crazy bitch."

James drove back to the cabin at breakneck speed. There was no one on the dark country road this time. He found the firemen already beginning to clean up.

He checked with the few remaining onlookers, asking about Shay, but none of them had seen a woman of her description. Every negative shake of a head made his gut twist. Where could she be? With all the commotion of fire and people, she must know it was safe to show herself, unless she was unable.

He block-checked that thought. She was hiding, and he and Bogart would find her. End of story.

The older fireman waved James over when he saw him. "We saved a good part of the structure. Of course, the living room will have to be rebuilt. Damnedest thing. Looks like the fire started under an easy chair. And it wasn't sparks from the fireplace. The hearth is cold."

James tucked that information away. Right now he needed to start the search for Shay. "I'll check with you later. There's a missing woman out here somewhere."

With Bogart on the leash, he went first to Shay's car door. James frowned when he saw the paper patch on the driver's side. He tore it off, swearing inventively when he saw the word etched into the paint. He had more to make up for than he thought. It made him want to go back and assault an unarmed man.

But the thought of finding Shay pressed him harder.

He opened the car door and picked up a sweater he found lying on the passenger's seat. He held it up to his nose and inhaled. It smelled of Shay. And, just maybe, forever.

When he'd given his partner a good sniff, too, he gave Bogart the command to search. *"Such!"* He made a motion with his hand. *"Voraus! Such!* Shay!"

Bogart circled the trampled yard in some confusion. Many feet and vehicles had passed through the open area because of the fire.

James held his impatience in check but it was hard. He had to trust his partner. He did trust his partner. He gave him more leash, letting him form his own opinion of what to do next. They were in the dark at the edge of the grassy lawn when Bogart's tail went up.

James grinned and came running up behind him. *"Such!* Shay!"

Bogart took off.

He was glad he worked out regularly. The terrain was mostly flat but the trail led through woods with shriveled vines and boulders, and without the aid of his high-beam flashlight the going would have been very tough. Shay knew she was running for her life when she traversed this maze. That thought kept him from giving a damn about how hard he was breathing and how much he wanted to smash things. He only wanted to hold on to her until she understood she was the best thing in his life.

Bogart paused a couple of times to sniff and consider but mostly he was taking them straight through the woods.

They came out the other side to a night full of stars. So silent and still it seemed as if they had popped out on the other side of the world. Except that Bogart was pulling him forward. Straining on his leash, he was determined to get to the bottom of a shallow ravine into which a dozen pipes had tumbled.

James couldn't figure out why Bogart was so interested in them but his interest was good enough reason to check them out.

Bogart didn't pause until he had nosed into a pipe that was up against a tree trunk on the other side of the shallow ravine they'd waded through.

James hunkered down and shined his flashlight inside.

Shay was in there, lying absolutely still. He couldn't breathe in or out. Didn't want to know the answer to the question beating through his pulse, if it wasn't the right one.

Bogart dove in past his partner. Usually he didn't like tight places, instinctively avoiding them as all dogs do. But this time, he was on duty and his goal was someone he knew. He grabbed one booted foot in his mouth and began backing out, dragging Shay with him.

She stirred and whimpered. It was the best sight and sound James had experienced, maybe ever.

James reached in when Bogart had pulled her close and patted Bogart's back, his voice full of praise. "*Gute Hund! So ist brav!* Such a good boy!"

When Bogart had backed out, James reached in and slid her the rest of the way out. She was groggy and her face was bloody. She was wearing only jeans. But she smiled when she recognized James's face. A really big all-happy smile.

"You came."

He grinned at her. "You knew I would."

"Yes."

Bogart moved in close and, nudging James's shoulder, stuck his snout in between them to lick Shay's face.

She smiled weakly and reached out to scratch him behind his ears. "My Prince."

James's heart contracted hard as he picked her up and hugged her to him. She was frighteningly cold to the touch and there was blood on her, but he could tell by the way she reached up and grabbed his neck and held on tight that there was a lot of fight still left in Shay Appleton.

CHAPTER TWENTY-NINE

James stood her in the shower and bathed her. There was nothing erotic about it. She was much too tired and sore, and drained from the volcanic overload of her ordeal, and still vibrating from the events of the night.

An ambulance had taken her to an emergency room in Roanoke Rapids where her wounds were assessed. She'd been grazed by a bullet, leaving a searing grooved burn on her upper arm that hurt like hell. There was also a nasty laceration on her right brow, made by a blow from the assailant's gun. And a black eye. Her torso was scratched in a dozen places from her run half-naked through the woods.

During the exam, James stood by her, absorbing every telltale detail of her ordeal, his face a stoic mask. Beneath that façade, he was feeling helpless and furious, wishing he had not been so by-the-book with the asshole who had done these things to her. Several times he had had to take a deep breath. On his job, he had come across bastards like the one who'd terrorized Shay. They raped and tormented for the pure pleasure of it. But he didn't want to add fuel to her nightmares. Some things a man kept to himself.

Which is why he was also a tiny bit glad he had not known all she had been through when he and Bogart tracked the suspect down. Shay needed him here, not arrested for assault.

Deputy Ward showed up at the hospital, after handing over the suspect, to take Shay's preliminary statement. But he didn't push when James flashed him a look that said, *Not now.*

After a thorough examination to determine that nothing else was seriously wrong, the doctor had stitched her brow, dressed her wound, and given Shay antibiotics and a sedative. He recommended that she remain overnight for observation. She was suffering from slight hypothermia caused by exposure and trauma.

But Shay, frustrated and on meds, became loud and downright uncooperative. She only wanted to go back to the cabin.

James didn't have the heart to tell her that her refuge was a burned-out husk. The compromise was a hotel room across the street from the hospital.

Too wired from what the doctor called an atypical reaction to sedatives, Shay had paced the floor of their room until James persuaded her out of her clothes and into the shower. The warm fall of water did the trick. Her heart calmed, her pulse stopped racing, and she began to breathe more easily.

Though she was much too tired to respond, Shay was very aware of James as he bathed her. She absorbed the careful passing of his hands over her body with pleasure. She luxuriated in how tender he was as he shampooed the blood from her hair while keeping the water from soaking the bandage on her brow. The feel of his strong fingers working the washcloth as he soaped her shoulders and back and then her breasts and stomach seemed to smooth out some of the pain of the many scratches.

Too tired to do more than follow his instructions, she braced her hands on his shoulders and balanced first on one foot and then the other on the edge of the tub as he washed her legs. His touch was impersonal but thorough.

They didn't talk. Yet she was vibrantly alive to the emotions running beneath his surface calm. Fully aware of his tenderness, and of a barely contained anger he didn't voice but she knew would remain a good while. He had failed to protect her. That was all he'd said to her about the ugly volatile feeling. The misery in his eyes made her want to cry for him. But she wasn't ready to carry that burden yet. Maybe she wouldn't need to.

He stopped every so often and just held her for a moment.

He hadn't undressed. His tee and pants were soaked by the time they were done but she supposed he was letting her know without words that this was not an erotic encounter. He understood she was much too exhausted in body and spirit for that.

She would have to give a statement to the deputy, the state police, and the fire department before she would be allowed to head back to Raleigh. But all that could wait until the morning.

She didn't need the look on James's face each time their eyes met to tell her how lucky she was. But she had survived. And nothing was wrong with her that time, sleep, and peace wouldn't cure.

When he was done washing her, he toweled her down until her skin tingled and quickly ran a comb through her hair as she sat on the commode. He had brought in a medic kit from his cruiser. After checking the bandages on her arm and brow to make certain they were dry, he applied antibiotic and new bandages to the minor cuts and abrasions the emergency room staff had not bothered to dress. She wondered briefly if taking care of Bogart had made him such an efficient groomer, but she was too tired to tease him about that. He produced a tee from his duffel and dressed her in it before tucking her into bed.

Maybe she said thank you. And maybe she went out like a light. What she remembered was that sometime later, he slid into bed beside her. And Bogart, who'd kept watch over the whole bathing routine, slept at the foot of the bed.

She felt safe. Cherished. And happy.

"You're beautiful."

"I'm a mess. I have a black eye, a bruised chin, and five stitches above my eyebrow."

"You're beautiful, anyway."

James leaned over her and kissed her very lightly, afraid that even the pressure of his lips might be too much for her bruised body.

They were in her bedroom, in her bed. It was late afternoon. She'd slept away most of the day while he'd been in and out.

After her interviews with law enforcement the day before, James had wrapped her up in two blankets, buckled her into his cruiser, and brought her back to Raleigh. She didn't remember returning to her apartment, or really much of the rest of that day. She slept and ate a little when he pressed her, and slept again. Bogart, who evidently had been put on guard duty, never left his post at the foot of her bed.

This afternoon, she'd awakened to late autumn sunshine slanting in through her blinds and felt, well, close to normal.

James told her everything he had learned from Jaylynn, and what he had pieced together on his hellish drive from Charlotte to Raleigh, and then up to Gaston Lake.

When he was done, she filled in what he couldn't have known.

Other than to ask for occasional clarification, he listened to the story of her ordeal at the cabin without comment. But the expression on his face told a different story. It was by turns stern, and sympathetic, and more than once she glimpsed his quiet anger surge into a white-hot rage that frightened her. No one had ever been that angry or hurt on her behalf.

When she reached out for him, he pulled away a little. She saw it in his eyes, the emotional retreat, and wondered.

"I failed you." Judging by his expression, that was the most difficult sentence he'd ever uttered.

That's when she understood. And it nearly broke her heart. He was shouldering responsibility, blaming himself for things he might have done differently when it had been impossible to know everything that was going on.

She lifted a hand to his cheek, forcing him to look at her. "You didn't fail me. You saved me."

She watched him struggle with her gratitude, shadows of doubt darting in and out of his sky-blue eyes. "Without you, no one would have come to look for me for a long time. You came, even after I told you to stay away. You saved me."

He blinked first. And then he pulled her toward him, kissing her with all the warmth she could ever hope for. When he let her go, she knew that once more, the hurt and pain was in her rearview mirror, and this time it was receding fast.

"Pizza?" Shay said suddenly.

James laughed. "You have me in your bed and you want pizza?"

Shay smiled. "Fill me up with pizza and I promise to think of a really nice way to repay you."

He wasn't gone long but he returned with more than pizza. He tossed a copy of the day's newspaper on the bed. "Check out the headline."

"Bank Executive Dismissed for Misuse of Funds." Below the headline was a picture of Eric Coates. The article stated Eric Coates had been fired after an employee—not her name but another woman's!—accused him of sexual harassment. It went on to say that during the initial investigation other concerns had come to light, including misappropriation of bank funds, as well as other instances of violations of bank ethics. The matter was being further explored to determine if legal action should be taken.

James tapped the picture. "You know anything about that?"

Shay met James's inquisitive stare with a sly smile. "I haven't had a chance to tell you everything that happened while you were gone."

She related her last confrontation with Eric. And how she'd decided to risk everything and take her accusations of sexual harassment and misconduct to the bank president, Mr. Cadwallader Jones. To judge by the article, either her accusation had caused someone else to come forward, or Cadwallader Jones knew more about Eric's activities than she thought, and her accusation was simply the catalyst to oust Eric.

By the time the only things left in the pizza box were crumbs and a smear of sauce, the subject had turned once again to Shay's more immediate worries.

"I can't believe I burned the cabin down."

"It's not a complete loss." James pulled a string of cheese off her chin and ate it. "The living area will need a lot of repair. But the fire didn't take the roof."

"Small comfort. The contents are ruined. I have no

idea how I'm going to repay my uncle and aunt for the damage."

"We could rebuild it for them."

Shay didn't dare look at him. Her emotions were too close to the surface. "You would help me do that?"

"Yeah. It would give us something useful to do while we argue."

The tears came quickly, spilling out over her lashes.

James put an arm around her, surprised that she should break down now, but pleased she had turned to him instinctively for comfort.

After a moment, Shay pulled back so she could meet his gaze. She didn't ask the question forming in her thoughts but stared at him because the answer was already there in those blue eyes. He wasn't going anywhere anytime soon.

"You're sure?" Okay, the woman in her needed to hear the words.

"Shay, I owe you—"

Shay put out her hand to stop him from speaking. But the moment her fingertips touched his lips a frisson of emotion raced through them to travel deep inside her. She took her hand away. After all they'd been through, he was what she wanted most.

After only a second, his sky blues crinkled at the corners and his mouth lifted in a smile. Enough said.

For the first time in her life, she wasn't afraid of the future. She didn't want to hide anymore.

She brought his head down for a kiss at the same time she arched up under him so there would be no mistake about her intent. She wanted to be Shay Appleton, completely open and alive with lust and love and tenderness for James Cannon.

"Your head and body," he murmured against her mouth.

"Hurt like hell," she whispered back. The words vibrating on their lips were sexy as hell. "Make it better."

His lips spread in a smile on hers and then he deepened the kiss.

They kissed for a long time, trading happy little intimate chuckles as they learned what sort of kisses were fun, and which were even funner.

She liked the way his hands smoothed over her shoulders and down her arms. It was much like when he bathed her. Only this time, there was heat in his palms and an urgency in the curl of his fingers. She practically purred when his hand moved to her waist and slid up under her tee. Her tummy quivered under the stroke of his fingers, and then he reached higher, tracing the curve of ribs in a lazy back-and-forth that rose higher and higher. Yet he was very careful not to press too firmly or move too roughly.

The shuddery sigh she let out broke their kisses but not their concentration.

His hand moved over her so carefully she finally grabbed his neck. "I won't break."

"Want to bet?"

She met his eyes, just inches away, and saw a smile of mischief.

She grinned back. "Do your damnedest."

He palmed one breast, using his fingers to tease the nipple. And then he moved over her, his hand dragging the edge of her tee up to give him access. He tongued her nipples until they stood shiny wet and hard, and she squirmed against the sheets.

He shifted again, this time so his hand could slide down into the front of her pj bottoms.

She did not try to be coy, she opened her thighs in welcome.

"Oh!"

She felt his fingers move inside her, slow and easy, his thumb grazing the apex of her folds with each stroke.

Wanting to be as brave and bold, she reached down,

pushing her hand into his jeans. He sucked in a breath and she went deeper and found his erection. For a while, each rode the pleasure of the other's hand.

When she thought he must be a master at holding back, he whispered, "I think you've won, Shay. I need to . . . now."

A little choke of laughter escaped when he pulled a condom from his pocket.

"What?" He looked at her in doubt.

"You were a Boy Scout, right?"

He grinned. "It's more a case of hoping like hell."

He slid into her like silk, if silk were long and thick and hard. Or maybe she was silk. All she knew was that he fit. And the throbbing inside her worked both ways, each stroke a gasp of pleasure and a promise of more.

Taking his weight on his elbows and knees, he rode her with long easy strokes, like swells on a lake, gliding in and up then down and out until his command slipped. Their climax was like dropping down a waterfall, a deep incredible drop where the rush and ripple overtook any hope of staying in control.

CHAPTER THIRTY

"You're going to love my family."

Shay dodged James's smile.

They were sitting in a burger place, eating out for the first time since Shay had recovered enough to go out. James had driven in after work to meet her in Greensboro, where she had come for a job interview. Perry had set it up for her. He said he hated to lose a good employee but she deserved to have a regular paycheck, and the position with the tech company was a perfect fit for her. It was a bonus that it would be an hour closer to James.

"Mom's already set a place for you at the Thanksgiving table." He dangled a fry but when she opened her mouth he snatched it back. "And she doesn't like to be disappointed." He offered it again, and this time let her grab it in her teeth.

When she had swallowed the fry, Shay sent him a doubtful look. "I don't know. This all seems kind of fast."

"My mother has been known to invite complete strangers to Thanksgiving dinner that she met in the checkout line the day before." He gave her a look that went all over her to pulse in several intimate spots. "You're hardly a complete stranger."

She shrugged. "You've got a lot of family, right?"

"Three sisters. All married. Nephews. Nieces. The family news is, there's a new girl on the way."

"I'm not accustomed to a lot of family."

"The Cannons qualify more as a horde. There will be so many folks there, they won't know you're not related to us."

Shay swallowed a lump. "It feels early."

James knew better than to answer that one directly. "You are sort of required to be there because I told my sister Allyson that you make the best fried oysters ever."

"What's that got to do with Thanksgiving?"

James looked down and picked up an extra-long French fry, dangled it before her nose. "Nothing."

It was possibly the best Thanksgiving meal ever made. Certainly the best Shay had eaten. James's family seemed to accept her without asking a lot of questions about her past or her family, or anything else she didn't want to talk about just yet. She suspected James was the reason for that. He told her he had already explained her ordeal, and the reason for the stitches and still smoldering black eye. Even so, she felt conspicuous and more than a little intimidated.

It wasn't until the pies and cakes were cut that she noticed his sister Allyson staring at her with a calculating eye. Was that because she had finally noticed that Shay and James had been playing footsie under the table for the past hour?

"I've got a bone to pick with you, Shay."

"Allyson, be nice." James's mother flashed Shay an apologetic smile.

"No, we need to establish some things right up front."

Allyson folded her arms. "I've heard about your reputation and I don't care what the family says about being polite. I don't think I can ignore it."

Shay stiffened and jerked her foot away from James. "Okay. I know you must have heard a lot about me, not all good."

"I don't know about that. What I'm talking about is my brother bragging on your ability to fry oysters. That's my claim to fame in this family. The best oyster fryer in North Carolina. What do you have to say about that?"

Shay glanced uncertainly at James. Grinning, he folded his arms and leaned back in his chair, clearly enjoying the confrontation.

Shay turned back to Allyson. "I respect your position in your family. However, if we're talking best ever—"

"Ouch! You've been dissed, baby." Allyson's husband, Mike, seemed to find this very funny.

"Sounds like a challenge that needs to be met." That comment came from James's dad.

Allyson's two sisters just sat and smiled very satisfied smiles while various other members of the family more or less ignored the culinary challenge in favor of dessert.

Allyson sized up her opponent with the barest hint of calculation. "Tomorrow is Black Friday so that's shopping and leftovers day. But come Saturday, you're on, if you're up to it."

"I don't know if I'll be here Saturday." Shay didn't dare look at James.

"Oh, so you're backing down?"

"No. I'm just saying, I might have to bring in my own oysters."

"I volunteer to drive to the coast tomorrow to buy gallons of oysters." James's father looked remarkably like his son when he smiled like that.

Shay shrugged. "Sure. I'm going to need a few secret ingredients. I'll get those. And stuff for slaw."

"You'll make hush puppies, too?" James looked very eager for a yes.

Shay glanced down at Bogart who was napping on the floor between their chairs. He had already wolfed down his part of the Thanksgiving meal. "If you promise to keep Bogart out of the oysters this time."

James grinned. So, Bogart had eaten hers that first evening. She'd offered him what was left, and lied about the fact. She'd been protecting Bogart and looking after his handler, even when she claimed not to even like him. Shay Appleton was a mystery that might never be completely solved. But that was okay. Because he planned on having all the time in the world to figure her out.

"Did everyone hear about James's ex?" Allyson smiled slyly.

"Now, Ally," her husband cautioned.

"Oh, but you all will want to hear this. She dropped that lawsuit against our little brother and Shay. Which I say is great news. She told reporters she had been misinformed and regrets any embarrassment she might have inadvertently caused."

Shay stared so hard at her serving of lemon meringue pie it should have caught fire. *Inadvertent*. That meant unintentional, unplanned, accidental. Jaylynn's lawsuit had been the exact opposite.

"Jaylynn also announced she's been offered a new job out of the state."

"What's she going to do?" James's tone was not a particularly encouraging one.

"That's the best part. She said it's with a morning show in Mobile, Alabama. But the girl who does my hair also does Jaylynn's. She says Jaylynn confessed it's as a weather girl because she couldn't find any other openings."

Shay lifted her gaze to Allyson.

Allyson met it and smiled. "Sounds to me like Jay-lynn's a sore loser liar who needs to get out of town before the truth gets out."

"More pie, anyone?" James's mom held out a sweet potato pie.

A little later, when they had a moment alone while washing up, a job they volunteered for, Shay nudged James aside with her hip as she moved to rerinse a glass he'd left soapsuds on.

"Your family's different."

James nodded. "They like you, too."

"They like confrontation."

He grinned that irresistible smile. "Cannons love a challenge."

She grinned back. "So that's why my attitude didn't scare you off."

"No, this is why." He kissed her, quick enough not to get caught but long enough to be a promise of much more later. "The attitude was just familiar."

He turned back to the dishes but Shay was tired of hiding her feelings. She slid between the sink and him, and slipped soapy hands behind his neck. She kissed him again, long enough to reveal that she would be more than holding her own later, and quick enough to keep him from taking her on his mama's kitchen floor.

James nuzzled her neck, measuring the odds of getting caught versus assuaging the new hunger that had just sprung up.

She really did smell like forever, but he wasn't going to tell her that for a while, maybe in a few months. Maybe sooner.

Bogart padded in and gave a bright bark.

Shay looked over. "Someone needs a walk."

"Come with me. There's a park at the end of the block with a wooded area on the other side."

Shay turned and saw that the invitation in his eyes included more than a stroll. She smiled. "I'll get my jacket."

"I'll bring a blanket."

James winked at his partner who barked again then gave him what he would swear was a great big lolling-tongue doggy grin.

Don't miss the second book in the K-9 Rescue series

FORCE OF ATTRACTION

Coming Spring 2015

And look for the K-9 Rescue e-Book novella

NECESSARY FORCE

Available now!